this just in

OTHER BOOKS AND AUDIO BOOKS
BY KERRY BLAIR:

The Heart Has Its Reasons

The Heart Has Forever

The Heart Only Knows

Closing In

Digging Up the Past

this just in

a novel by

kerry blair

Covenant Communications, Inc.

Covenant

Cover photo © 2004 by Don Kovalik

Cover design copyrighted 2004 by Covenant Communications, Inc.

Published by Covenant Communications, Inc.
American Fork, Utah

Printed in Canada
First Printing: September 2004

10 09 08 07 06 05 04   10 9 8 7 6 5 4 3 2 1

ISBN 1-59156-623-1

Dedication

To every woman who believes

If I make the lashes dark
And the eyes more bright
And the lips more scarlet;
Or ask if all be right
From mirror after mirror,
No vanity's displayed:
I am looking for the face I had
Before the world was made.

—William B. Yeats; 1890

And to the Blair and Wolfe granddaughters: Kimberly Dawn, Hilary Lynn, Jessica Joy, Caitlyn Mae, and Megan Elizabeth —you are truly jewels in your ancestors' crowns.

Author's Note & Acknowledgements

Eskiminzin and Lozen are real people. The stories of their lives as told in this novel are true and based on historical accounts. I have made every attempt to relate their experiences accurately, and to portray them as the people of strength and integrity I believe them to be. Aside from historical references made to these two people and their associates, all other situations, characters, and their relationships to persons living and deceased are products of my imagination.

Special thanks to Lauren Pettit who graciously allowed me to raid her webpage (www.thefrugalface.com) for great makeup tips; and to Bishop Paul R. Machula, a gentleman and a scholar, who kindly corresponded with me about Eskiminzin. His research, writings, and personal experience regarding the great Apache leader and his descendents are without peer. (View his outstanding webpage at www.geocities.com/~zybt/index.html.)

Other sources I used include *Enju, The Life and Struggle of an Apache Chief from the Little Running Water* by Sinclair Browning (1982, Northland Press); *On the Border with Crook* by John G. Bourke (1891); *As Long as the Stone Lasts: General O.O. Howard's 1872 Conference* (1994 Journal of Arizona History 35); numerous articles from *Arizona Highways* magazines (1964–2003); and priceless materials from the archives of the Arizona Historical Society. The care and attention of the docents at the society was invaluable and much appreciated.

Finally, my love and appreciation to Hilary Blair and Margaret Turley, who read the first draft and encouraged me to finish it anyway; Carol Hopper Holmes for an eye worthy of an eagle; Shauna Humphreys for kindnesses and encouragement beyond the call of duty; Angela Colvin who was once "only" my editor and is now a dear friend besides; my beloved fellow goosies—you know who you are; and, last but not least, Joan Sowards and La Merle Martinez, who first encouraged me to write, and who remind me that friendship, like love, is eternal.

chapter 1

Everybody says that a good beginning is the most important part of a book, and I've put a whole lot of thought into this one. I wanted to begin with "It was the best of times, it was the worst of times," because that would sum up my story perfectly, but my editor insists that line has already been taken. Since this is a memoir, my next thought was to begin with "I was born." That too was a no-go. (Can you *believe* the little Dickens took *all* the best openings? What do the rest of us wanna-be writers have to work with—great expectations?)

Never mind. You'll see for yourself why running for my life was the worst—and best—of times for me. And beginning with my birth would have started my story about twenty-five years too early. If this were a movie instead of a book (and I automatically convert all books into movies in my head, don't you?), we'd probably open to a scene of the bustling newsroom hours before someone set out to murder me.

That's me, center screen—Jillanne Caldwell, the perky blond reporter for NewsChannel 2's top-rated morning show, *What's Up, Tucson?* Every weekday between 7 and 9 A.M. I'm out covering everything Arizona has to feature, with "feature" being the operative word. Gila monster races, chili cook-offs, ostrich rodeos—I'm there. Though it's true that I'm never confused with Diane Sawyer, it might be because she doesn't have my flair for fashion and makeup.

If I look familiar to you non-Tucsonans, maybe you saw me in the Miss America pageant a few years back. I was the one who smiled for all she was worth, while the newly crowned Miss America bawled her perfect little eyes out. (There is something backward about that if you ask me, but nobody has.) As first runner-up, I got the in-the-event-Miss-America-is-unable-to-serve lecture, two dozen American Beauty roses, and a "Get into College Free Card." (It beats having *LOSER* written across your forehead in lip liner, but you don't realize it at the time.)

Anyway, if you *have* seen me on TV sampling chili or modeling a swimsuit, you've probably concluded that I'm as fearless as I am beautiful. Conclude again. I would never have gotten myself into those worst/best of times—lost in a desert canyon and being shot at by men who'd give even desperadoes a good name—in order to further my career. (Seriously, bullets aside, do you know what the Sonoran sun can *do* to fair skin?) I went into the wilderness to magnify my calling as a Primary teacher. I went because I love Connor Teagler. I went because, frankly, I'm impetuous and not very bright.

And that, dear reader, brings us to the opening scene of my story.

My first segment of the morning show had just ended and I was back in the newsroom when the report of a lost child came in. Gene, the news director, rushed into the room while I was applying fresh lipstick before I went back out to shoot a special. (The world's largest kiss-in was about to be held at the university and nobody was better qualified to cover it than I was.) Gene waved his arms, scattering interns as he bellowed that a U.S. senator's little kid had gone missing.

I froze in mid-pucker. You don't have to work for CNN to know that there are only two senators from the great state of Arizona, and that one of them hadn't had a child in the house since the Eisenhower administration. Gene must mean Alexander Teagler. I flung my lip brush aside.

It isn't easy to run in high heels, but I'd had enough practice to almost master it. I gained on Gene before he reached the bank of television monitors and lunged for his shirtsleeve.

"Senator Teagler's son?" I gasped. I couldn't stop him, but with my nails stapled to his shirtsleeve, I at least slowed him down a little.

"Tell Dirk to get that helicopter up!" he hollered, dragging me along unnoticed behind him. "Put Kaysie on it."

"No!" I moved my nails from fabric to flesh to get his attention. "Me, Gene! Send *me* with Dirk."

Gene glanced back at last. He seemed genuinely surprised to see a pretty blond feature reporter attached to his arm. He swatted at my hand as if to discourage a mosquito. "This isn't a kiss-in, Jill. It's real news."

"It's Connor!" I said. "Connor Teagler. Isn't it?" My breath came in gasps, but it wasn't from exertion as much as it was fear at the thought of Connor being lost in a place as vast and terrible as the desert mountains north of the city. "He told me his family was going—"

The words brought Gene to a complete halt, so the remainder of my sentence was mumbled into the back of his shirt when I ran into him. He turned and grasped my shoulders. "You *know* Connor Teagler?"

"I'm his Primary teacher," I said. "Last Sunday we were supposed to be learning about how music blesses our lives, but Connor kept interrupting 'If You're Happy and You Know It' to tell us about the trip his family was taking out to their ranch, and . . ." The look on Gene's face told me that not only had "Primary" lost him, but I was also giving altogether too much information. (My propensity for narration is one of my "gifts"—much to the chagrin of everyone who knows me. My mother, who lives with me, tuned me out years ago. My current "boyfriend," who prefers his voice to mine, talks over me. The morning-show producer, who hasn't been able to change me, just cuts me off in mid-word to air commercials.)

I drew a breath to start again with shorter sentences and more pertinent information. "I go to church with Connor's family. I know his mother. She and I went to—"

Gene didn't give me a chance to tell him if Shar and I had gone together to girls' camp or the senior prom. I thought the answer—both—would surprise him, since who would expect a girl who looks like me to have trouble getting a date to prom?

"You *know* Sharon Teagler?" Gene pointed me toward the elevator and propelled me forward until we reached the shiny metal doors. Then he turned me back around to face him. "How *well* do you know her?"

Finally. "We went together to girls' camp and the senior prom."

Gene wasn't surprised. He was delighted. "Do you know where the helipad is?"

"On the roof?" It was a guess—I'd never seen the helicopter up close. Nobody but the pilot and a handful of cameramen and reporters are allowed to set their experienced derrières on its expensive seats. Still, it was an *educated* guess, since you can't exactly park a chopper in the basement next to the news vans.

Gene pushed me backward through the now-open elevator doors, but he didn't release his hold on my shoulders. I hoped his hands weren't sweating as much as his forehead, because perspiration is murder to get out of a raw-silk blouse.

"This thing'll go national," he said. With his eyes raised to heaven it seemed as if he were telling God rather than me. He muttered a few more things I hope God missed, and pulled me back out of the elevator. "I can't send Reporter Barbie to cover something this big."

I stiffened. It's not exactly a secret that the prettier one's face, the "fluffier" her assignments, but I *am* a reporter, darn it. So what if my tuition was paid by a scholarship from the Miss America Corporation? I graduated from the Walter Cronkite School of Journalism at Arizona State University with a diploma as valid as anybody else's. And so what if the most investigative reporting I'd done thus far involved detecting Slim Fast on the breath of a blue-ribbon greyhound? I'm willing to work my way to the top of my profession one dog-and-pony show at a time. Even Walter Cronkite couldn't become poster boy of the Fourth Estate overnight. And Mr. Cronkite had a few advantages: for one, he never had to wax off his mustache; for another, it didn't take him half an hour between assignments to fix his makeup. (On the other hand, *he* never looked as good on TV as I do. It was lucky for Walter that television was black and white when he started out.)

But even apart from my qualifications as a journalist, I had to convince Gene to let me go. So I did what I always do when my toes start to curl and I feel an anxiety attack coming on—I prayed. When you've prayed as many different prayers in as many different places and under as many different circumstances as I have, you get to where you can do it fast and fervently at the same time. Sometimes it's just one word—*please*. This time the word was *Connor*.

All history with his mother aside, I loved Connor Teagler more than anything. He was one of the only real things in my Barbie Dream House life. I stood outside that elevator and choked back tears as I remembered the first day Connor sat next to me in Primary. He'd stroked my long, lacquered nails with his chubby little fingers and asked, "Are they real?"

"Real acrylic," I admitted.

The next week he had asked about my highlighted hair, thick eyelashes, and full lips. He might have proceeded farther down if I hadn't clutched the lesson manual over my chest and steered the conversation back to Jesus wanting him for a Sunbeam. Week after week, Connor was full of questions, surprises, and surprising insight. I'd sit in the classroom after Primary thinking that if I could become as *this* little child, maybe I could figure out, at last, why a girl who apparently had everything wanted something else.

But today Connor was missing, and whether it made sense or not, I somehow felt it was up to me to find him. The first step to following that spiritual prompting was to get through Gene onto that helicopter.

My smile is often called "perky," which would not get me what I wanted at the moment, so it was good that the face I raised to my boss was unhappy. I straightened the front pleats in my designer skirt and wished it were an inch or two longer and that my tousled hair was upswept instead. I would have to rely on my manner to convey dignity and competence.

"Shar Teagler will talk to me," I told Gene firmly. "She won't talk to another reporter."

It was a bold statement, considering the fact that Shar had barely spoken to me since her wedding day. I hadn't seen her, in fact, until serendipity—and a lucrative modeling contract—put us both back in the same ward. (At least for the months she and her senator husband spent in Arizona.)

I thought when I first saw her at church that our reunion would be something like the one in *Beaches*, but the reality was more like *Ice Age*. After being frozen out of Shar's social circle at one ward social, two Enrichment Nights, and a Primary Activity Day, I finally (if resentfully) accepted my new role in her life. I no longer co-starred as the best friend of the young, impeccably styled wife of Arizona's fastest-rising political star. I had been recast as an extra—the Primary teacher whose one minor scene ends up on the cutting-room floor.

That whole movie-as-life-metaphor was the way Shar and I had coped with our poverty-stricken adolescence. The year we turned eleven—old enough to command the respect of infants and young children—we founded KidSitters in the housing project where we lived. For the next seven years we invested every dime we earned babysitting in the nearby dollar theater. On Wednesdays, dollar movies showed for fifty cents, which was within even our limited budgets. If a flick was worth seeing, we saw it. If it was really worth seeing (meaning Val Kilmer or Chris O'Donnell or somebody equally attractive was in it) we saw it twice. Or thrice. Or . . . you get the idea. When we weren't sitting in the theater, we were waiting to be discovered by boys and cast in glamorous starring roles in romances of our own.

All things considered, it was an idyllic life. With Shar at my side, I didn't notice that my father was gone and my mother was depressed. (Although it did occur to me that Mom took too many pills and lost too many jobs.) Shar and I were inseparable. At least we were until we did what too many best friends do—we grew up and let a man come between us.

Six years later, I looked Gene square in the eye and repeated, "Shar will talk to me." After all, it *might* be true. Maybe this *was* the day Shar would put the bad part of our past—the part where she'd met and married Alex Teagler—behind her and remember instead all the really great years that had gone before.

Gene looked at me as if he were standing before an all-you-can-eat buffet that displayed nothing but raw squid, chopped liver, and chicken gizzards. At last he closed his eyes and released the delicate fabric of my blouse. "Go, Jillanne," he said, pushing the "roof" button in the elevator. "Don't come back without a Pulitzer."

Thankfully, neither of us knew then that I almost wouldn't come back at all.

A Personal Note from Jill: *Surprise! You probably picked up this book thinking you were getting a great adventure story—and you are!—but little did you dream you'd also get fantabulous tips garnered from my years of experience with fellow pageant contestants, professional makeup artists, and extensive perusal of just about every fashion magazine printed in the English language. (Plus some things I thought of as I went along and just had to throw in!) I hope you like the idea because, frankly, my editor isn't sold on it. She's worried that guys will see my "advice columns," decide this is a chick book, and toss it aside. But I know better. I mean, you men are smart enough to just turn the page and get on with the drama, right? I knew it! All my male readers may now be excused to go on to Chapter 2. Meanwhile, ladies, you're in for a treat!*

Jill's Tips for Luscious Lips

Even when you have every intention of keeping your lips to yourself, you want them to look luscious enough to kiss. Here are some tricks of the trade:

Like me, you probably know women who swear by a certain expensive brand of lipstick, but I say the lipstick itself isn't nearly as important as the way you use it. I buy my lipstick at the corner drugstore because I figure why pay $30 or more for one lousy shade when you can get ten lipsticks for the same price and mix them together to create colors that are uniquely your own? To do this, put tiny portions of two or more sticks into each compartment of a small, plastic pillbox. Pop it in the microwave for just a few seconds and then mix with a toothpick. Voilà! Now you have seven colors nobody else can buy. They not only look great, they're easy to take anywhere!

The style now is to skip lip liner, but this won't work if you have a blurry lip line, thin lips, or if you have dark hair and fair skin and don't want your lips to seem to disappear. To provide definition, use a pencil to apply the liner first in a thick line, making it wide on the sides of the lips, particularly the bottom lip. Then blend the inside edges into your lips with a dry brush and apply the lipstick, keeping it only on the center where there is no liner. Blend well. (I learned this from the girl who placed third at the Miss America pageant. It's guaranteed to make your lips look shapely instead of flat like hers.)

A couple more things you should know: to make your teeth look really white, mix up a lipstick in a blue/red or wine/plum. Shades with too much brown can make even white teeth look dingy. Use different lipsticks to add the illusion of fullness. (This is why you buy cheap and get more.) Apply the darker base to your lips, and then use a little light lipstick on the bottom center. You can also use light lipstick in the lower center of your top lip (near the bow) to make your lips look larger and fuller.

Does this sound complicated for something that will only last a few hours at best? It is! But makeup is an illusion, and nobody ever said magic—or glamour—is easy. If you're on your way to the store or to school, I say gloss and go. But for a photo, a special night out, or those once-in-a-lifetime pageants and kiss-ins, luscious is a look you'll like!

chapter 2

Come to find out, I hate helicopters.

Sure, they get you up in the air fast, but this is not an advantage when you're a girl who's lost more than one partially digested corn dog on a Ferris wheel. And while they cover a remarkable amount of ground in remarkably little time, you can't actually *see* any of it. (Unless the blur I saw was just my life passing before my eyes.) But the worst thing about them has got to be the *transparency* of the things. I felt like Glinda the Good Witch of the North, except my bubble didn't float tranquilly over a yellow-brick road. It bobbed wildly around skyscrapers and satellite antennas before roaring out over the freeway.

I probably screamed, but there was no way to know for sure, since I went deaf about the time the pilot started the engine. I thought I might have gone blind, too, but then I realized I just hadn't opened my eyes since the moment we'd almost creamed that poor, myopic pigeon.

When Dirk Hadden, NewsChannel 2's Guy in the Sky, tossed a combination headphone-mic into my lap, I finally opened my eyes to regard him dumbly. Then I looked down at the gizmo and wondered how much it would cost me to replace the piece of equipment when I slimed it with the thick goo that churned in my stomach and rose to my throat. (Of all the times to leave behind my tranquilizers, this was the worst.)

"Put them on," Dirk mouthed through the roar of the chopper.

And let go of these metal bars? Not likely. Clearly, my contribution—clutching the underbars of my seat and pulling upward with all my strength—was the only thing keeping us airborne. If I let go we would spiral out of control like an overgrown dragonfly and splatter across the windshields of who-knew-how-many semis on the interstate below.

"Put them on," he shouted. "You'll need to hear this."

I ignored him. I knew I wouldn't be able to hear over the pounding of my heart anyway. But when Dirk released the control stick to reach for the headphones himself, I reconsidered. One of my white-knuckled hands shot up and plunked the headset over my ears (careless, for once, of my hairstyle) before returning to its death-grip on my seat.

"Having fun, Babe?" Dirk asked, guffawing at his own warped sense of humor. He pulled the chopper into a wide arc that left my stomach heading north for Phoenix while the rest of me veered east toward the open desert.

Silently calling Dirk a jerk—and a few other nice-girl expletives—I gaped at the mountains. At this distance the Galiuros still looked blue and purple. With ragged peaks jutting into the blue, near-autumn sky, they looked incredible. But while they made a great postcard picture, they were the worst place imaginable for a little boy to be lost.

A native of the area, I had heard enough history to know that for the better part of a century, bands of renegade Apaches led by men whose names had passed into history—Victorio, Cochise, and Geronimo—had used these mountains to elude cavalry forces that often outnumbered them more than a hundred to one. Bravely, stubbornly, savagely they held on to what little they had, often relying on a labyrinth of hidden caverns to conceal themselves from their enemies, and sparse desert vegetation to sustain their lives. Even the hardiest men raised in these mountains struggled to stay alive in them. How could a frightened little boy who grew up in a mansion possibly survive out there for more than a few hours . . . especially all alone?

The fresh wave of fear was pushed from my mind as a familiar voice came over the headphones. Gene gave Dirk instructions and then told me to listen carefully to an upcoming feed from the reporter already on location. Senator Teagler was about to make a statement.

Dirk gunned the engine as though he thought he might be able to get the chopper down before the senator said his first word. I closed my eyes again. I had no doubt we'd make it back to the ground—I just didn't believe it would be in fewer pieces than the average jigsaw puzzle. My hair began to turn gray one silky blond strand at a time.

Then it hit me.

"There's a reporter there already?" I managed to squeak around the lump in my throat. (The goo had hardened into cement.) *How did somebody get there before us?* I wanted to ask. *And why couldn't I ride with him instead of you?*

"There's a slew of reporters on-ground," Dirk responded. "Teagler had a press conference scheduled before his kid disappeared this morning."

"Huh?"

Dirk laughed, again. (And it wasn't *with* me, if you know what I mean.) "Don't catch much news, do you, Babe?" he said. "This is the day Alexander Teagler was set to announce his primary candidacy."

Primary candy see? I didn't see at all. His words made no sense. (It's very hard to think rationally when you're bouncing around in a plastic bubble, two minutes and five hundred feet away from a particularly unattractive death.)

"He's running for president of the United States," Dirk said. It didn't escape my attention that he said it in the same tone of voice I use to talk to Sunbeams.

"And he's announcing it in the desert because he wants the rattlesnakes to be the first to know?" I asked, forgetting for the moment the significance of Alex standing on the front porch of his ancestral estate.

I have a bad habit of speaking before I think. One of my former boyfriends used to say it's because I'm blond, but I seriously doubt it has all that much to do with my hair color, as almost-natural as it is. As soon as I heard my own dumb question, I knew the answer. Teagler's ancestors were among the original settlers of the area, unless you include the American Indians. When you add the Apache and Tohono O'odam to the equation, the Teaglers were several thousand years too late to add "original" to their title of "settler." While most Tucsonans living in the 1800s huddled within the relative safety of the town and relied on General Crook, et al, to preserve and protect their "right" to the Indians' ancestral land, the Teagler family staked out a sizeable ranch on the best bottomland and spent generations fighting hostile Apaches to keep it. (At least, that was how I'd always heard the story.) Anyway, since Alex Teagler had begun his political career in Tucson, it was probably obvious to everybody else in the nation why he'd returned home today to announce the furtherance of it.

In the next moment, the headphones over my ears filled with static, followed by Alex's rich, sonorous voice. Even though his only child was missing, his voice didn't waver. He was a born public speaker. Heck, he was a born politician. Alexander Teagler had it all—big smile, big hair, big head, and only a passing familiarity with the meaning of integrity.

I listened as Alex thanked the local dignitaries, the press, and the search-and-rescue teams for being there. (It sounded like he was addressing the last session of a stake conference. I almost expected him to add, "Now, be courteous as you're out there looking for my son. We don't want any accidents on the way home.") Then he said regretfully that, although there had been another reason for asking the media to come, their presence was providential in that it afforded him the opportunity to ask the nation to join him in prayer for the safe return of his little boy. He referred to the picture of Connor that he was holding and said what a joy he was. At that point, his voice broke. Finally, he explained that he was appearing alone because his wife had locked herself inside the ranch house, distraught over Connor's disappearance because she felt it was her fault.

"My wife is young," Alex explained to the press corps. "And inexperienced. I blame myself for not bringing our au pair along with us last night."

It was clear to me—though knowing his luck, it probably wasn't to the million other people listening in on headphones, radios, and televisions all over America—that Teagler didn't blame himself at all. He blamed Shar.

I let go of the seat and clutched my plastic-encased ears instead. "Did he say—?"

Dirk cut me off with a wave of his hand and pointed to his own headpiece to show me he still wanted to listen to the senator even if I didn't.

Suddenly, the helicopter couldn't move fast enough to suit me. I needed to find that little boy and take him back to my best friend.

(As crazy as it sounds, at that moment I not only felt I *should* find Connor, I believed I *would.*)

Before I could tap my little red three-inch heels together thrice, my wish was granted. We swooped down toward the sprawling ranch just as I was about to start muttering, "There's no place like home." Almost falling off the seat brought me back to reality.

There were at least six helicopters and two light planes already on the ground or circling the area. I recognized a few of them from other news stations in Tucson and Phoenix, but the rest were law enforcement, search-and-rescue, and—my heart skipped a beat—MedEvac. I closed my eyes and told myself that the latter was only a precaution. They'd never need it. After all, the long, circular drive already flickered with red, blue, and yellow strobes from emergency vehicles. Already, hundreds of people had arrived to search for Connor Teagler. He'd be safe before sunset. He had to be.

"I'll set you down there," Dirk said, heading toward a recently vacated spot on the ground. "I'll be around, but catch a ride back to town with one of the ground crew, would you?" He tossed a small station bag into my lap. I knew it contained a radio, tape recorder, and other tools of the trade, but I didn't catch it. My hands were once again glued to the bars under my seat. Petrified, I watched it fall between my shaking knees and onto the floor at my feet. I left it where it lay.

A new voice snickered in my headphones. It was Art, the cameraman wedged into the small area behind the seats. He was already at work, feeding live panoramic views to the studio anchors that had undoubtedly interrupted the soaps with the more-dramatic news of a lost child. I hoped all those viewers wouldn't agree with Alex's implication that Shar had been negligent, but I hoped they would take in the view of the miles and miles of barren desert and remember to pray for Connor.

The helicopter took a dip more sudden than a runaway elevator, but still I managed to turn my scream of terror into one of protest. "Wait! I don't want to be put down!" I told Dirk. I could scarcely believe the words myself—I definitely didn't relish staying aboard this roaring bubble of doom. But I heard myself continue, "I want to help look for Connor."

Despite his lack of good sense and common decency, Dirk might well be the best pilot in the business. A Marine reservist, he's fearless, tireless, and willing to play a hunch. Since news stations afford them more eyes in the sky, law enforcement agencies are generally tolerant of news-chopper jockeys, but they *like* Dirk. He stays professional, stays on top of the scanner, and is willing to take the risks. More often than not, he's the guy (in the sky) who gets the job done. I knew staying with him might be my best chance of finding Connor.

"Take me with you!" I pleaded.

"No can do, Babe," he said affably. His grin told me he had taken the mechanical bug down faster than was technically necessary, just for the thrill of seeing my face fade from parchment-colored to paste to bleached bone. "Your job is to make nice with the kid's family. Mine is to find the kid."

I felt the helicopter's landing gear—or whatever you call those parallel strips of flimsy aluminum—scrape into the desert floor as if into my spine. The copter shuddered to a stop, but the blades at the top of the craft kept whirring.

No wonder they call them choppers, I thought. *It's like sitting beneath the spinning knives of a giant food processor.* I shrank down in my seat.

"Duck on your way out," Dirk advised.

"Aren't you going to turn it *off*?" I gasped.

Dirk's grin widened as he shook his head.

Sadist.

From behind my seat, Art reached forward and opened the escape hatch. Then he undid my harness.

I leaned tentatively out the door to look up at the chopper blades. I decided they were probably too high to lop too much off my recently styled do. Then I looked down at the ground and wondered if it would be unprofessional to kiss the terra firma once I'd fallen down there on my knees and all.

Dirk retrieved the station bag from the floor and looped one of its straps over my head. Then he started to reach for my headphones, but paused at the sight of another chopper coming down nearby. I heard his low whistle through the earpiece. "They brought in the top gun," he told Art, motioning toward the new helicopter.

The craft was still more than a hundred feet in the air, but the side door had opened and a pair of long, jean-encased legs swung over the side as it continued to descend. I held my breath as an athletic man with dark hair grasped a slender line with one hand and dropped to the ground. Landing agilely, he pulled the strap of a leather bag more securely over his broad shoulders and sprinted toward a long white van with the words "Pinal County Mobile Command Center" printed prominently on its side.

"Who's that?" I asked. Except for the lack of cape and cowl, I figured it might be Batman. (Or at least a darker, better-looking version of Val Kilmer.)

"That's Clay Eskiminzin," Dirk said through my earphones. "Steer clear of him."

"Why?"

"He hates reporters," Art supplied. I wanted to ask why he hated journalists. I wanted to know why Dirk called him "the top gun." Most of all, I wanted to find Connor and go back home—slowly and by land vehicle. But meanwhile, as shallow as it sounds to come right out and admit it, I really wanted to meet Batguy up close and personal. Unfortunately, I wasn't given enough time to come up with a plan.

"So long, Babe." Dirk pulled off my headphones as he pushed me from the helicopter. "Good luck. You're gonna need it."

He was right about that last thing.

Jill Answers the Hairy Questions

Unless you're Alex Teagler, you probably don't have perfect hair. Nobody does. At least no women do. At any given moment, most of the women in America fervently believe that their hair is too thin, too thick, too dark, too light, too dry, too oily, too long, too short, too curly, too straight, and/or too ugly to be seen by anybody except a professional dog groomer. To advise you to remember that everybody else thinks you look better than you do yourself, is the best beauty tip I can give you. But since you won't believe me, here are answers to some of the "hair mail" I've received at the station.

How often should I wash my hair? As often as needed to maintain body, shine, and bounce. This is different for everybody because everybody's hair and scalp are different. You might be surprised to know that over-washing is worse than under-washing because you're using chemicals to strip all the natural oils from your hair and then trying to replace them with more chemicals. As if that's not enough, after you shampoo your hair, you probably dry it with air hotter than a Sahara wind, and then wrap it around a rod that could be used to brand cattle. The result of all this abuse can be hair that looks like it belongs to one of your old Barbie dolls. (And you know the one I mean.) For your hair to look its best, shampoo only as often as you really need to and let it air dry as often as you possibly can. (When you do shampoo, be sure to tilt your head back to keep the shampoo from running onto your face. The chemicals in it are much harsher than what you use to wash the sensitive skin under your eyes.)

How do I get the red, blue, green, pink and/or purple streaks out of my hair before my concert, prom, graduation and/or interview with the bishop? Frankly, girls, the best idea is not to put them there in the first place. Those little packages of bright-colored powder were designed to make punch, not hair dye. But once you've done it—and, really, who hasn't?—the best damage control is in your kitchen. Take about a tablespoon of mild liquid dish soap, mix in a teaspoon of baking soda, and then massage it into your damp, Technicolor locks. You may have to do it a couple of times. Follow it up with a shampooing and the very best conditioning treatment you can find.

What is the very best conditioning treatment I can find? Good news! It's probably already in your refrigerator. My mother used to do a treatment on me she calls her "Saturday Night Special." First, she rinsed my hair and applied a raw egg directly to the scalp. She rubbed it in thoroughly, rinsed it out, and then applied a mousse of mayonnaise, paying close attention to the sun-damaged ends of my long, blond locks. After we ate tuna-fish sandwiches (the mayo was already out on the counter, after all) she applied a tiny dollop of baby shampoo and rinsed my hair very well. On Sunday I had hair softer than a baby's and twice as lustrous. This is still my favorite at-home treatment!

chapter 3

Fortunately, I've had quite a lot of experience landing on my feet, so the only thing injured when Dirk pushed me from the chopper was my pride. I didn't give him the satisfaction of a glare or even a backward glance. I didn't have time. Dorothy had an easier time walking through the tornado than I did stumbling through the dust storm raised by those chopper blades. After all, this wasn't a Kansas wheat field, it was the desert. I didn't see any witches fly by, but more than one cactus came uncomfortably close to restyling my hair and adding body piercings in places almost nobody would consider.

When I finally fought my way to the outer edge of the maelstrom, I continued to ignore Dirk and Art—and their advice. I headed in the direction Batguy—I mean Val—I mean Clay What's-his-name—had gone.

"Pretend you're on a runway," I told my knees as they threatened to give out several steps from the burley deputy sheriff who came to meet me. It would have been easier to make believe if the "runway" had been level and not littered with stones.

The deputy's eyes were on my stylish, teetering heels, but they didn't stay there long. They rose slowly to take in my ankles, calves, and then the rest of me. I could tell from the look on his face that I had at least one thing going for me—even with my chopper-styled hair, I was easily the most attractive reporter to arrive thus far.

I gave him my best Miss America smile and hoped he didn't notice the sand that must surely be stuck between my teeth. "I'm Jillanne Caldwell," I began. "I'm here to fi—"

The deputy didn't give me a chance to finish the word, let alone the sentence. Instead, he steered me toward the press corral. It was harder now to pretend I was in Atlantic City. The other stations had thus far sent their political correspondents, all of which happened to be men. Sure, some of those guys had bigger teeth and better hair than me, and most of them might beat me in a pageant judge's interview, but when it came to the evening gown and swimsuit competitions, I was sure to take the tiara. Too bad nobody here was giving out tiaras—or even points—for pretty.

When I tell you I was being led to a press corral, I mean it. The media's base of operations was a dry, dusty open space about the size of a bus terminal. It was ringed by news vans and private vehicles around a fence of ancient mesquite branches stuck in the desert floor and looped together with barbed wire. It was rustic, and, considering the locale, possibly attractive. It was also a cattle pen. I couldn't help but wonder if it were being used today out of convenience, or if it was an expression of somebody's not-so-subtle opinion of the press. I eyed the enclosure and dug in my heels.

"I'm not a reporter!" I told the deputy as he tried to herd me in there with the news bulls. When his eyes lighted on the NewsChannel 2 bag in my hand, I moved it behind my back. "Really, I'm not. I'm a friend of the Teaglers. I only rode out on a station helicopter to get here faster. Have you ever been in a helicopter? They're horrible! They're noisy and fast and almost entirely transparent. And the way that pilot flies! I thought—" I was doing it again, talking too fast and giving too much irrelevant information. I took a deep breath.

"I'm not a news reporter," I repeated more calmly. "I'm a friend of Shar—Sharon—Teagler. If you'll excuse me, I'm on my way to the ranch house . . ." I edged hopefully in that general direction.

The lawman grasped my upper arm with a strong (and not particularly clean) hand. That settled it. The cleaning bill for this blouse would be on Gene's desk tomorrow morning.

Clearly, the deputy was a man of little trust. But at least he was willing to investigate. He called, "Hey, you!" to a guy in the corral who carried a bag identical to my own.

I tried not to make an unattractive face, for fear it would freeze that way, but the man he called was Sean. Sean covers the political beat for NewsChannel 2 and considers everyone else's assignment inferior—particularly mine. The chauvinistic camera hog does like women on his arm, if not at his side. I'm probably the only station employee in a skirt who's refused to go out with him, and I do it with the same diligence I take vitamins and do Pilates—daily.

Sean swaggered over to where we stood. (But then, Sean swaggers everywhere he goes.) He didn't look happy to see me. He would undoubtedly want to keep such a big story for himself.

I held my breath and uttered another of my super-economy prayers. There were dozens of ways the deputy could word a question to Sean, and almost all of them would land me in this bull pen with nothing more constructive to do than fend off the advances of the livestock.

Being a man of few words—and possibly divinely inspired besides—the deputy asked, "She a news reporter?"

One corner of Sean's mouth curled disdainfully. "Not that I've ever seen."

It was the one and only time in my life that I could have kissed him. It was the best break I could have asked for, and I took it. "The pilot asked me to give you this," I said, flinging the station bag into Sean's midriff. I didn't stop to think I might have to file a report later, or that the time would come that I'd have traded my Rolex for that cell phone. Before Sean could tack on a disclaimer, I dodged around the deputy and ran toward the ranch house. ("Ran" being a relative term, considering the aforementioned wobbly knees, loose dirt, and three-inch heels.)

I was down to the last fifty yards of my dash before I realized how foolish and futile my efforts were in the first place. Alex Teagler stood on the wide front porch surrounded by lawmen, his cronies, and the minor party dignitaries who'd come out expecting to see him throw his cowboy hat into the ring. The chance of the senator greeting me with anything more cordial than an epithet was slim. The chance of him letting me see Shar was nil. The chance of him evicting me from his property was almost a sure thing.

Maybe I've already mentioned this, but Alex and I never saw eye-to-eye—despite being almost the same height. I'm 5'8" (which is almost perfect by runway standards) and Senator Teagler isn't a centimeter taller. Sure, he looks tall on TV, but that's only because he stands on risers for speeches, sits on Thoroughbred horses for political commercials, and the rest of the time surrounds himself with staff and associates who are even shorter than he is. His wife is about the size of the average porcelain doll, and even daintier. In other words, Alex is a man who has a gift for fashioning the world according to Teagler. It was him manipulating Shar—trying to *own* her is more like it—that came between me and my best friend in the first place.

Shar and I had been on the lookout for the perfect man since we were old enough to notice God had created two sexes. Shar thought she'd found Mr. Right at eighteen, but I was still shopping at twenty-five. I like humorist Jean Kerr's observation that a husband is like something you see in a department store window that you think you're just going to die if you don't have. You pick one up and take him home and move him from here to there, until you realize he doesn't go with anything you already own, and you can't figure out what you were planning to do with him in the first place. Anyway, that's the reason the guy I sometimes refer to as "my boyfriend" is still my boyfriend instead of my husband or even my fiancé. He looks great through windows—we both do—but looking good together is all there is to our relationship.

This is *still* healthier than the relationship Shar has with Alex. I tried to warn her before it went too far, but she was smitten. When they first met, she was a few months away from turning nineteen and he was thirty-four, but it wasn't the age difference that bothered me. It was the way he actually came right out and told her that he only dated significantly younger women because he wanted a wife he could "mold into a perfect helpmeet." Most girls would hear those words and run away as fast as they could. (Heck, if they were smart, they'd forget running and charter a jet.) But Shar wasn't most girls. Shar was in love. Or perhaps she was desperate.

The thing you probably need to understand is that although she is much prettier than I am, Shar is petite and curvaceous—the kind of girl most men want, but most magazine-cover editors don't. A year out of high school, I was modeling and picking up scholarships here and there on the pageant circuit, but Shar was working at Wal-Mart full-time to scrape together enough money for community college. She had big dreams, but little opportunity and less moola. In her eyes, Alexander Teagler had it all: a huge fortune, a tiny Ferrari, and enough fame as a gung-ho state legislator to get his name on the ballot for senator. Alex, Shar thought, was going places, and she wanted to go along. He proposed to Shar at a gala fundraiser and reaped coast-to-coast coverage, not to mention the votes of every romantic in the state. (Every romantic except me.)

Of course, given his relative political youth and inexperience, nobody expected him to win the election. Nobody but Alex, that is, and his mentor, Eliot Fuller. If Alex is a genius when it comes to self-promotion, it's because he learned it from the master. And when a scandal was uncovered in the office of the incumbent—quite conveniently at the end of October—Mr. Teagler went to Washington.

Six years later, it had been a new election but the same story. Alex was still a golden boy who always seemed to be in the right place at the right time. Shar still wore what Alex told her to wear, said what he told her to say, and did what he told her to do. One of the things he was most adamant about her doing (and he first told her this as they left the wedding reception where I was her maid of honor) was staying away from me. I figured it was because I was one of the few people who could see right through senator-elect Teagler—and didn't like the view.

I still didn't. I skidded to a stop in the thin desert soil and executed a perfect turn on the balls of my feet like any well-trained pageant princess. My new plan was to go around to the back of the house and hope the servants were more congenial. Of course, I'd only pull it off if Alex didn't see me first.

He saw me, but either he didn't have any hounds, or the dogs must have been otherwise engaged. The senator looked drawn and anxious, as would any man whose son was lost in the Sonoran Desert. I thought I saw a moment of hesitation cross his face before the tall, patrician man at his side leaned down and spoke into his ear. (It was Eliot, of course. Nobody who had ever seen that man, even on television, forgot his face.) In the next moment, Alex called his bodyguards, or Secret Service agents, or whoever the heck it was who had the dubious privilege of seeing to his well-being.

"Take her off my property!" he commanded the two men. The "and shoot her" wasn't vocalized, but clearly implied by his tone of voice.

My fight-or-flight reflex must have been broken in my ignominious exit from the helicopter. I stood frozen to the spot. Out of the corner of my eye I saw the gorgeous guy who'd jumped so gracefully from his own helicopter now exit the command center. It was gratifying to note that he looked on with at least a modicum of interest as the apes-in-suits rushed forward and grasped me by the elbows, further ruining the delicate fabric of my blouse.

No cleaning bill now, I thought. *The station will just have to replace it.*

"I'm a news reporter!" I called out. (I felt guilty about the deputy catching me in my little fib, but my mission—if not my life—was on the line.) "I represent the people! You can't let them cart me off!"

Without meaning to, I'd addressed my words to Mr. Tall, Dark, and Muscular. He didn't look away, but he didn't come immediately to my rescue, either. It was only then that I remembered Art's words about Batguy hating reporters.

"I'm a Primary teacher!" I hollered at him in desperation as the suits picked me up off my feet. "I'm trying to magnify my calling here!"

Attractive little creases formed at the corners of Batguy's eyes and he took a step forward. I never knew if he'd have come to my defense, because at that moment an upper window of the house opened and Shar Teagler's auburn curls appeared above her ashen face.

"Jillanne!" she cried. "Oh, Jill!"

The creases that formed on Alex's face were not nearly as attractive as Batguy's. "I'll take care of this, darling," he called up to her. (The emphasis, I might add, was not on "darling.")

But Shar had already left the window. Before the Suits could decide whether to put me down or carry me off, Shar was at the front door. Alex made a grab for his wife as she flew across the porch, but he missed. (Not only is Shar small, she's fast.)

When a senator's wife is wrapped around your neck, most of your troubles are over. Suits 1 and 2 backed off sheepishly, while the *honorable* Mr. Teagler stood rooted to the porch surrounded by cronies and tried to affix an indulgent smile to his pained expression. There wasn't much else he *could* do with his wife clutching me and sobbing her guts out in front of a cattle pen full of cameramen. I mean, it would have been a really inopportune moment for a politician to commit murder, though it probably topped the list of things he *wanted* to do.

I held Shar close and sobbed right along with her. At times like this, even girls like me forget about their mascara and ignore the tear stains on raw-silk blouses. "I'm so sorry!" I managed at last. I meant our separation and my barging back into her life uninvited, but most of all, Connor's disappearance.

"It's my fault Connor's lost!" Shar wailed.

I didn't believe that for a second. I didn't want Batguy to believe it either—even in the midst of all the emotion, I'd noticed when he moved closer. I wanted to think he moved in to be ready to defend me if the bodyguards took a renewed interest in my disposal, but I suspected he was just nosy.

"What happened?" I asked Shar.

"We were playing outside." Her words were still drenched in tears, but mostly intelligible. "Alex wanted me to get Connor's wiggles out so he could stand still with me and look good for the press conference. You know how Connor is."

After the past few months of Primary, I did know, and it tore at my heart.

"So we were playing cowboys and Indians. Connor was his famous grandfather defending the family fort, and I was a marauding Apache that . . ."

Like me, Shar doesn't know how to tell a *short* story. I noted that Batguy focused on the mountains in the distance as she embellished the tale of hostile Indians and heroic Teaglers, but he was listening.

"Then I got a phone call," Shar continued. "Alex's aide came outside to tell me. He said it was important and I should take it. I *told* Connor to wait for me on the porch. He always does as he's told."

I'd never met a four-year-old who always did as he was told, especially Connor, but my experience with children was limited to about seven hours a month, so I nodded.

"I wasn't away from him three minutes," Shar said. Her voice rose and I knew before many more words were out it would be a wail. "But when I came back outside he was *gone*! It's like he disappeared." Her grip on me tightened as if she were clinging to a life raft, or maybe the last little bush at the very edge of a steep cliff. "Oh, Jill! Connor is *everything* to me! If it could be me out there lost and dying instead of him, I'd do it. I *would!*"

"Nobody's going to die!" I gasped, moving her to arm's length so I could meet her eyes. When I saw how haunted they were, I regretted the action and pulled her close again. "Shar! It's going to be okay." I shook her a little, but more for my sake than hers. "They're going to find Connor. They'll bring him back to you." In desperation I turned to the guy with the great hair and inscrutable face. "You'll find him, won't you?"

The average all-American hero would have given me a modest, "We'll sure do our best ma'am," but Clay Eskiminzin wasn't average in any respect. He looked from me to Shar with the most heart-stopping blue eyes ever granted a mortal man and said, "I'll find him." Just like that.

But the oddest part was that Shar and I believed him.

Jill Dishes on Dating

First let me say to the guys: If you haven't turned the page already, stick with me on this one. I mean, dating is something that only works if you have a girl AND a boy. Secondly, let me say that I realize this column will come a little too late for many of you. You've already been to that metaphorical department store to pick out that spouse, and you couldn't be happier with the choice . . . most days. But you stick with me too. Even if you can't use the tip yourself, you can always pass it on.

Thirdly, you probably know by now that you can trust me on hair and makeup, but DATING? All right, already. I've fessed up to being something less than an expert on the subject despite my years of painful experience. Fortunately, I can read, and while I might not be the sharpest eyeliner in the case, I'm smart enough to read the right things.

So here's my best advice. Go to any bookstore in town and check out the shelves for young—and sometimes not-so-young—adults. You'll find dozens of books and magazines full of advice on dating and falling in love and getting married. Now go home without buying anything. Open the "For the Strength of Youth" pamphlet. (If you don't have one, ask any LDS bishop or branch president. Tell him I sent you.) On pages 12–21 you'll find everything you need to know about dating . . . and a few other important tidbits besides.

Isn't it fantastic? Now you can use the money you saved by not buying all those ridiculous how-to-date books to get yourself a whole new outfit and to-die-for shoes to match! Better, you have the word of the Lord to guide you.

And just who do you know who gives better advice than God?

chapter 4

For a guy who'd promised a grieving mother that he'd find her little boy lost in the desert, Clay Eskiminzin seemed to be looking in all the wrong places. First he had ignored the political caucus on the ranch's front porch and spent ten minutes examining the edifice as if he suspected Connor might have slipped beneath a stray floorboard. Then he walked down the stairs and around the ranch house once, then again, and then in ever-widening circles until he was maybe a hundred yards away. If he continued the spiral pattern, I figured he might eventually stumble upon the child—though at the rate he was moving he'd need that strange walking stick of his for support by then, and the Connor he brought back would be middle-aged. Thank goodness there were other people out in helicopters and jeeps and on horseback and foot. While there was no denying that this "top gun" was attractive to observe, I was about to conclude that we couldn't count on him to find his own shadow.

"What is he *doing*?" I asked the deputy impatiently. It was the same guy I'd lied to about not being a reporter, but since it turned out I'd told him the truth about Shar, I think he figured it evened out.

Mrs. Teagler and I had sole possession of the front porch now—with the deputy and Suit 1 to keep the press at bay. Alex had been unsuccessful in prying his wife from my side. Either my friend had finally grown a backbone, or the horror of losing her child had put her in a state of shock deep enough that she scarcely noticed her husband, let alone his artfully crafted attempts to get her back upstairs. Alex had retreated within to lick his wounds while Shar suffered her raw agony in stoic silence without. We sat side by side in a rustic double swing on the porch, half listening to muffled voices from a dozen different radio frequencies reporting to the command center, and watching Batguy waste precious minutes he should have been spending looking for Connor.

"You mean Eskiminzin?" the deputy asked, as though there was somebody else standing stock still, staring into the foothills. "He's the best," he informed us almost reverently. In his circle, this man must be more legendary than Batman.

"The best what?" I asked with more than a little sarcasm.

The deputy looked surprised. "Tracker," he said. "Guide. Ranger. He knows the Southern Arizona mountains better than any man alive."

Then why was he staring into the Galiuros as if seeing them for the first time?

"He's a full-blooded Apache," the deputy offered. "The great-great-great-great grandson of an Apache war chief. Born and raised in the wilderness. The things he can do . . ." the words trailed off in a shudder of admiration. "Spooky."

A latter-day Apache chief? That might explain Batguy's self-possession and his stunning bronze skin and thick, dark hair—but where did those heavenly blue eyes come from? For that matter, where'd he get his height? I'd always thought Apaches were short and stocky, but this guy was 6'2" if he was an inch. I stared out at Eskiminzin and tried to work out the incongruities in my head. The only thing I knew for sure was if that "full-blooded" Apache was turned into a marble statue, he'd be more likely to be mistaken for Adonis than Geronimo.

It suddenly occurred to me that the woman at my side had ceased breathing and was clutching her throat with one perfectly manicured hand. Before I could remember if I even knew the Heimlich maneuver, let alone how to administer it, Shar managed to gasp, "I told him all about our game." The eyes she turned to me were large and anxious. "You know, Jill—the part about me pretending to be a bloodthirsty Apache. No wonder he won't look for my little boy!"

I set my jaw. What kind of "hero" would let an innocent remark like that—even a culturally insensitive one—keep him from doing everything he could to save a child's life? I wanted to march across that yard and grab handfuls of Clay Eskiminzin's hair in both my hands. (To be perfectly truthful, this wasn't the first time the thought had crossed my mind, but this time I didn't want to run my fingers through it—I wanted to yank it hard enough to make it hurt.)

But before I could do more than daydream about getting his attention, Batguy turned. The way he strode back toward us told me this man could cover ground when he wanted to.

"They say he can hike fifty miles in a day," the deputy whispered as the ranger approached.

He took the porch steps in a single stride and crouched in front of Shar, putting his face at her eye level. I'm used to men looking at *me*, but this one didn't spare me a glance. I wish I could say I shared his aloofness, but the more I looked at Batguy, the more it began to dawn on me that he probably used that strangely carved stick of his to beat off women prettier than me.

Shar's fingers were over her mouth and her beautiful green eyes had filled with tears. Through her fingers she whispered, "I'm sorry for what I said."

His thick brows knit together as he waited for her to compose herself enough to continue.

"About . . . about the . . . the Apaches, I mean. I didn't know you . . . I mean . . . I . . . I didn't know."

Batguy glanced over his shoulder at the deputy as if gauging what the man might have told us about him. Then he turned his full attention back to Shar. "I didn't take offense, Mrs. Teagler."

"Then you will find Connor?" she breathed.

"I'll find him," he said. "But I need your help. I need to ask you a few questions."

Shar swallowed her tears as best she could and nodded.

"How would you characterize your immediate family?" he began. "Are you intimate?"

I started. In the first place, I'd expected him to ask what Connor was wearing when he disappeared, or the last place she'd seen him play—something useful. In the second place, I couldn't help but wonder at the way the guy talked. What kind of born-and-bred mountain man used words like "characterize" and "intimate"?

The only one more interested in Shar's answer than me was Alex's hired Suit. It showed on his face. He seemed to be torn between running straightway to his master to report the question or waiting around long enough to hear Shar's answer. He waited.

"We're . . . we're very close," she said. Clearly, she didn't know what Batguy was trying to get at any more than I did.

"No marital difficulties?"

"Of course not!"

Eskiminzin nodded, but not as if he necessarily believed her. "How much of your son's day-to-day care do you provide?"

"I don't know what you mean," Shar said. "We have an au pair who lives with us . . ."

The ranger waited patiently for her to continue.

Patience might be on his list of virtues, but it wasn't on mine. "Shar's a perfect mother!" I told him. As soon as the words were out, I realized I had no idea if they were true. The only place I'd ever seen her with Connor was at church. A lot of women look like perfect mothers at church. But my outburst had one positive result. It made Batguy spare me half a glance.

"I don't doubt you're a good mother, Mrs. Teagler," he told Shar quietly. "It's apparent that you love your child. I'm asking if you're the one who most often supervises Connor's activities on a day-to-day basis."

She shook her head miserably. "The nanny does."

"Did you have younger brothers and sisters growing up?"

Again Shar shook her head. Like me, she's an only child. Batguy opened his mouth to ask another question, but Shar wailed, "I *know* it's my fault!"

He laid a gentle hand on her shoulder. "You have no reason to blame yourself."

I blinked. Hadn't he just established that Shar was inexperienced enough to have lost her child? It was almost as though he were interrogating her on a witness stand. Now I couldn't figure out if Eskiminzin was acting like the attorney for the prosecution or the defense.

He leaned back on his heels with his carved stick across his knees. This rescue ranger possessed an inherent grace that people who walked down runways would kill for. "I'm sorry about questioning you at such a difficult time," he said, "but these are things I do need to know so I can find Connor."

His voice was so calm, compassionate, and confident that Shar not only blinked the tears from her eyes, she managed a half-smile.

"With so many people in the area for the press conference," he continued, "I know it's impossible for you to be sure, but do you remember seeing any strangers talking to Connor this morning?"

"No. Alex is very careful to keep both Connor and me out of the spotlight as much as possible."

"Was anyone watching you play together?"

"I don't think so." Shar looked nervously at Suit 1 and he shook his head. "No. Nobody else was around."

Batguy regarded Alex's henchman a whole lot longer than he'd looked at me. I tried not to take it personally.

"Last couple of questions," he said, turning his attention back to Shar. "Who was up here with the family this morning when Connor disappeared?"

He might as well have asked Cecil B. DeMille to name his extras. (Mr. DeMille *was* the director famous for his casts of thousands, right? In the days before most of the hordes of "people" became computer graphics, I mean.)

"The bodyguards," Shar began. "They follow me everywhere." She cast a quick glance at Suit 1 and amended, "I mean, they go everywhere with us. For our protection."

Eskiminzin pulled a single sunflower seed from a front shirt pocket. (It occurred to me that notebook and pencil would have been handier.) But he didn't put the seed in his mouth. He just held it in his hand. "And?" he prompted.

"Our cook," Shar said. "Elsie. And she brought her daughters up to help make the beds and get everything ready last night."

A nod. And another sunflower seed.

"Our au pair didn't come," Shar offered.

"Why?"

"She was getting a cold," Shar said. "Alex thought it would be better if she wasn't around Connor. He catches colds so easily." Shar began to cry again, but softly this time.

"I know how hard this is," Batguy said.

I wondered if it was a well-intentioned platitude or if he *did* know what it was like to worry about a child because he had a "little bat" of his own at home. He wasn't wearing a wedding ring. (Not that I looked specifically at his ring finger. We reporters are just naturally observant.)

He urged, "Who else, Mrs. Teagler? Friends of your husband's, maybe?"

Suit 1 took a step forward.

She wiped at her eyes and nodded. "Kent—he's Alex's campaign manager—came up with his two assistants. And Eliot, of course."

I was beginning to think I'd have to change Batguy's name to Birdguy. He pulled out a third and fourth sunflower seed before asking, "Eliot Fuller?"

"Yes. He's . . ." her words trailed off. She seemed to be trying to decide what to say in front of the well-dressed ape that hovered at her side. "Eliot's my husband's . . ."

"Keeper?" I suggested. At the startled look on her face, I consulted my in-brain thesaurus. "Handler? Trainer? Rasputin-in-Residence?"

I thought the last was particularly apt—Eliot Fuller was the only person I'd ever heard of that was even fuller of himself than Alex. And if you asked me, he might have posed for the caricature of the czarina's pinched-faced advisor in *Anastasia*. On the other hand, I mused, perhaps I had the wrong movie. Even though Fuller didn't fit the handsome Dr. Frankenstein role, he'd sure as heck created his own monster.

"He's Alex's political advisor and mentor," Shar decided. If she'd been reading my mind, she'd left out the best parts.

Eskiminzin palmed another seed. "Anybody else?"

The tears increased along with her frustration and confusion. "Yes! There are people *everywhere*. I don't know *who* they are!"

"I understand." He was still calm. *Too* calm, if you ask me. "Let me ask you this, then. Has anyone who came up with you last night, or anybody you know who arrived this morning, since left the area?"

I drew in a breath, but it wasn't a gasp. Not exactly. Alex had told authorities, and reiterated in the press conference, that Connor must have wandered into the desert alone. It's what Shar believed. It's what I had believed. Was this guy implying that the disappearance was no accident, that Connor might have been kidnapped?

"Think carefully, Mrs. Teagler," he urged.

I could see that Shar *was* thinking carefully, and was terrified of where her thoughts led.

"You should be talking to the senator," the Suit interrupted. "Mrs. Teagler, I'll have to insist you not say anything more until your husband joins you."

Batguy looked up at him again with interest. "Are you their attorney?"

Suit 1 frowned and headed for the front door.

"He's on my husband's security staff," Shar explained, looking after the man with worried eyes. I guessed that the creep had finally reminded her of how closely Alex guarded her every word. "I . . . I should probably go inside to be with Alex." She looked at me with a mixture of apology and panic. "I don't know what I was *thinking*. It's been such a difficult time for him . . . for me . . . for . . . oh, Jillanne! I'm so sorry!"

Shar stood up so fast she sent the swing in a backward arc before I could grab her arm. My fingers only brushed her wrist, then she was gone.

I scrambled to my feet as quickly as I could, but Eskiminzin had also risen and was blocking my way.

"Move!" I told him with a very unladylike jab at his upper arm. I had to catch Shar before she could disappear back inside Teagler's lair where I might never see her again. He didn't move, but I didn't hit him again either. I might as well have punched granite the first time. The impact hadn't exactly hurt my hand, but it didn't feel very good either.

"Let her go," he said. The words were so quiet I almost didn't hear them.

But he heard my response. Everybody within a two-mile radius probably heard my response. "You're crazy!" I yelled at him. "You don't know what's going on here! You don't even know what you're doing! You're supposed to be some kind of hotshot. A top gun, my foot. Why aren't you out there looking for Connor?"

Rather than regard the woman raging in his face, the ranger's eyes had sought a spot on the mountains and held it. "Because I can better find him if I first figure out where he is."

Like that made sense. I tried to stare him down, but he wouldn't meet my eyes. Despite myself, I finally glanced over my shoulder to follow his gaze. There was something hypnotic in the way he focused without blinking. Nobody could see him stare and not try for themselves to see his point of interest. At least I couldn't.

I was still searching for whatever it was he was looking at when he said, even more quietly than before, "She'll come back to you."

I whipped my head back around, but he was still regarding the mystical spot of nothing. His eyes, I noticed, were a deeper blue than the sky, but much clearer. My voice disappeared with my anger and I whispered, "How do you know?"

"Because I saw who she went to when she most needed comfort." Eskiminzin blinked once and the spell of the mountain was broken. He nodded farewell and turned away.

He was down the steps before I put two and two together and came up with a sum that made me shiver despite the warmth of the day. I scrambled down the stairs to catch up to this tall Apache with the Ivy League vocabulary. "What are you saying?" The note of desperation in my voice made him pause, but he didn't reply.

I planted my heels in the dirt in front of him. "You said Shar turned to me when she needed comfort," I blurted out. "And you said she'd come back to me again. But you also said you'd find Connor," I reminded him. "You did! So if you promised to find him, but you still think Shar will need me, then are you saying . . . ?" I couldn't get the rest of the words out. I couldn't ask the question because I didn't know if I would be able to bear hearing the answer.

I heard it anyway, from a man who couldn't keep his eyes off those stupid mountains long enough to look a person in the face. He said, "I can't promise to find him alive." Then he walked away as my heart broke into about a zillion throbbing pieces.

Jill's Fashion "Wins" for the Shapes We're In

The first part of this is only for the strong of heart—or perfectly proportioned. (And I'll bet there are lots more of the former out there than the latter.) Ready? Find a full-length mirror in a private, soundproof room (for when you scream) and exchange all your clothes for an old swimsuit. Now turn on the lights and open your eyes. (Yes, you have to.) In the next three minutes you'll be able to pinpoint with absolute certainty the parts of your body that you hate. But it's the three minutes AFTER that that are important. Spend this time looking for things you DO like. (Yes, you do too have some great features.) Maybe you have lovely shoulders or really terrific ankles. Everybody has something to be proud of. Take note of it and glow a little while you get dressed. Finished? Then let's talk about how to play up your good features and play down your not-quite-as-good ones.

If you're tall, your skirts should reach mid-kneecap to just below the knee since anything shorter will add height. (Of course, I know you'd never consider going much shorter anyway.) Full, soft lines help diminish height, and contrasting colors in separates also help shorten a tall figure.

If you're short, you'll look best in separates of compatible tones—or the same color with minimal waist and neck detail. Wear your shirt collars open and avoid fussy, high necklines. Hemlines should hit the bottom of the kneecap, and pants shouldn't be worn shorter than ankle length. (I know, I know, capris are in. Try to remember that unlike commandments, fashion rules are made to be broken.) Jackets, vests, etc., should be short, hitting at the waist or just below, and all your accessories should be proportionate to your petite figure.

An overall large frame looks smaller in darker solids. Keep patterns simple and avoid extremes that can make you look like upholstered furniture. (No, Cousin Eunice, of course I don't mean YOU. You look simply stunning in that orange-flowered muumuu you're so fond of.) Entice the eye inward with decorative belt buckles, detailed lapels, and necklaces with pendants worn just below the hollow of the throat. Proper fit at shoulders, waist, and hips is essential.

An overall small frame is less likely to be overlooked when you dress in bright or light solids with neutral, small accessories. Again, pants should be slightly long, with fitted waists to add dimension to your figure. Avoid bold prints, patterns, and stripes as they tend to overwhelm a small frame.

No matter what shape we're in, we can like what we see in the mirror (when we're fully clothed, at least!) if we take the time to research the colors, styles, and fabrics that make the most of the beautiful bodies God gave us. Remember, even better than looking pretty is looking pretty amazing! Anybody can handle that.

chapter 5

I never thought anybody would hear these words from me, but there are times when fashion doesn't count. This was one of those times. I'll explain in a minute. Clay Eskiminzin, child-rescuer extraordinaire, might have given up on finding Connor alive and well, but *I* hadn't. I was more determined than ever.

There's a remarkable thing about hearts—they're much more resilient than you think they are. When at last I gathered the pieces of mine back together, it told me Connor was still alive and could be found. The same little voice that had spoken to me in the newsroom told me so, and added that I should be out looking for him.

Of course, that was hard to do in an A-line skirt and three-inch heels. But just when I thought it was hopeless, I caught a break so big it could only be filed under *M* for "miracle." I was on my way back to the press corral (hoping to avoid the Suits) when it happened. Right there at the edge of the ring of vehicles appeared the blessed NewsChannel 2 van in all its splendor! It wasn't just *any* station van, mind you. It was Mobile Unit 2, the one that had picked me up from the gym the day before because I had been late for an assignment. I'd changed clothes in the back on the way to the remote, but when our segment ended I caught a ride back to the station with the weatherman. (He's okay-looking, kinda funny, and unmarried. Since I seldom pass up the chance to window shop for a husband, I thought I should check him out and . . . but that's too much irrelevant information again, isn't it?) Anyway, the point is that the van parked outside Alex's ranch would still have my gym bag shoved under the front seat. See what I mean? They're usually around just when we need them most—miracles, I mean, not gym bags or news vans.

I crammed myself in the back of the van, barricaded the door, and shimmied out of my skirt. Although I regretted consigning it to the depths of a smelly canvas bag, I had no such qualms when it came to the ruined silk blouse. The slip, camisole, and pantyhose were the next to go.

I dressed quickly, breathing through my mouth. If my gym clothes smelled bad, I didn't want to know it. I bent over to reach for my socks and cross trainers and muttered to myself about the idiot whose idea it was to cram so dang much TV equipment into such a small space. Still, I was grateful for the two or three square feet, since my only other option of dressing rooms was a Porta-John. Talk about a place to hold your nose.

In a few minutes I was ready to rock and roll. I wore clothes no woman would be caught dead in outside of an all-girl gym: basic gray sweat pants offset by a lime-green T-shirt, accessorized with white cotton socks and a hot-pink terrycloth headband. (I go to an all-girl gym specifically so I don't have to dress in cutesy exercise attire. But today was a paradigm shift. I resolved that after this was over, I'd invest in something a little less "relaxed"—and bug-ugly. In the meantime, I'd have to devote my next eight or ten paychecks to paying off cameramen for any film they might shoot of me dressed like a down-on-her-luck teenybopper.)

I exited the van and circled the corral with more stealth than most secret agents. Then I sprinted for the command center. A couple of cameras flashed, but nobody tried to stop me. The Suits were back inside the ranch house and I had the poor deputy so confused by now that he merely looked the other way and whistled "Dixie." I'd reached a set of metal stairs that led to the open door at the end of the long white trailer, when I suddenly heard two male voices. I recognized one of them.

"The scene is compromised," I heard Eskiminzin say. "There are footprints and tire tracks everywhere. It's inexcusable."

"I don't make excuses to you," the other voice replied. "I'm in command here and you answer to me if you want to work."

"I want to find the child."

"And you think I don't?" The other voice paused before continuing, "You're not the one up for reelection, Clay." The man who must be the sheriff changed tack. "What's the problem, anyway? They say you could track a man if he walked on water."

"They say a lot of things." Clay's voice was flat. Frustrated. "Anson, I'm telling you, there *are* no tracks. I can see where Connor Teagler walked into the house with his father last night. I can see where he played with his mother this morning, but I can't pick up a single trail that shows him heading away from the ranch house and not coming back."

"Could you have missed it?" The sheriff was almost pleading now. "You said yourself the area's compromised—overrun with people and cars."

Eskiminzin didn't respond.

"Tell me you might have missed it," the sheriff said. "Don't make me call in a whole bunch of federal agents just because we didn't clamp down soon enough on the traffic. Clay, we both know the FBI'll only make things worse than they are."

"As you said, it's your call," Batguy said. "That's why they pay you the big bucks and me in mesquite beans."

Eskiminzin's voice was closer now. I retreated from the stairs and flattened myself against the metal wall of the command center.

"One more thing," the sheriff said. "You know Reporter Barbie?"

My mouth opened of its own volition. *It's not necessarily an insult,* I reminded myself. *Maybe the sheriff's complimenting my curvaceous form and great hair more than he's speculating on the emptiness of my little plastic head.*

"What about her?" Clay asked cautiously.

"The senator wants you to take her along. She's an old friend of his wife's and he's impressed with the way she came all the way out here to help."

Huh? Either Alex Teagler was lying through his capped teeth or he'd been out in the sun too long without his Stetson.

"Send her with somebody else," Clay said.

"He asked for you specifically."

"No."

"Clay, Teagler's a United States senator," the sheriff said. "He may well become the next president of the United States."

"Is that meant to impress me or intimidate me?" By the tone of Eskiminzin's voice, it clearly did neither.

My heart was beating so hard it must have knocked on the side of the command center. The next moment Clay leaned out the door.

"Come in," he said. "As you know, we're talking about you."

I knew my heart hadn't really beaten hard enough to attract attention. Discounting sonar, how in the world had Batguy known I was there? The deputy was right. This guy was spooky.

I straightened my shoulders, lifted my chin, and walked up the stairs with as much dignity as a poorly-dressed-eavesdropper-with-almost-no-makeup-left-on-her-face can muster.

Although he looked as surprised to see me as I was to be seen, the sheriff politely introduced himself and then Clay.

"I'm Jillanne Caldwell from NewsChannel 2's *What's Up, Tucson?*" I said. Obviously, neither of them were big TV-watchers or they'd have been impressed; we have some of the highest ratings in the Southwest. "Shar Teagler is my best friend," I continued quickly, "and I want to help find Connor. I *have* to help. I'm his Primary teacher, you see, and I was in the newsroom when the first reports came in that he was missing and I had to beg Gene—Gene's my boss, the news director, though I'm only assigned feature—*anyway*, I had to beg Gene to let me get on that helicopter. And it was terrible, just so you know. I hate helicopters! I thought I was going to die. But I knew I was supposed to come because when I first heard about Connor my heart turned over and the Spirit told me—" It was a new low in information overload, even for me. Still, I paused only because I had to either draw a breath or pass out cold.

My impromptu oratory had one immediate effect. From his expression, it looked like I had convinced the sheriff that I should never have been released from the rubber room, let alone be sent out into the desert.

Clay regarded me in silence for several seconds, then said the absolute last thing I would have expected. He said, "Wash up as well as you can, Ms. Caldwell, and we'll leave in a few minutes." To the sheriff he said, "I don't want to tell you how to do your job, Anson, but if I were you, I'd consider calling the feds, because I'm afraid you're going to need the forensics team before this is over. In the meantime, I'd get some dogs out here to cover the ground between the ranch and the road in. See if they can pick up a single track circling around to someplace a vehicle might have been concealed off that road. If they do pick anything up, radio me. I'll head toward the bluffs until I find something to go on."

When Batguy turned back to me I hadn't moved, breathed, or processed what he'd said. His dark eyebrows rose. "Are you coming, Ms. Caldwell?"

"Miss!" I exclaimed. I don't know if I blushed or blanched, but neither is attractive when you're as fair as I am. "I mean, yes!" I managed.

"There's a sink over there." He motioned with his thumb. "Use it quick and I'll meet you outside at the jeep."

This time I blanched for sure. I was mortified. Sure, I'd breathed through my mouth when I changed into my gym clothes, but I had no idea they smelled *that* bad. I wanted to die—not to smell like I already had.

Eskiminzin almost smiled. "You're wearing Red Door perfume, I believe."

I nodded dumbly. The deputy had been wrong, I decided. This guy wasn't spooky, he was scary. I didn't think even a bloodhound could distinguish between Elizabeth Arden scents.

"Wash it off," he said. "Or every insect in the desert will be attracted to you."

Even with motivation like that, there are only so many places on your body you *can* wash when you're standing less than five feet away from a male county sheriff. I scrubbed my neck and wrists until they were raw and then headed back outside, wondering why scientists can't design fragrances to attract more men and fewer bugs.

In the time it took me to damage my delicate skin with cold water and cheap paper towels, Eskiminzin had changed clothes and commandeered a small jeep. (Batman wasn't that fast, and he had Alfred and a Batcave.) The ranger now wore a long-sleeved knit shirt that bulged in all the right places, and lightweight pants with drawstrings at the cuffs and more pockets up and down the legs than a beauty queen's makeup case. Both articles of clothing were cotton and had a camouflage pattern of browns and grays that was repeated in the canvas hat he'd pulled onto his head. I figured the ensemble was designed to make him all but disappear in the desert foothills. If, that is, he closed his eyes. I was willing to bet that on a clear day those blue eyes of his could be seen from outer space.

I climbed into the passenger's seat and automatically felt for a seat belt. There wasn't one—the awful thing didn't even have doors or a roof—so I gripped the metal frame of the seat. "I'm ready."

He might only have been exhaling, but I thought he sighed. "Do you have anything else to wear?"

I wanted to say yes, since I happen to own more clothes than most women in the Western Hemisphere. But none of the rest of my wardrobe was with me, nor did I think GI Joe here would approve of anything from my closets anyway. (I'm generally heavy on raw silk and surprisingly light on cotton camouflage.) I said, "No."

It *was* a sigh. I was certain this time.

"Tuck your sweatpants into your socks," he said. He turned in his seat to retrieve the leather bag he'd been carrying when he exited the helicopter. "I'll see what I have in my parfleche." It wasn't enough that the guy was well trained, articulate, and stop-traffic gorgeous, he had to be charitable to boot.

"What's a parfleche?" I asked.

He hefted the bag silently. There are times I believe my head really is empty plastic, and this was one of those times. "It's a French-Canadian word," he explained politely.

I nodded mutely and pulled my socks up over the cuffs of my sweatpants. (It is not a fashion look I recommend.) While I was bent over, I noticed that the thin fabric of Batguy's pants was pulled tight enough to reveal a line at his knee that could only indicate he'd been through the temple. (And don't tell me *you* don't look. We all look, especially if we're single.) I might have only been inhaling, but I think I caught my breath.

Clay tossed a long-sleeved, tan cotton shirt onto my lap. "That's going to have to do. Put it on."

I could have put it on me and two or three of my friends besides. Not that I disliked it. It smelled like sunshine and leather and nice guy. (The makers of aftershave don't bottle it, but they should.)

Next he took off his hat. As he passed it over he said, "Please tell me you're wearing sunscreen."

"Always," I assured him. "I wear sunblock to bed." Of course, I had probably just scrubbed most of it off my neck in the command center.

"Put on the hat anyway." He stuck the key in the ignition. "I won't take you out very far, but I like to be prepared."

Clay Eskiminzin: part Boy Scout, part bloodhound, part Greek god. How was a girl like me going to impress a Batguy like him—especially dressed like an out-of-work scarecrow?

I pushed the thought from my mind. I hadn't come out here to impress men—even men who'd impressed me first. I had come to find Connor.

Jill's Good Sense for Your Good-Scents Cents

If you hope to attract something besides insects, being subtle in your use of fragrance is the best way to go about it. I think cologne is better than perfume. (And it's less expensive besides!) Even though it's lighter, you still shouldn't spray it on yourself like a disinfectant. Instead, reach as high above your head as you can and squeeze off a single, short spritz in front of where you're standing. Then step into the light spray. The result is a delicate fragrance on your hair and clothes that doesn't yell, "Here I come!" before you enter a room. You know women who smell stronger than Bambi's friend Flower, don't you? Try to drop them a subtle hint. Hey, I know what you can do! Buy them their own copy of my book and turn down the corner of this page. You'll be doing your fellow breathers a favor. (And no, Great-aunt Myrtle, of course I don't mean you!)

For a fun fragrance for free, take a cereal bowl and line it with a piece of cheesecloth, allowing the fabric to drape over the rim of the bowl. Fill the bowl with flower blossoms of your choice. Since I live in a state with lots of citrus, orange blossoms are my favorite! Any flower that is highly fragrant will work (lavender, lilac, honeysuckle, rose, plumeria, etc.). Cover the petals with a cup of water and let them sit overnight—at least 12 hours. The next day, use the edges of the cheesecloth to pull the blossoms out of the bowl. Pour the scented water into a small saucepan. (Be sure to squeeze all the water out of the cheesecloth.) Simmer the water until you have only about a tablespoon left—a teaspoon if you want it potent. Cool, and then pour into a small, pretty bottle. (I buy them at the dollar store.) Dab your perfume on your throat and wrists and enjoy feeling as feminine as you've ever felt in your life! You can use your custom scent every day for about a month before it starts to go bad, longer if you refrigerate it.

chapter 6

"Why did you let me come?" I finally asked Clay after more than an hour of silence. I'd been riding shotgun, obediently following his direction to "Scan your side of the landscape for anything that looks unusual." Give me a break. I'm a city girl. Everything looked unusual. The usual outdoors where I come from is buildings, concrete, and asphalt. Everything out here was rocks, dirt, and cacti—and I saw it all up-close and personal.

There'd been no reason to hold onto my seat after all. We hadn't moved any faster than twenty miles an hour since leaving the ranch. We hadn't talked, either. My companion drove with his right hand while most of the rest of him leaned out his side of the vehicle. The only difference between this and what I'd seen him do on foot was that now he did it in wide arcs instead of complete circles. But he did it with more concentration than the average Sho-Lin master.

As much as I hated to break Batguy's concentration, I hated the silence more. I'd never been this quiet for this long. (I even talk in my sleep.) The silence, as they say, was deafening. I searched the dashboard, but the only radios in search-and-rescue vehicles are two-way things. (Go figure.) I *had* to hear the sound of a human voice. First I decided I'd try talking to Clay. If that didn't work, I figured I could always put my fingers in my ears and sing aloud. Anything to block out the din of all that silence. Maybe he hadn't heard me.

"Why did you let me come with you?" I repeated.

To my surprise, the jeep rolled to a stop and Clay shifted it into park.

I should have kept my mouth shut, I thought anxiously. *Maybe he's going to take me back to the ranch. Worse, maybe he's going to leave me here.*

I gripped the seat frame in case he planned to push me from the jeep, but with his eyes released from the ground, he only scanned the vast skies over the mountains. I followed his gaze. "Helicopters," I observed quickly, to demonstrate I was doing my part as a member of the "team."

He nodded. "They scare away the birds."

Birds? I wondered if scaring them was a good thing or a bad thing. *Who cares?*

Judging by the look on his face, Clay cared. "Birds see more than all the pilots and heat-seeking devices in the world," he said. "They can tell you where there's water, or unusual activity, or—"

He cut himself off, but I knew he had been going to say, "Or a dead body." I let go of the seat to peer steadfastly at the ground out my side of the vehicle. "Let's keep looking for Connor."

"Drink some water first." He reached behind the seats and pulled out a canvas water bag.

The canteen looked like it had seen active duty with General Custer. It was pretty safe to assume it didn't contain Perrier. "No, thanks," I said. "I'm not thirsty."

"When you're thirsty, you're already dehydrated. Drink."

I gingerly unscrewed the cap and dribbled a little of the tepid liquid onto my tongue. It tasted better than any bottled water I'd ever sampled. Since I'd lied about not being thirsty, I put my lips to the rim and took a long drink.

"I let you come with me because you're honest," Clay said.

I coughed out the last swallow.

He looked politely away to give me time to wipe the spittle from my chin, then continued, "Maybe the word I'm looking for is *sincere*."

I suspected he might be smiling and I wished I could see it. But when he turned back to me, his face was sober. "Where do you think I should look for the little boy?"

"*You're* asking *me*?"

He nodded as if it made perfect sense for an ace tracker to consult a second-place beauty queen in matters of life and death. "You said you *felt* you should look for Connor," he explained. "You went to a lot of effort to get here. You're his Primary teacher, so you have some stewardship." Clay opened his hands. "And I have nothing else to go on. So, yes, I'm asking you. Where do you think I should look?"

It was a good thing he took the canteen from my hands when he did, because my fingers had turned to plastic and it seemed to be spreading. I'd never felt more like Barbie in my life because, frankly, unless the activity is dress-up, I'm pretty much useless. Reporter Barbie *nothing*—I'm more of a Fashion Princess doll at heart. I wished I had a pretty pink box to hide in.

"Let me tell you about a great Apache warrior," he said, raising the canteen to his lips. After he had swallowed he said, "Her name was Lozen, and they called her the warrior princess. She was the sister of Chief Victorio. When he was killed, she threw in her lot with Cochise and Geronimo." He screwed the lid back on the canteen and lowered it to his lap. "It was a bad time for the Apache. The worst. Most of the Aravaipa and their sister tribes had been exterminated or imprisoned on reservations. The small band of Chiricahua that was still free was hunted like a pack of rabid coyotes."

I had no idea what this had to do with me, or with Connor, but I was enraptured by the story—or at least by his telling of it.

"Some say the band survived as long as they did because the One God, Usen, gave Lozen a gift—the gift of seeing that which was not yet there." He leaned over to return the water bag to its place in the back of the jeep. "Don't look so surprised. We may call Usen by a different name, but there's only one source of truth and inspiration."

I nodded.

"Lozen went often to the mountains to commune with Usen. When she came back to her people, she would know where their enemies were. Her little band would move before they could be found and killed." He flicked off the ignition. "They say she was never wrong." Batguy looked at me—really looked at me—for the first time. "Why don't we follow a good example, Sister Caldwell? After we've prayed, you can tell me where to look for Connor."

To say I was surprised wouldn't cover it. *Dumbfounded* wouldn't cover it. *Stupefied* might have come close. I was still frozen in my seat by the time he'd circled the vehicle.

"You *were* telling me the truth about teaching Primary, weren't you?"

I nodded and he smiled. As I had suspected, it was a sight worth seeing. "Then you're familiar with the custom of prayer?"

"Of course!" I said. "I just . . . I . . ."

He made a motion inviting me to join him on the desert floor. Meekly, I climbed out of the jeep and knelt across from him.

"Since you're at a rare loss for words," he said, "shall I go first?"

Clay offered a prayer that told me at once where he got his confidence and charity, and probably most of his job success as well. When I had recovered from the power of his ability to talk to God, I breathed, "Where did you go on your mission?"

"Tucson, Arizona."

I shook my head. (I'd have shaken it harder if I really thought the act would clear it any.) "But I thought you were born and raised in these mountains."

"I was born in Maryland." He looked bemused. "But I probably didn't really grow up until I came out here."

"Then you're not an Apache?"

"Yes," he said, "I am. By half of my lineage, that is."

There were approximately sixty-two million more questions I wanted to ask him. Before I could ask even one more, Clay bowed his head again and said, "Your turn."

Fortunately, even I am smart enough to know that praying aloud isn't a category in a beauty pageant or speech competition. It's a good thing, too, or I might have been too intimidated to speak after Clay's Enos-esque example. I believe that while people around you might hear you stumble over a word or accidentally slip in a "you" where you meant "thee," God doesn't hear the mistakes—he's too busy listening to your heart. So I did what I teach my Primary children to do. I told Heavenly Father how much we loved Him, and thanked Him for blessing us thus far, and then asked Him to please, please, please help us in our time of need. I asked Him to bless Connor and to lead us to him. Some way. Any way. The way He knew was best.

Clay was quiet after the "amen." When I started to speak he said, "Listen for the answer."

I listened for all I was worth. At first I thought I didn't hear anything. Then, after almost a minute, I heard the "chop, chop" of a distant helicopter, the "shh" of a hot gust of wind, and the gentle sighs of Clay breathing at my side. I thought of Elijah in his desert cave and how the word of God wouldn't come to me from the wind or a helicopter or even an Apache guide, good as he might be. It would come to me in a still small voice only I could hear.

Or else it wouldn't come to me at all.

More minutes passed. I knelt and prayed silently and listened until my eyes began to fill with tears of frustration. I was no warrior princess. Lozen saved all her people, but I couldn't help to save one little boy.

Before I could sob, a disembodied voice cut through the near-silence and made me jump. It wasn't the voice of God. It was only the sheriff hailing Clay on the radio in the jeep.

Sheepishly, he rose and returned to the vehicle to respond. I sat back in the dirt, trying not to feel grateful to the sheriff for calling at such an inopportune time. Maybe, I rationalized, I could convince myself that his call interrupted my meditation at just the wrong moment. Maybe it was *his* fault I didn't hear the answer. I didn't want to believe I wasn't hearing anything because I wasn't worthy of inspiration.

"Sorry," Clay said from the jeep after he'd talked to the sheriff. "Anson wanted me to know the dogs arrived."

A helicopter—a different one than I'd seen before—appeared from behind one peak and disappeared behind the next. "How many people are out looking for Connor?" I asked.

He shrugged. "A hundred . . . probably more."

"If he'd really just wandered off, wouldn't they have found him by now?"

"Not necessarily," Clay said. "In the first place, there's a whole lot of land to cover and they're just getting started. In the second place, little kids have a tendency to hide when they're lost and afraid. They often won't answer even when they hear searchers call their name."

"But the dogs can pick up his track and lead rescuers to him."

"Maybe." The way he said it made it sound like two words.

I sat back and wrapped my arms around my legs. "You don't think Connor wandered off."

"I don't know."

"But that's why you were walking in circles this morning. You were looking for Connor's footprints heading off into the desert by himself." I hugged my knees to my chin. "You didn't find any."

"I'm not infallible," Clay said. "Despite what you may have heard, I *can't* track people who walk on water."

I mustered a weak smile. "I'll bet you haven't tried. Nobody's done it in two thousand years."

He was staring off into the mountains again. I knew I wouldn't see anything if I looked, but I looked anyway. They hadn't changed much since the last time we'd stared at them.

Then it occurred to me that Clay hadn't asked me again where I thought we should look for Connor. He must have read the discouragement in my face and was too kind to wound the pride of someone with an already-broken heart.

That's the moment I realized he was married. He had to be. There wasn't a Mormon in existence who was that nice, that good looking, and that *male* who wasn't sealed forever in the bonds of holy matrimony. So what if he didn't wear a ring? He didn't even wear a watch.

"It's about eleven o'clock," he said.

I jumped. If this guy could read minds, I hoped he hadn't bothered with much of mine.

"Hungry?" he asked.

"No," I said. This time it wasn't a lie. I was discouraged and sad and scared to death for Connor, but I wasn't hungry.

"We should eat," he said anyway.

I watched him rummage around again in the back of the jeep and decided he probably had a year's supply tucked away in there somewhere. Prepared? This guy was prepared for everything from an afternoon outing to Armageddon.

"Sandwiches," he said, holding up two waxed-paper packages. "Courtesy of the Pinal County Sheriff's Office." He looked from one to the other, but didn't move either toward his nose. "Turkey or roast beef?"

"How well *can* you smell?" I asked, remembering how he had identified me outside the command center by a whiff of my perfume.

"Not as well as I can read," he said, jumping effortlessly down from the jeep and walking back to where I sat. He handed me the sandwich marked "turkey." "How's my guess?"

"Right on." I took the package and asked, "But how did you know what fragrance I was wearing?"

"Are wearing," he corrected.

Since my throat and wrists were still raw, I frowned.

"My sister uses the same brand." Clay unwrapped his food and bit into it, but he didn't sit down. His eyes were on the ground, sweeping toward the horizon in slow arcs. I wondered if he looked for people in his sleep, or if he slept at all when someone was missing.

I rose, thinking he'd want to get back in the jeep and resume our drive, but he didn't move. He studied the barren terrain and chewed.

As I've said, I'm not the silent type. Nor has subtlety's name ever been confused with Jillanne. Since his sister wasn't the relation I wanted to confirm, I ever-so-casually inquired, "And what fragrance does your wife wear?"

There was a pause before he said, "I'm not married." His tone was that of a man who'd been coerced into saying it a thousand times before and was tired of the sound of it.

Suddenly I felt like the kind of woman everybody tries to avoid at singles conferences. I jumped to my feet and headed toward the jeep. I might not be inspired, but I had just nailed insipid.

I hadn't taken two steps before Clay grabbed my elbow and pulled me back into his wall of a chest. "Watch it."

The "it" he told me to watch was the largest, mangiest, most terrifying tarantula to ever scrabble across the face of the earth. I'd never imagined anything like it in my worst nightmares. (And, as a card-carrying arachnophobe, I'd had some doozies.) This spider was about the size of a Pomeranian, but hairier. I have no doubt that people in inner-city Detroit heard me scream and got up to close their windows. With my fight-or-flight instinct now completely reengaged, I tossed my sandwich toward Canada and would probably have crossed the Mexican border before sundown if Clay had relaxed his grip on my arm.

"Take it easy," he said. "Breathe." Motioning back toward the spider, Clay added, "He has enough problems without you scaring him."

"Me?" I choked. "I . . . him . . . you . . . oh my heck!" I am very strong when I'm terrified. I managed to bulldoze Clay back ten or twelve feet before the thought crossed my mind that maybe tarantulas travel in packs and might even now be surrounding us. I froze.

"There's another one," he said.

They do travel in packs! I turned to scale up Clay's chest in order to reach his broad shoulders. I might have gotten up there, too, if he hadn't taken a firm grip on my shoulders first and turned me back around. "See?"

"We're not watching the Discovery Channel," I squeaked with my eyes tightly closed. "We're *in* the desert. I don't *want* to see!"

"That's his mate," Clay told me. "She'll stay with him until he dies."

Something in his voice sounded so much like admiration that I had to open my eyes. *Two* big, ugly, hairy, horrifying spiders trekked to who-knew-where. You can't imagine how fervently I wished I'd used the Porta-John outside the press corral before leaving the ranch. Thank goodness the disgusting duo moved *away* from us.

"A tarantula hawk got the big guy," Clay said. "That's why he looks so bad." When I didn't reply he added, "The hawk is a kind of insect. It preys on tarantulas with a paralyzing bite and then deposits its eggs into the spider. When the larvae grow, they feed on the host."

In other words, they eat him alive. My stomach and I were both glad I hadn't unwrapped the sandwich. I muttered, "And I thought *I* was the one who always gives people more information on a subject than they ever wanted to know."

"This desert is the most beautiful place on earth," Clay said. His hands slipped from my shoulders. "But it's also the most unforgiving."

I turned to see his eyes fixed on the mountains. I knew he was thinking about Connor. My breath caught in my throat.

When Clay finally looked down at me, his eyes seemed full of trust, but it was more likely that what filled them so completely was faith; faith in Someone lots more omniscient than me. In a voice scarcely above a whisper, he said, "There isn't much time to find him, Sister Caldwell. Tell me where to look."

To my surprise I didn't panic. I didn't even hesitate. Instead, I released the breath I'd been holding and felt one of my arms rise as if it were attached to a helium balloon. I pointed to the foothills at the base of the greatest of the majestic Galiuros. "I think we should go that way," I said. As soon as the words were out they felt right. I took a step forward and wondered if Brigham Young had been as sure as I was now on the day he'd declared the Great Salt Lake Valley home.

"Clay, I think that's the place."

Jill Nails Down the Facts of Life for Fabulous Fingers

Whether we're pointing out the Promised Land or clinging to the edge of a cliff by the tips of our fingers (Or is that getting ahead of myself in my story?), every woman wants to have hands that say, "Hold me."

For hands so soft he'll never let them go, try this routine at home. First, to slough off dead skin cells and remove discoloration, massage a rub of 1 tablespoon sea salt mixed with 1 teaspoon lemon juice into your hands. Rub vigorously for about five minutes. Rinse well. While your hands are still damp, apply a mixture of 1 teaspoon of honey and 1 teaspoon of olive oil. Slip your fingers into plastic or rubber gloves and then into cotton gloves. (I use gardening gloves.) Leave on for thirty minutes. The warmth from the double gloves will help the treatment penetrate. Rinse your hands again, dry gently, and then run find somebody's hand to hold.

To paint or not to paint? Now, while I think nail polish looks very pretty sometimes, I'd vote to take it off the "required" list for good grooming. To me, it's more of a special occasion thing. If you do polish, go light on the remover and give your nails a chance to go au naturel every other week or so. I promise you they'll be happier and healthier and will reward you by growing longer and splitting and chipping less. Besides, natural is in right now, especially in my line of work. You'll never see long, red nails in the Miss America pageant (nor black or green or purple or chrome). And next time you watch the news, pay attention to the hands of the anchors and reporters. Not one in fifty women wears a colored polish. (For that matter, the men don't use it much, either!)

chapter 7

It took another hour or so of careful, silent observation, but I finally determined that the Clay Eskiminzin model was marginally defective after all. He'd been shipped to mortality with only one speed, and it wasn't fast forward. Despite his belief that Connor was in danger (and my newfound certainty that I knew where to find him), another hour had passed and we still weren't looking. At least we weren't hiking up into the mountains calling Connor's name like I thought we should be. Instead, we'd only gone as far as the foothills when Clay started to do that little drive-back-and-forth-while-he-leaned-from-the-jeep thing he was so fond of. And did I mention he drove *slowly*?

"Is that a tortoise gaining on us?" I asked.

"I doubt it," he said. "There aren't many desert tortoises left out here. Besides, they'd be looking for shade this time of day."

Sarcasm is wasted on some people.

Most people would bite their tongue at that, and lapse back into the silence he obviously preferred, but I'm not most people. I tend to be chatty when I'm irritated. "How did you get to be an expert on desert flora?"

"Fauna," he said without lifting his eyes from the ground.

I bit my tongue after all. I *knew* that. How many times had I seen *Sleeping Beauty*? Aurora's three fairy godmothers are Flora, Fauna, and Merryweather. Flora is the one who makes flowers come out of her wand.

"What makes you an expert on the *desert*, then?" I asked, determined to press on despite my fairy faux pas. "There's none of it in Maryland where you grew up." I hoped this last bit was true. The only thing I knew for sure about Maryland is that most of a continent separates it from Arizona.

"I never said I was an expert," he replied.

"Other people say you are."

"People say a lot of things."

I'd heard that. Now I wanted to hear if any of the things they said were true. "People say you're a direct descendent of an Apache chief."

He finally raised his head, but he looked up into the mountains instead of at me. (Who could have predicted *that*?) "And if I am?"

"You have an Apache chief for a grandfather?" I said. "How romantic is that?"

"You've seen too many movies. There wasn't much quixotic in the first Eskiminzin's life—the *real* one—unless you think lice and hunger are romantic." His eyes returned to the ground. He'd resumed the quest, but I still didn't know what he—we—were looking for. "They tend to leave dysentery and a multitude of other daily humiliations off the big screen."

If you think a little rebuff like that would shut me up, you haven't been paying attention. "What do you mean, the *real* Eskiminzin?" I asked. "Isn't that your name?"

"It's my legal name," he said.

"You mean you changed it? Why?" Maybe it was something mysterious and romantic. Maybe it was an alias. Maybe he was in the witness protection program because his father was a mobster. Maybe—I remembered what he'd just said about romance and stopped speculating. My scalp has a tendency to itch if lice are mentioned twice in the same conversation.

He said, "I wanted to honor my heritage."

"Then shouldn't you have kept your father's name?"

The pause was longer now. I thought he wasn't going to respond, but then he said, "My great-great-great-great grandfather was the last full-blooded Apache in our family. When he was taken to the white man's school, they gave him a white man's surname. It's been our family name ever since. I merely changed the faux name I inherited to one of a forebear I admire."

If nothing else, Batguy was too polite to ignore a direct question. Add that to the fact that I make a living doing interviews, and it was clear that in no time at all I would know as much about this man as he knew himself. I smiled. "So you came to Arizona to dig up your roots?"

"I came to Arizona because I was called by a prophet of God," he reminded me.

Oh! Right. The mission to Tucson. (So much for Interviewing Rule #3: Before you ask a follow-up question, try to recall the answers to the ones you asked before it.)

"The rest was serendipitous," he added.

There he was using Ivy League words again. "Were you living in Maryland before your mission?" I asked suspiciously.

"No, I was at Harvard law school."

"Aha!"

The "aha!" may have been a little over the top. Clay was out of the jeep before I realized we'd come to a stop. My instinct was to follow, but when he jogged over a low ridge, I wondered if perhaps he'd been summoned by nature, so I sat where I was and looked up at the sky. There were no helicopters this far out, but no buzzards circled the peaks, either. There were only a few fluffy, silvery clouds stacking themselves up one on top of the other in the south. They were very pretty.

Clay was back in almost no time. He swung the jeep in a wide arc and headed back toward the ranch, but at a different angle than we'd come before and much, much faster than I thought this jeep could go. Or *should* go. Apparently it wasn't nature that had called him after all.

I hung on for dear life. Apparently, we were out to break a record for the amount of dangerous, rocky land that could be covered by a maniac driving an open jeep without seat belts. (Frankly, if I was going to go into a record book with him, I'd much rather have done it at a kiss-in.) Although letting go was a dangerous proposition, I used one hand to pull his hat down more securely over my head, then returned to my death-grip on the seat.

I didn't know if we were still scouting at this point, but figured we probably weren't. Even Clay Eskiminzin couldn't have distinguished the flora from fauna from rocks at the rate they passed outside where his door should have been. But he was still leaning out and taking it all in as if he thought he could.

"Look out!" I cried. With his eyes on the ground to his left I knew he was certain to hit the low outcropping dead ahead. I was right. I lost my grip, sailed up off the seat, and realized at once why a roof isn't standard issue in this type of vehicle. After a minute or two I landed back on the seat and wished I'd taken a nature stop myself. "I like helicopters better than jeeps," I whimpered. "And I hate helicopters."

"Hold on," was Clay's only response.

"To what?" He had a steering wheel. I didn't even have a door handle. Or a door. But I renewed my grip on the seat, and after what seemed like an eternity, Batguy displayed the intelligence and good sense of a crash dummy by whipping the car into a 180° turn and heading back toward the foothills from whence we'd just sped.

"Have you lost your mind?" It was more of a cry than a question—I'd long since lost interest in interviewing him.

"We've picked up some tracks," he said. But the words were mostly lost in wind that was rushing by faster—and hotter—than it comes out of my blow dryer.

Tacks? Good. I hoped punctured tires would impede this joy(less) ride long enough for me to catch my breath to scream. But we didn't slow down any. So much for my theory that this guy only had one speed. Was I ever destined to be right?

We sped on for another mile or more and then suddenly skidded to a stop, spraying loose gravel on the flora and causing any and all fauna in the vicinity to flee in terror. Clay retrieved binoculars from behind the seat and stepped out onto the hood of the jeep before I could ask him to pass me the moisturizer and the motion-sickness pills. (Surely he stowed them back there with everything else.)

His binoculars slowly panned the horizon. About the time I began to suspect he didn't know where we were any more than I did, he lowered the glasses, jumped nimbly to the desert floor, and examined the crushed rock beneath his feet.

I climbed from my seat and tried to stand. Newborn colts come equipped with legs steadier than mine were at that moment. After an awkward step or two, I draped myself over the hood of the car and tried to look more fascinated than frazzled. "What are we looking at?"

"It's an ATV," he said.

But what he pointed at was no three-wheeler. It was run-of-the-mill Sonoran soil with about six inches of tire tread imprinted on it.

"A unicycle?" I guessed in amazement. (In my defense, there was only one tread.)

He glanced up with a perplexed look, but it disappeared quickly. "Three-wheeled Yamaha Z60, carrying about 250 pounds."

"You know that from one little scratch in the dirt?"

"It's more than a scratch." He looked back in the general direction of the ranch and then off toward the foothills. "There was no sign of it at the house."

He was lost in his thoughts. I gave him a little while to find his way back out, but when it didn't look as though he'd ever return, I asked, "What does it *mean*?"

"It means you were right, Jillanne."

He'd said I was right. *And* he'd called me by my given name. I could stand up now. Heck, I could probably float. "*I* was right?"

He nodded and headed for his side of the jeep. "I've got to get you back to the ranch. I don't like the look of those clouds."

"You mean those pretty, puffy ones?" Who wouldn't like cotton-candy clouds? These looked as though they might literally have a silver lining. Or at least pewter. They had grown darker since the last time I'd admired them.

"If the storm breaks before I get back here, I'll never pick up the trail again."

I returned to my side of the vehicle, but I didn't get in. My head wasn't so far in the clouds that I'd missed the fact he wanted to dump me. "I'm not going back to the ranch," I said. "I'm going to help you look for Connor."

"No, you're not." He was in his seat with his hands on the wheel, clearly impatient. When I didn't climb into the jeep, he added, "It's dangerous."

"Like riding with you *isn't*?" Clay Eskiminzin was about to find out just how wide my stubborn streak was. "So far today I've braved a stressed-out news director, a helicopter jockey with a death wish, two senator's goons, spiders escaped from Hades, and Mr. Toad's Wild Ride." I crossed my arms over my chest. "I'm going with you. I'm not afraid of anything." That was true—I'm pretty much afraid of *everything*. "Just so you know," I added.

He was too polite—or too humorless—to laugh in my face. "These are professional, scary people, Ms. Caldwell."

I didn't have to know what the first part implied to know by the "Ms. Caldwell" that he meant business.

"Please get in the jeep," he said.

Men that strong are used to being obeyed. I wondered how far his innate chivalry would stretch before he picked me up and tossed me in the back with the rest of the extraneous gear.

"It's got to be thirty minutes or more back to the ranch," I pointed out. "Even if you drive like Batman on a good day, you'll lose more than an hour of search time right off." Something like a gas pain flitted across his face. "Plus, all those people back there will ask you where you went and what you found. Even if you can avoid them, what about me? Reporters are notoriously bad at keeping secrets."

I may not have known for sure what I threatened, but I knew when it worked. The pain on his face was mixed with something I could only pray was grudging admiration. Still, for a person in a hurry, Clay was slow to make up his mind.

I gazed up at the sky. "I don't like the looks of those clouds."

"Get in the jeep," he said, resigned at last.

I scrambled up beside him and clutched my seat while he once again followed the elusive scratches in the soil. He reached for the radio to report our position to the sheriff.

I was relieved to hear the sheriff's voice answer from the dashboard. It hadn't escaped my attention that we were the only searchers as far as the eye could see, and had been for some time. I was glad that would change now that we had a lead to report. Forget relying on watch birds for help; it would be comforting to have a few whirlybirds overhead, increasing our chances of finding Connor quickly. And it would make this vast wasteland seem more . . . civilized.

"You're going to have to ground the choppers," Clay said into the radio.

If I'd been chewing gum I would have choked on it. Or I might have spit it at him. What did he mean, *ground the choppers*? We *wanted* choppers. And more searchers. And dogs. Where were the dogs, anyway?

"No dogs yet," Clay said into the handpiece. "We don't want to spook these people. Let's keep a real low profile until we know for sure what we're looking at."

I was the one spooked. What *were* we looking at? I'd signed on to look *for* something. For Connor. And, I didn't want to keep the glory all to myself. I wanted help, and I wanted it now.

Jill's About-Face

Since my father was once a boxer, he used to tell me as a very little girl not to lead with my chin. It was one of many things he was wrong about. Unless you're a pugilist, your face will precede everything else about you. That's why it's important to care for it as best you can. I'm sure if you're older than eleven, you already know the basics of skin care, so I'll skip that and share a few things I've told people who've written to me with special questions.

What do I do about these awful crow's feet if I can't afford cosmetic surgery? One of the best wrinkle treatments you can find outside a dermatologist's office is Thompson seedless grapes. Really. Cut one in half and gently crush it into your face, paying close attention to those rotten crow's feet around your eyes. Leave on for twenty minutes, then rinse and moisturize. If you do it every day, I guarantee you'll be amazed at the results.

I have a date/interview/recital in an hour and a pimple on my face that's about the size and color of a maraschino cherry! What do I do? First you panic. (At least that's what I always do.) Then you run to the medicine cabinet and grab that tube of stuff Grandpa uses on his hemorrhoids. (I know it sounds awful. Do you want to shrink that zit or not?) Dab it on and watch it work a minor miracle. The swelling and discoloration will decrease enough for you to conceal the place with an extra dab of foundation. Be careful not to use it around your eyes, and always wash it off after the event has passed. Medicate your face with whatever you use for blemish control, and then pray it doesn't happen again. (It will. Pimples are the only thing in life as certain as death and taxes.)

Do you have a tip for great-looking foundation? Of course! I have a tip for everything. In the first place, tap the foundation onto your face with your fingertips or a makeup sponge. (Some women look like they use a trowel. Oh, no, Hortense. Of course I don't mean you!) Open your mouth while you apply it to your jawline—it will help you avoid leaving an obvious line. When you've finished, if you want a fabulous, dewy-fresh finish, saturate a gauze pad with witch hazel, and then barely tap it against your skin. It will remove the matte finish and leave your face simply radiant.

What do you use to take the makeup off your face? Frankly, I use the gentlest, cheapest products I can find at the drugstore. After a cleansing wash, I pat my face dry, apply a toner, and then moisturize. If, however, you're out of eye-makeup remover, petroleum jelly, baby oil, or even yogurt will work equally well. I also sometimes substitute witch hazel for my regular toner. As for moisturizer? Hey, you've got to splurge somewhere!

chapter 8

"Listen, Jillanne," Clay began. He'd signed off with the sheriff and then spent several minutes listening to my demands that he get back on that radio and call in the cavalry. He'd waited until my harangue had worn itself out before speaking.

"Jill," I interrupted. "My boss calls me Jillanne. The bishop calls me Jillanne. My mother calls me Jillanne when she's put out with me." I wanted Batguy to think of me as Jill.

"Jill," he repeated patiently. "This is serious business."

"I'm a serious person." (I didn't deserve the look he gave me. I really didn't.)

We were moving even more slowly now that we'd progressed from sandy, rolling foothills into more rugged terrain. There were still cacti and rocks, of course, but there were also bushes and small scrub oaks, stunted by the harsh conditions.

Batguy drove with one hand on the wheel, using half his attention to dodge the obstacles ahead and the other half to follow tracks only he could see. He did both effortlessly. "How much have you figured out?" he asked.

I hesitated to admit that the only thing I knew for sure was that he was better at carrying on conversation while multitasking than he had heretofore let on. The shrug I gave him was meant to convey a nonchalant I-know-everything-of-course-but-go-on-and-talk-if-you-want-to kind of thing.

It was impossible to tell if that was the message he got. "You know by now that there's a very real possibility that Connor didn't wander off?" he asked. "A probability, at this point."

I may have known it, but I didn't want to admit it. The only thing I could imagine that was worse than Connor being lost and alone in this wilderness was him being held—and perhaps hurt—by a kidnapper. "But if you think he was taken, why isn't *everybody* over here looking?" I blurted out. "Isn't that the theory behind Amber Alert? The more people looking for the kidnapper, the better! Why did you tell the sheriff *not* to send help?"

"This isn't a random abduction," Clay said. "These people know what they're doing." When I didn't respond . . . *couldn't* respond . . . he continued, "They must have set it up well in advance. They've probably been following the family for weeks, if not months. They knew how preoccupied the parents would be with Senator Teagler's announcement today, and they knew how many people would be in and out of the ranch because of it."

"Wouldn't all those extra people make them more cautious?"

"No," Clay said. "It's the break they were waiting for. With all the politicians and press around, nobody knew anybody else very well, and nobody knew who had charge of Connor and who didn't. Someone could have carried him down the road on their shoulders and nobody would have thought anything of it. Perhaps not even Mrs. Teagler, had she seen it. She would have thought he was just playing with one of her husband's several aides."

"Shar is a good mother!" I said sharply.

"I'm not saying she's not a good mother," he responded. "I'm saying somebody took advantage of the commotion going on at the Teagler ranch."

"Why didn't somebody spot the ATV? Why didn't you see the tracks?"

"It wasn't parked within a mile or more of that ranch," Clay said. "I think somebody carried Connor to the edge of the driveway and then took him by car far enough down the main road to safely transfer him to an accomplice waiting with a three-wheeler." He shook his head. "It was very well done. With all this land and the way that bike circled wide and kept mostly to the rocks, it could have taken me days to pick up the trail. If I ever did."

I was too miserable to glow with pride for pointing us in the right direction.

"They took such a circuitous route," he continued, "because they were counting on the fact that the first assumption would be that Connor had wandered off on his own. Everybody knows a little boy could never get as far as they've taken him; ergo, nobody is looking for him way out here."

"Nobody but us."

"Right."

Clay skidded the jeep into an abrupt halt and my heart skipped a beat. We were within six feet of the edge of a canyon. It wasn't much by Grand Canyon standards, but it was canyon enough to roll a little jeep ten or twelve times before we finally smashed to bits at the bottom. Except for the canyon, which obviously went down, the rest of the land headed almost as abruptly up. I didn't find the Galiuros quite as lovely now as they'd seemed from a safe distance, but there was no doubt they were one of the most impressive sights I'd ever seen. (I was way out of my comfort zone—which extends from the upscale fashion plaza in south Tucson all the way up to the factory outlet stores north of town.)

"End of the road," Clay said.

He'd turned in the seat to look through his Batbox of goodies. I wished I'd held onto that bag from the station instead of pitching it at Sean. I didn't know what all had been in it, but at least I'd have something of my own to rummage through. I felt silly sitting idly in the seat with nothing to do but contemplate how close we'd come to annihilation. I considered taking off the hat for a quick finger-combing of my hair while Clay's back was turned, but decided not to risk it. If there is anything less attractive than a windblown blond scarecrow, it's a windblown blond scarecrow with hat hair.

Clay placed several items in his parfleche and flung it onto the ground outside the jeep. Then he removed his walking stick and leaned it against the side of the vehicle, dropped the canteen next to it, and finally turned to me with both hands concealing a small object still in his lap. "Have you ever fired a gun?" he asked.

Do I look like Jane Bond? The closest I've come to Annie Oakley, even, was when I sang a jazzed-up version of "Anything You Can Do I Can Do Better" with Sean at the office Christmas party.

The anxiety attack that had been hovering at the edge of my consciousness since I first heard Connor was missing began to take over. (Whenever my eyes start to twitch and my toes start to vibrate, I know it's time to take the anti-anxiety medication the doctor gave me in Atlantic City. But those little orange pills were still in the makeup case, which was still on my desk, which was still at the station.) I blinked rapidly to cover the tics and curled my toes up in my tennis shoes. "Does laser tag count?"

"Did you hit anybody?"

"No."

Frowning, he turned a palm up to show me a small black revolver. "It has snake shot in it," he said. "You won't kill anybody with it, but you might slow them down. Aim for the center of the body. You have six shots. If I hear you fire, I'll come back as fast as I can."

Aim for the body? Snake shot? Come back? I didn't know which of the thoughts jangling through my mind was worse: maybe having to shoot a person, maybe having to shoot a snake, or maybe having to stay in this jeep all by myself. Horrified, I put my hands behind my back and used my curled-up toes to push myself away from the gun as quickly as I could. The result was that I lost my balance and fell out of the jeep.

"Jill?" Clay scrambled over the seats and peered down at me in concern. (Or maybe it was amazement—I have trouble telling the difference even though I get the look all the time.) He said, "Are you all right?"

"No," I replied with utmost sincerity.

"Don't move."

How he managed to exit the vehicle without stepping on my face is a mystery, but he did it. He knelt at my side, put his fingers just behind my ears, and then moved them carefully down toward my shoulders to determine if I'd broken my silly neck in the fall. I lay perfectly still, stared into his incredible eyes, and marveled that hands that looked so strong could be so gentle.

"You're shivering," he said—with genuine concern this time.

Yeah, I was, but it was only at his touch. Suddenly remembering where we were and what we were supposed to be doing, I sat up in embarrassment.

"You're okay?" His hands were still on my shoulders and his eyes were locked on mine.

Not only was I okay, I'd made a breakthrough that could set pharmacology on its ear. Little orange pills don't stop anxiety near as fast as a sudden, mortifying fall and the tender ministrations of a really nice guy. "I'm okay," I said. "But I'm not staying here by myself to shoot snakes." I looked nervously around, but no reptiles were in sight. "Or people," I added. This time my shudder had nothing to do with Batguy's touch.

"But I have to go in on foot."

"I have feet. Take me with you."

Clay shook his head. "There's nothing out here that doesn't prick, sting, or bite." He paused meaningfully. "Or worse."

"I've figured out that you think whoever brought Connor out here hasn't left yet," I said. "But you also said the ATV carried about two hundred fifty pounds. If forty-five pounds on it was Connor, then there can't be more than one guy with him, can there? Surely *you* can take one medium-sized guy. I'll stand back and watch."

Although I think I might have impressed him a little with my analytical thinking, he still wasn't sold on us as a dynamic duo. He rose and said flatly, "There are at least two men involved. Besides, I can move quieter and faster without you."

"Not if you have to drag me." I gripped his nearest ankle with both hands to prove that I intended to be a more faithful follower than Ruth. (Sure, my motives were less altruistic than hers, but whither Clay wentest I sure as heck was going to goeth too.)

"Jillanne—"

His tone indicated he might be nearing the end of his patience. I let go of his ankle (it *was* a little juvenile, now that I thought it through) and rose with my dignity hanging in shreds. "I'm sorry," I said. "That was silly." I brushed the desert off my rear and repositioned his hat over my ruined do. "I think the fall scrambled my brain."

He was too gallant to say, "No, you've been this way all along," but I could see that he thought it. He said, "Wait in the jeep. You have water. You have food. You have a radio and you have the revolver. You'll be fine."

I climbed back in the jeep and folded my hands in my lap while he went around the vehicle and gathered up his gear. I even managed a cheerful little wave to send him on his way. He'd gone about two hundred yards toward the side of one of the mountains before I leaped from the seat and ran after him.

"Hi," I said. It was all I could manage between puffs.

Clay didn't respond. He didn't even turn in surprise. He just kept nosing around a thick growth of bushes like he'd lost something in them.

After a moment or two I asked, "What are we looking for?" (*We* is such a warm, inclusive word, don't you think? It's at least twice as nice as *I*.)

Clay pulled away a piece of mesquite tree that had looked like it was rooted to the ground, but wasn't. "This," he said.

It was a three-wheeled ATV with "Yamaha" printed on the side. It didn't say "Z60" anywhere I could see, but I'd have bet my sunblock Clay was as right about the model as he had been about everything else. He knew what he was doing. If I wanted to help him—to help Connor—I'd be quiet and get my *I* back out of his way.

I turned silently back toward the jeep, but couldn't take more than a single step—my toes were curling up something fierce. "I get anxiety attacks sometimes," I whispered to a lizard sunning itself nearby. "I left the station so fast this morning that I didn't think to bring my medication." I sat on the ground but maintained my beauty-queen posture, determined not to dissolve into a pitiful heap until Clay was out of sight. "If you don't mind the company," I continued, "I'll sit here quietly." The reptile probably thought I was winking at it, but it was just those darn eye tics.

Clay's shadow fell over me and startled the lizard. It disappeared under a rock. I wished I could do the same.

One of his bronzed hands was wrapped around his walking stick, but he extended the other. "I've been thinking," he said. "Maybe it's a better idea for us to go into the canyon together, after all."

To this day I don't know whether Clay Eskiminzin really wanted me to participate in his new plan, feared I'd mess everything up if he left me alone, or only pitied me because I was pathetic. Nor do I care. I took his hand and let him pull me to my feet. My toes uncurled a little, but my eyes kept on winking.

"Take this," he said, handing me his stick, "and walk back toward the jeep."

I glanced back over my shoulder every few seconds to make sure Clay followed. He did, walking backward and dragging a large branch of some kind of bush along as he went. At last it dawned on me that he was covering our footprints, so that a person returning to the place he'd hidden his ATV wouldn't know anybody else had found it.

"Here's the thing," Clay said when we got back to where we'd parked. "It's vital that whoever has Connor doesn't suspect anybody's on to them."

"Why?" Although I'd determined to be a silent partner from here on out, my curiosity has always been stronger than my determination.

"Kidnappers are generally in it for the money," he said, "but they also tend toward cowardice. Not even a million dollars is worth their lives." He looked out across the canyon. I'd noticed that while Batguy didn't sugarcoat things, neither would he meet my eye when giving it to me straight. "There are thousands of places to hide a body as small as Connor's if this thing goes south. They know that without Connor or his body, we'd never get a conviction."

"You think they'd kill him?" I gasped.

"In a heartbeat." He caught the walking stick I dropped before it hit the ground. "That's why there are no helicopters, no deputies, and no dogs. There're only a couple of city slickers out for an afternoon hike."

I didn't know if the kidnappers would believe Clay's scenario, but I was willing to. I'd believe *anything* that would let me look for Connor and not stay all alone in the middle of nowhere.

It's a funny thing about being nowhere, especially if you've never been there before. It gives you a crash course on your importance in the universe. Nowhere is so *big*, and you feel so small . . . and so helpless. I'd never admired a lizard before. Now I knew that whereas it could spend an entire lifespan in my backyard and thrive, I probably couldn't survive a whole day alone out here in its world.

Unconsciously, I moved closer to Clay.

"Come on, Jill," he said.

They were the three sweetest words I'd ever heard in my life.

Jill's Anxiety Tics Aside, The Eyes Have It

There's no denying it—a woman's eyes are her greatest asset. Who doesn't admire eyes that are bright and shining? Probably the most dramatic and meaningful way to enhance your appearance and add sparkle to your eyes is to read Alma 5:14–16. When you've done that, we'll open the makeup case.

Eye makeup is a work of art. (I should know. I started using colored markers as eye shadow about the time I turned three. Bright orange is not, by the way, a look I still recommend to my friends.) As with lipstick, you can pay more for eye shadow and get less. I like to buy the sets of a zillion colors you can get for cheap in the after-Christmas sales. They not only last me all year, but I almost always find a shade that instantly becomes a new favorite. At any rate, you should include three basics in your shadow palette: pale, shimmering highlighters for just beneath your brows; classic, neutral matte tones for your eye lids; and deep, intense colors for glamorous contours at the crease.

Choosing an eyeliner and mascara is simple. Mascara should be compatible with your natural eyelash color—either brown or black. (The only exception I'll make is for very young women with blue/gray eyes. They can look simply stunning in that bright blue stuff.) To avoid globs, just pull the brush from the tube and apply. Despite what some women think, pumping it up and down like a tire pump hurts more than it helps. If you're in an emergency situation (almost out of mascara, I mean) you can dribble a couple of drops of contact solution into the tube. Although this won't work with waterproof mascara, it will give you an extra three or four uses of regular mascara. FYI: It's not a good idea to keep a tube of mascara lying around too long, nor should you ever share mascaras with your friends. Eye infections are easy to pick up, hard to get rid of, and never attractive to look at.

As a general rule, eye-defining pencils should match the basic color of the eye shadow you're using that day. To make your eyes seem a little larger and more wide-set, line only half of your bottom lids. (Start at the center of the pupil and move outward toward the corner of your eye.) As with the top, blend the liner to blur the definition. The Cleopatra look went out about the time she raised those asps to her bosom.

The rest is up to you. You can pick the colors, the combinations, and the intensities. Just make sure that the end result will make staring into your eyes the stuff of that special guy's dreams!

chapter 9

I believe in the Law of the Harvest. Or maybe it's the Theory of Relativity I believe in. The Law of Averages? Murphy's Law? At any rate, I believe in the law that says it's always best to be honest and to choose the right, because when you do, the Lord can bless you, and when you don't, it will come back to bite you in the rear when you least expect it.

Let me illustrate. When you were a kid, did you ever pretend to be sick because you didn't do your homework or you wanted to miss a test? And then did you get sick for real on the day of a field trip or something else you didn't want to miss? Well, sometimes it happens that fast. But sometimes it's years before the long arm of the law catches up to you. In my case it took a whole decade.

Confession: when I was fourteen years old, I twisted my ankle just before the third-year hike at girls' camp. (I was truthful about the twisting thing; I merely left out the part about how I'd used my own hands to twist it and that I could walk just fine.) So, while my friends and leaders hiked and sweated and developed character, I sat in the craft tent blissfully gluing sequins on a ball cap. Now, ten years later, not only had the lie finally caught up to me in a desert canyon, I wished I had the sequined hat. Ugly as it was, it beat the too-large commando look I sported courtesy of the Apache ranger. Still, being unglamorous was the least of my problems; being a liability to Clay as he searched for Connor was the greatest of them.

Not that I was out of shape. Flamingos carry more body fat than I do. It's mostly that girls' camp never did teach me to hike. And I don't walk either. For exercise I work out on fancy little machines set on polished floors. I drive to work, to church, and to my mailbox. If it weren't for shopping malls, my feet might never touch the ground.

Clay, on the other hand, probably walked from Maryland to Arizona. With him it was an art form. Despite the fact that his boots were big enough to have been worn on a lunar expedition, he never made a sound with them and he always seemed to know where he put them even when his eyes were raised to the mountains.

It seemed as though we walked for months, although it was probably more like a week. (Clay said it was just over an hour, but I was skeptical.) His instructions had been clear: I was to follow in his footsteps. Literally. While I knew it was to keep me from twisting my ankle for real or—horrors!—stepping on a rattlesnake, it was easier said than done. Not only were Clay's feet much bigger than mine, his legs were longer. At first I felt like I was playing Mother-May-I-Take-A-Giant-Step. Then I settled on Follow the Leader and scrambled along after him as best I could. I suspected we looked something like a gooney bird trailing a gazelle.

It wasn't long before I knew that (a) I should have gone on that hike at girls' camp ten years ago, and (b) I should have stayed in the jeep today. But since I couldn't change either decision, and with Connor's life on the line, I was determined that (c) no matter what, I wouldn't complain; (d) no matter what, I wouldn't slow Clay down; and (e) no matter what, I couldn't keep up. I would die in this canyon. I looked around for a suitable rock upon which to expire.

"You okay?" he asked over his shoulder.

"Great," I wheezed, figuring I'd be dead long before that lie caught up to me.

Clay stopped abruptly. With my eyes busy searching for snakes and/or potential death biers, I butted into him.

"Whoa," he said, turning in time to catch me by the elbows before I fell backward. (Even during all that pageant training, nobody ever called me "Grace" and meant it.) He righted me before pointing at the ground. "Look at that."

Instinctively, I closed my eyes. I'd already seen enough terrifying desert fauna to last well into my nursing-home years.

"Do you recognize it?" he asked.

I cautiously opened one eye. No spiders. I opened the other and looked closer. "Yes," I said. "I recognize it. It's dirt."

He crouched on his toes and used his index finger to point to what might have been a triangle stamped next to a square in a dusty patch of otherwise rocky soil. "Cowboy boots," he said. "Child-sized."

"Connor!" I gasped. "He loves his cowboy boots. He wears them to church with this little gray suit and looks just . . ." For once, I hadn't the heart to share more needless information.

Clay nodded. Though there were mountains overhead to stare into, this time he scanned the walls of the box canyon.

Having written that, I wonder if maybe "box canyon" is something I read in a Zane Grey novel that stuck in my mind, but doesn't fit the description. You decide. One side of this place rose almost perpendicular to the basin and you'd have to strain your neck to see up to the mountain peak that formed its upper rim. The far side was similar, but didn't look quite as steep or as high. Although I could say we stood next to a "canyon wall," it and the fourth side that adjoined it were really more like mountainsides broken up by occasional sheer rock faces which could be scaled only by insects. In other words, though I wouldn't recommend it, you could only hike two sides of this canyon if you knew what you were doing and used a series of long switchbacks.

(If this still doesn't give you a very good picture, I suggest you peruse an issue of *Arizona Highways.* Any issue should do. And try to remember I'm a city girl, would you? I prefer my canyons civilized, with paths maintained and labeled by the National Park Service.)

We had cut back and forth across this particular wall so many times on the way down that it felt like we were pacing. I didn't know if it was to make the hike easier for a rookie (me), or if Clay was looking for tracks. I assumed it was a little of both.

"They stopped here," he said.

Forget where they'd stopped—I was more concerned with where they'd gone. It began to occur to me that my impetuosity and love for Connor had gotten me into more than I had bargained for. What business did Reporter Barbie have tracking hardened criminals? What would I do if we found them—interview one while Batguy sneaked up on the other from behind? I was only slowing Clay down and probably risking his life and Connor's. My eyes began to tic. In another minute I'd probably be flicking Clay with tears.

"I lied to get out of a hike at girls' camp!" I cried. (Of all the things swirling around in my head that I could have blurted out, I had to choose *that* one?)

When he finally realized he was staring, Clay closed his mouth and looked carefully away.

"It's the Law of *Something!*" I explained. "It's irrevocably decreed in heaven." Clearly, he still didn't understand, so I expounded. "It's like when you tell one guy your aunt died because you want to go out with a different guy on Friday night, then the guy you *do* want to go out with doesn't ask you."

He was trying to understand; I could see it on his face.

"Or when you lie about being sick," I added. "Or—" It suddenly occurred to me that at this point Clay might be wondering just how much experience I had with lying. "Not that I lie a lot," I amended quickly. "Really. That's the truth." I sank down on the nearest boulder. It was as good a funeral bier as any.

Clay swung the water bag from his shoulder and extended it. "I think you've been in the sun too long."

I accepted the bag and took a drink. The water tasted great. The rock felt warm and wonderful beneath me. It was a great place to die.

"Sit a few minutes," Clay said. As if I had any intention of ever rising again. He probably had another sixty or eighty miles in him, but he lowered himself politely into a crouch.

I moved over a little to make room for him on my bier. "You couldn't possibly be comfortable like that."

"You'd be surprised," he responded. "My Apache ancestors could sit this way for hours. Days if they had to."

"But it looks like you're ready to jump up any minute." As soon as the words were out, I knew that was the point. I also knew that if I tried it myself I'd fall on my face, so I sat tight. "How long did it take you to learn to do it?"

Clay smiled. (Or was it the sun peeking from behind the heavy clouds?) "It doesn't take long to learn, but it takes years to master."

"Who taught you?"

"A man named Chee," he said. "A shaman." After he'd taken a drink of water he added, "A shaman is the medicine man, or the wise man, of a tribe. The position's often passed down from father to son.

Chee's line persevered and recited the old ways, even on the reservation. Since the Apaches had no written language, all that is remembered is what was told by the elders. When it was possible, Chee's father brought him back to the Galiuros to teach him. Chee revered the ways of these mountains all his life, but he never had a son to leave his knowledge with."

"Until you," I said.

"I'd like to think so." The tracker's eyes were on the mountains. (I realized now that when he looked at them he was seeing something I didn't. Probably lots of things.) "I knew when I came to Arizona that one of my father's ancestors had been Eskiminzin's child of his old age. But until I met Chee, I never knew what it meant to be Apache."

"Where did you meet him?"

One corner of Clay's lips turned upward. "Would you believe I was tracting? I spent the last quarter of my mission on the San Carlos Reservation. On my next-to-the-last day in the field, I happened to be in the same place at the same time as Chee." The way Clay said "happened" told me he didn't consider it a coincidence—maybe one of the greatest blessings of his life. "I went back East long enough to see my family and withdraw from law school for good, and then I came back here."

"How did your parents feel about that?" I asked.

He shrugged. "My family would probably trade me straight across for Alex Teagler. Grandfather, especially."

"They aren't proud of their heritage?"

"They're proud of it all right, but mostly my mother's—the side that came over on the *Mayflower*. We save my father's Apache ancestry to entertain people at cocktail parties." He stood. "As disappointed as they are in my so-called career, they're not surprised. After all, I was 'foolish' enough to join the Church during my senior year at Harvard. They pretty much wrote me off when I put in my mission papers after one year of law school."

"But you still see them?" I pressed.

"Sure. Thanksgiving. Mother's Day. Whenever Grandfather's up for reelection."

Reelection? Harvard and the Mayflower? Who is this guy?

Before I could ask, he tossed me his walking stick. "Use this," he said. "We'll go a little slower from here on out."

"I'm fine."

"Humor me."

I'd already learned that Clay didn't talk and walk at the same time. At first I had assumed that, like lots of the best-looking men I'd dated, he couldn't. Only after some time and careful observation did I realize how many things he was doing while I had to concentrate solely on not falling down the canyon. He walked without making a sound, maybe because there were so many things he wanted to listen to . . . look at . . . smell. He probably got more news out of his surroundings than most of us glean from the *Tucson Citizen*.

After another thirty minutes or so, he again stopped abruptly. This time I was paying more attention and managed to avoid running into him.

"Did you hear that?" he asked.

"What?"

He shook his head, straining to hear.

"Thunder?" I guessed. There was a good reason Clay hadn't liked the looks of those clouds. I didn't much like them myself now. Forget cotton candy—these things had turned into steel wool. But their color was off; even I knew that. Thunderclouds are black, gray, and silver. These clouds tended toward brown and copper at the bottom. They were rusty steel wool—strange and more than a little scary.

"No," Clay said. "It's not thunder."

As much as I strained, all I could hear was the rising wind, the cry of birds I couldn't identify, and the rush of blood in my ears as my heart beat faster at the look on Clay's face.

He stared up at the canyon lip from whence we'd come. His eyes narrowed and fine lines of concentration etched his bronze skin. In a moment he had come to a decision. In the next moment the parfleche and canteen were at my feet and he was ten feet back up the canyon wall. No switchbacks or meandering now. Clay climbed the mountainside in a straight line and did it with almost as much ease as the average mountain goat.

"Get out the radio," he called back to me. "Tell the sheriff we're in Del Gato Canyon, about twenty-five miles southwest of the ranch. Tell him the dust storm will be here within the hour, so he'd better get those choppers grounded now. When it's blown over, the tracks will be gone, so we'll either have to bring in the dogs or wait out the kidnappers. Got it?"

I stared up at him dumbly.

Another fifty feet up, he paused in his climb to look down at me. "See that overhang?" he yelled. "Climb under it and wait for me there. Get out the radio and the gun. Tell the sheriff we're in Del Gato Canyon. Whatever you do, don't move from that spot." As an afterthought he added, "Check it for scorpions first."

It's amazing how fast dumb can turn to dread. "I . . . Clay . . . I can't . . ."

"Yes you can," he said. "Do it now." He climbed a little farther before turning back. "Jillanne!" he hollered as if speaking to Lot's wife, post-pillar. "First, get under the overhang, then use the radio. *Do it*!"

I did. At least I tried. I approached the overhang with less excitement than I would've a headstone with my name on it. Check for scorpions, he'd said. Sure. I knew how to do that. *Not.*

"Okay, scorpions," I yelped. "Allee-allee-out-come-free."

Nothing came out. Either there were no scorpions under that ledge or they didn't know how to play hide-and-seek.

I used Clay's stick to prod the dirt and sweep the corners. Nothing moved.

I sat down and ever so gingerly edged myself backward under the rock, fully expecting a centipede to race up my leg or a scorpion to drop down my back. I had to bite my lips to keep from screaming. Finally, I settled in cross-legged like a wild-eyed Buddha figure and reminded myself to keep breathing.

It was several minutes before I could force a coherent thought through the haze of *Oh-my-heck-I'm-all-alone-in-the-desert-and-I'm-going-to-hyperventilate-from-all-this-deep-breathing*. At last I remembered the radio. I crawled far enough out of my den to grab Clay's bag and drag it back in with me. I untied the thongs that secured the flap and fumbled around inside without looking. Fortunately, the walkie-talkie was on the very top so I didn't have to see anything else that might have been in there—though the thought of a snake-bite kit came to mind. Why hadn't Clay told me to check for *rattlers*? I almost bolted from my seat until I remembered that snakes are bigger than scorpions. If I hadn't seen the one, I probably hadn't missed the other.

I turned my attention to the radio and tried to remember what Clay had called this canyon. *Bell Grotto? Del Monte?* I didn't know. I only hoped I'd come close enough to the name for the sheriff to know where I was talking about.

What I didn't know was what I'd say if he asked me where Clay had gone, or why he'd gone there so fast. I leaned out from beneath the overhang and saw that Batguy was already two-thirds of the way back to the top of the canyon. As fast as he moved, I knew it wasn't nature beckoning, if you know what I mean.

As it turns out, my ability to work a radio is roughly on par with my ability to search out scorpions. I turned a knob. Then I turned another. Then I found a little button to depress and pushed it so hard I broke my thumbnail.

Maybe it's a newfangled voice-activated thing, I thought. Optimistically I called into it, "Can you hear me, Sheriff?"

He couldn't.

I turned another dial. "Somebody answer me!"

They didn't.

After fiddling with it for another ten minutes with no success, I whacked the little piece of equipment against the rock at my side. "Work, will you?"

It wouldn't.

I threw it out of my cavelette in frustration and clutched Clay's bag to my chest.

"I will not panic," I told myself. "I will not panic. I will not panic." A little tic began in the corner of my left eye, so I closed both eyes tightly and curled my toes into my shoes while I prayed. No super-economy prayers this time. I figured I had the rest of my life—all thirty minutes or so of it—to talk to my Heavenly Father.

Miraculously, more than thirty minutes later, sometime after the ninth or tenth *Thank you for there being no scorpions or snakes in here and please bless Connor*—probably about the time of the second *And please forgive me for lying at girls' camp*—I fell asleep.

Jill's Motto: If You Don't Snooze, You Lose

There are only a few things in life to which I'm really dedicated. The gospel of Jesus Christ is number one. Good, clean romantic comedies and sleep round out the top three. A good night's sleep—not to mention catnaps now and again—offers a plethora of beautiful benefits. It can make you feel more alert and alive. It can increase your energy level. It can even provide an instant "face-lift" by helping to eliminate those under-eye circles and bags more efficiently than any concealer on earth.

I can "power nap" anywhere, anytime and wake twenty minutes later feeling like Aurora right after Prince Philip's arrival. Here's what you do. (1) Make yourself as comfortable as possible. (Personally, I prefer my soft, chintz couch at home, but if rocky ground is the only thing available, I make do.) (2) Clench every muscle in your body. Concentrate. You have more muscles than you think you have. (3) Now, starting with your face and jaw, slowly begin to relax every one of those muscles. It's harder than it sounds. Keep practicing until you can do it without effort. (4) Inhale slowly. Your tummy should rise and you should feel light as a balloon. As you inhale, say to yourself, "I am utterly relaxed." (5) Exhale slowly. Expel every bit of air from your lungs. As you do, say to yourself, "I will wake in twenty minutes, refreshed and invigorated." (6) Repeat the breathing exercise. As you do, visualize the most beautiful place you've ever been. See every detail. Smell the breeze. Feel the sand between your toes. (Or the grass, or thick carpeting, or whatever you love.) Hear the surf or your favorite music wafting softly nearby. If a thought comes to you, let it drift away like a puffy cloud. (7) Wake to the remarkable automatic alarm clock in your body, exactly twenty minutes later, feeling fabulous. Try it. You'll like it. (But don't try it right now—you have a book to finish!)

chapter 10

"Jill?"

You know what it's like when you're having the most wonderful dream in the world and you wake abruptly to discover it's only half true? (You *are* with the dream guy, but you're *not* on a white beach a thousand miles away from any and all scorpions and kidnappers.) That's how it was when I opened my eyes and saw Clay Eskiminzin bent over, peering in my little cave. Conking my head on the low overhang brought me to my senses before I wrapped my arms around his neck, buried my face in his chest, and sobbed out my relief that he'd come back for me.

"You okay?"

"Yes," I breathed, scuttling forward like a crab.

"Don't come out," he said.

It was only then that I realized that while there was sand everywhere, just like in my dream, this sand wasn't beneath us—it was swirling madly in the air accompanied by a roar that sounded like a diesel truck. This was ten times worse than being under the whirling blades of a helicopter. I pulled the canteen into my lap with the bag and scooted over as best I could to make room in the small space.

Clay edged in next to me. "It's the jeggo."

"The what?" But I didn't really need a definition, since I'd already figured out that *jeggo* must be the Apache word for "the end of the world."

"It's a Pima word for 'the wild wind of the desert.'" He took the parfleche from my lap and retrieved two pieces of flannel from it. Passing one to me, he said, "Hold this over your face and breathe through it. One thing about these storms, they don't last very long."

I had only been awake for three minutes, but that was already too long to face this. The air was so charged with static electricity that I felt the hair rise on my head and arms. I clutched the cloth over my nose and mouth in gratitude. I'd never particularly liked the few freckles that dot my otherwise flawless complexion, but that didn't mean I wanted them sandblasted off.

"Cover your eyes, too," Clay instructed. From beneath his piece of red flannel, he said, "The wind blew. Dust it blew along the ground and cast it upon my face." It was a minute before I realized he was reciting an ancient Apache poem. "Twigs and gravel it blew along the ground and tangled them in my hair," he continued. "It was my wind. The wind of my people. Behind me it came whirling. The standing trees it went shaking. The desert rubbish it went piling high. The coyotes they ran to their covers."

"It's beautiful," I said when he had finished.

"The jeggo was one of the Apache's greatest blessings," he said.

It amazes me what some people can survive, let alone what they'll feel blessed by. The wild wind of the desert was very low on my list of things to appreciate—below cacti, although certainly above snakes and scorpions. "What in the world did the Indians like about it?"

"Mostly the fact that it obscured all traces of their trails," Clay replied. "And sent the coyotes running to cover. The coyotes were the white soldiers who pursued them so relentlessly." Before I could respond he said, "It's not a blessing for *us*, however. Our blessing is the modern technology you used to tell the sheriff where we are right now."

I released the flannel. Clay caught it in the split second before it blew away and let go of his own face covering to hold mine in place. I worried that when I confessed that I couldn't even work a radio, he'd use the cloth to strangle me instead.

"I couldn't work the radio," I murmured into his hands, almost hoping he wouldn't hear me. I was out of luck.

"Where is it?"

I pointed out into the howling dust storm, grateful not to be able to see his face.

"Hold this."

When I raised my hands to the fabric to comply, I felt him move away from me. In the next second he was gone. "Clay!"

I don't know if he couldn't hear me, couldn't answer because all the dust and dirt choked him, or if this time he had left me for good. Not that I blamed him.

I think I will forever define eternity as the time Clay was out in that storm. When he finally heaved himself back down next to me, I lowered my piece of fabric in relief.

"Put it back," he said at once. "One of us has to be able to see when this is over."

It only took a glance to see that his eyes were red from irritation, that his dark hair was almost gray from grit, and that he had sand in every crevice of his face. Dirt caked the corners of his lips. He looked wonderful.

"Did you find the radio?" I asked.

"Yes." He didn't bother to explain how he'd done it in zero visibility.

I waited to hear what he'd say to the sheriff. Funny thing was, Clay didn't seem in any hurry to use the thing now that he had it. I nudged him. "Aren't you going to call?"

"Did you get any static?" he asked in reply.

"No. No matter what I twisted or pushed, nothing happened." I heard his long exhale of breath even above the wind and lowered my flannel an inch or so, just in time to see Clay knock the radio against the wall. "I already tried that."

He scowled.

"Could it be the batteries?"

"I don't know."

"Can't you fix it?"

"Believe it or not," he said tersely, "small appliance repair wasn't one of the things Chee taught me, nor Harvard for that matter."

The wind screeched and moaned and grated on my already-raw nerves.

"Stupid. Stupid. Stupid," Clay said.

I wondered if he meant me or the radio.

In the next moment, I knew he meant himself. "I should have checked it. I always check it. But I've never had a problem with Anson's equipment."

I didn't want to ask, but I had to know. "Does this mean you're going to have to climb that cliff again to use the radio in the jeep?"

It was a long time before he responded. "The jeep isn't there."

I moved my fists away from my ears, certain they had muffled my hearing.

"The sound I heard earlier," he continued, "was somebody taking the jeep."

"Wow," I said without thinking. (It's a gift, remember?) "I wonder why they wanted it. It's not much of a car."

He muttered something, but mercifully I missed it. I pulled the flannel more securely over my face.

In a few minutes, with the storm showing no signs of abating any time this century, Clay leaned back next to me. Despite my embarrassment at my stupid remark—despite everything—there was something very comforting in the feel of his arm against mine. "Do you think Connor is out in this?" I asked.

"I hope not."

After another interminable silence I said, "Who do you think took the jeep?"

"I don't know."

"Don't know or won't say?"

Clay stretched out his legs. A guy his size needed more room than we had available. "I don't think it was a random theft by joyriders, if that's what you mean."

"Then the kidnappers know we're down here?"

"Somebody does."

I pulled up my knees to try to give him more room. "But not the sheriff?"

"No. The last place I checked in with Anson was ten miles from here."

Ten miles didn't sound too bad. "So is that where they'll start to look for us when the storm ends?"

"No," he said. "They'll start to look wherever the jeep is left for them to find. Probably thirty miles from here." He considered, and then added, "There's something else you should know. They won't start looking anytime soon. A storm like this decreases visibility to almost nil and the effect lasts for hours. By the time they could get the choppers back up it will be fully dark."

Even with my eyes closed—especially with my eyes closed—I had a pretty good picture of our situation. Somebody, probably the kidnappers, knew we'd followed them here, so they waited until we were well in the canyon and then they took our jeep. They'd leave it miles and miles away to make sure anybody who came looking for us would think we'd gone another direction. The storm would obliterate any tire tracks we might have left behind. We'd have to spend the night—if not the rest of our abbreviated lives—in this canyon.

I said, "Why don't they just shoot us and get it over with?"

You'd think he'd have heard of a rhetorical question, what with graduating from Harvard and all. "I'm sure it's occurred to them," Clay replied. "My best guess would be that they don't have silencers on their guns, and don't want to risk attracting attention. In clear weather, a gunshot can echo fifty miles or better."

"When the storm ends we'll fire your gun!" I exclaimed, surprised he hadn't thought of it himself. "Somebody will hear it and come rescue us!"

"If we do that," he said, "what do the bad guys have to lose by shooting us?"

I simply *had* to start thinking before I spoke. "Then, what *are* we going to do?"

He'd apparently already made up his mind and was just waiting for me to ask. "We're going to do what Geronimo did."

Attack a wagon train? Bedevil the U.S. Cavalry? Surrender and spend the rest of our lives on a reservation or the Wild West Show circuit?

Before I could decide, Clay scooted forward. "We're going to disappear into the bottom of the canyon," he said. "Then we're going to find them before they find us." When I lowered the cloth from my face, I saw him carefully folding his own into a long strip which he tied around his forehead under his longish hair. "Apache warriors wore red flannel for luck," he told me.

I began to fold my fabric as I had seen Clay do. Not only did I want to feel like Lozen, the Apache warrior princess, I had a very strong feeling that we were going to need all the luck we could get.

A Personal Note from Jill: *By now, you're probably looking forward with bated breath to whatever helpful hints I might have to offer next. (Or else you're turning the page really fast when you come upon one of my columns.) Either way—surprise again! Fom here on out, I won't have something to say between every chapter. I'll only include my tips when something in my story reminds me of something that I just have to share. Toward the end, when I get really wrapped up in telling you about how we almost died, the tips will probably disappear altogether until after the thrilling climax. Just so you know.*

chapter 11

"Apaches could disappear," Clay explained. He'd put the canteen in the bag with the worthless radio and shouldered it. "They did whatever they had to. Sometimes they'd strip and wrap themselves in yucca shoots. Then they'd drag their naked bodies across the desert floor over rocks, cactus, whatever."

"Oh . . . my . . . heck."

Even in the rust-colored gloom I could see him almost smile. "We're not going to do that."

"Thank you," I murmured sincerely to the heavens.

"But we *are* going to move out."

"Now?"

"Now."

I squinted out into the maelstrom. "We're just gonna walk right out there into that storm?"

"Yes. The kidnappers probably know where we were when the storm blew in. We don't want them to know where we are when it passes. We'll use the jeggo to cover our tracks." Before I knew what he was doing, Clay tore a two-inch strip from the bottom of his long, tan shirt—the one I happened to be wearing at the moment—and wrapped it around my hot-pink sweat band. Then he looped it around my head just below my eyes. Next he secured my piece of flannel under it so it covered my mouth and nose and plopped the hat back on my head. "You're ready."

"Do I look like a beautiful, mysterious harem girl?" I asked hopefully.

"No." (Count on a Harvard-educated, desert-trained, blue-blooded Apache RM if you ever need brutal honesty.) "But you don't look so much like a sitting duck, either."

That was something.

"Hold onto the back of my shirt," he said, "and stay as close behind me as you can. It'll help cut the wind in your face." I was going to ask about his face, but he'd already pulled the collar of his knit shirt over his mouth and nose and crawled out of our shelter. "Keep your eyes closed as much as possible. You don't have to worry about watching for snakes. They've all headed for cover under the overhangs."

Suddenly, I was much happier to leave our rock pile than I'd been the second before. I grasped a handful of Clay's shirt and pushed him forward.

In no time at all we'd fallen into a routine for traveling through dust-storm purgatory. Clay pushed through gale-force winds by sheer power of determination. I stumbled along behind, tripped over a rock (or a branch or a bush or my own two feet) and fell into Clay. He paused long enough for me to right myself against his back, and then we moved on.

"It's letting up," Clay said after my fifty-third fall. (Give or take a dozen. It was easy to lose count with the wind ripping thoughts from my head before I could think them.) "We need to pick up the pace. I want to be at least a couple of miles from here before the storm's over."

Over? I had no idea where he got the idea that this storm would ever end. Or even let up. The known world extended no more than a couple of feet in any direction. Beyond that, everything was a mass of whirling, screaming, scratching dirt and debris. I remembered a story my grandfather liked to tell about the devil taking a vacation in Arizona. Lucifer left after an hour or so, the story goes, saying he preferred Hades—it was cooler and they had more water and less wind besides. Who knew Grandpa's story was *true*?

"Hold on," Clay said as he walked a little faster.

It was needless advice since the average vise has a looser grip than I had on that man's clothing. There was no chance whatsoever he could leave me behind. "Can you see where you're going?" I called up to him.

"No."

Hadn't anybody ever told George Washington up there that there are times when a person might *appreciate* a little lie? "Then how do you know we're going the right way?"

"We are."

"What if we fall off the side of a cliff?"

"We'll save the bad guys a lot of effort."

That made me feel better. (I don't know about you, but when people are out to kill me, I hate to make it any easier on them than absolutely necessary.) Still, mine was not to question why. Mine was but to follow Clay or . . . die. I followed Clay.

"Here's where it gets tricky," he said after we'd covered more wilderness than Lewis and Clark saw in their combined lifetimes.

I let go of Clay's shirt and collapsed into a done-in, discouraged, and *dirty* heap. My shoes were full of sand. My clothes were full of sand. Even my mouth, ears, and eyelids were full of sand. At this point I figured I weighed about a ton. A hundred and ten pounds of me was Jillanne Caldwell and the rest was the native soil filling my pores. At least the buzzards wouldn't eat me when I died because I'd be too gritty.

"Not to be a spoilsport," I gasped, "but I don't like the sound of 'tricky.'"

Clay turned and used his stick for balance as he did the crouch-thing beside me. It was only when he didn't immediately blow on top of me and crush me flat that I realized the wind *had* let up. Still, visibility was as bad as he'd said it would be. With no rain to follow the wind, the dust particles would be airborne for hours.

"You okay?" he asked kindly. "You've done great."

Ha! He could lie with the best of them! If I hadn't been about to perish I'd have called him on it. "*Please* don't tell me I look as bad as you do," I managed at last.

"Okay." He looked away. "Why don't you rest a few minutes before we go on?"

"Go on? I'm not going anywhere until you define 'tricky,'" I said. "It doesn't have anything to do with yucca shoots, does it?"

"No."

"You promise?"

"On my honor."

"What do you have in mind?"

"See that chimney?"

The one with Santa Claus on it, no doubt. The jeggo must have made my companion loco.

"A *chimney* is a climbable crack in a rock face," he explained after my silence.

Thank you, Mr. Webster. Now, if only I knew what that had to do with me. Too soon, I found out.

Clay pointed down at the ledge onto which he'd led us. "We need to go down."

I leaned over to look—very carefully. Visibility was better than I thought. It was probably a hundred feet to the bottom of this ledge and I could see every rocky inch of it. "Way down there? From all the way up here?" I scooted away from the edge in horror. "No way."

"There is no other way," he said patiently.

"You're telling me the kidnappers went that way with Connor?"

"Of course not. We're trying to avoid the kidnappers until we're ready. Remember?"

I shook my head. I couldn't remember my telephone number. Not that I'd ever need it again. If, by some miracle, I survived this, not even my agent would call me. My face was surely pockmarked by sand, and my eyebrows had probably blown off. I'd never be able to appear on TV without eyebrows. With no real job skills besides looking good on camera, I'd be unemployable. I'd lose the condo and have to live on the street . . . with my mother! And as if that wasn't bad enough, the Lions Club would have to give me somebody's old cast-off glasses so I could see well enough to beg for spare change.

I reached up to feel if I still had ears to hook the glasses on. I did, but they were below a tangle of fur that would have done credit to the Cowardly Lion, pre-Emerald City. Somewhere along the forced march I'd lost both Clay's hat and the cloth he'd given me to cover my face. All I had left was the fabric-wrapped sweatband. Even though I knew it probably wasn't responsible for the throbbing in my temples, I yanked it off my forehead and tossed it into a bush.

I knew I was already toeing the line of hysteria, so I kicked reason aside and plunged over it.

"This isn't the way it's supposed to *be*!" I cried out. Clay paused in opening his bag to regard me curiously. "I mean, this is just *wrong*, Batguy! Don't you see that?"

He didn't respond, but the curiosity on his face changed to incredulity.

"I've seen my share of action-adventure movies," I continued irrationally. "They're my current boyfriend's favorite. I like romantic comedies myself, so we take turns. On Friday we go to one of his movies and on Saturday we rent a chick flick. I've seen at least one movie a week since I turned eleven years old." I knew I wasn't only sharing irrelevant information now—I was raving—but I didn't care. I'd lost it. (Or, more accurately, it had been blown away.) Besides, Clay clearly wasn't getting my point. "Do you know how many movies that *is*?"

"Uh, hundreds?" he ventured cautiously.

"*Whatever*! The point is that in not one of all those movies—*not one!*—does the leading lady end up looking as horrible as I do right now! *Her* mascara never runs, *her* lip gloss never fades, and if *her* hair gets messed up she only looks *more* adorable! It's not fair, Clay! It's not! I've seen women in movies hacked into itsy bitsy *pieces* and *still* end up looking better than I do right now!"

Then I cried. At least I tried to. All that really happened was that globules of mud formed in the corners of my eyes and I made a sound reminiscent of a Sea World walrus.

Batguy was brave, I had to grant him that. Instead of sprinting off in the other direction, he approached with only a canteen with which to defend himself. He retrieved my discarded sweatband, poured water onto the still-pink terrycloth, and used it to carefully wipe the mud from my eyes. When I could see again, I liked what I saw. Though Clay was at least as dirty as I was, the only thought that went through my mind was, *Viggo Mortensen doesn't look half that good in movie makeup and soft lighting.*

"Take a drink of water," he said, offering me the canteen. "As much as you want, but drink it in sips."

Since I was horribly thirsty, and since I couldn't snivel and sip at the same time, I stopped crying and took the canteen.

As he watched me drink, Clay's frown gradually disappeared. "Better?"

Finally at a loss for words, I nodded. I don't know if it was the coolness of the water in my raw, parched throat, or the closeness of the man who ministered to me, but I did feel better. Much better. I thought if only Clay would kiss me now I'd feel better than I'd ever felt in my entire life.

He didn't kiss me. He moved away. But as he screwed the top back on the water bag he said, "You don't have to be in a movie to look terrific, Jill."

My breath caught in my throat. He might have just given me the most meaningful compliment I'd ever received in my life. On the other hand, he might have meant the "you" in general, meaning nobody had to be in a movie to look good, rather than in the personal sense that I looked good even though I wasn't in a movie. If only I knew how to properly diagram that sentence!

Then it occurred to me that maybe it didn't mean anything. Maybe it was just words designed to get me to stop gibbering about my looks and my addiction to B-movies and—I swallowed—my boyfriend. I rose to my knees "About that boyfriend-thing . . . it's meaningless. He . . . I . . . we . . ."

Clay wasn't listening. He'd returned to his bag and removed from it a lightweight nylon rope. The ominous sight of that rope was probably the *only* thing that could have jarred my mind into another gear, and reminded me I was perched on the lip of a sheer cliff, but it did the trick. "I'm not going down that chimney," I told him, scooting farther away from the ledge. "Not now. Not on Christmas Eve. Not ever."

"We'll loop the rope around your waist," he said (as if I wasn't nearing hysteria again), "and—"

"The only place I'd consider looping that rope around is your neck!"

He didn't stop uncoiling it, but this time he didn't come any closer, either. "Didn't you rappel at girls' camp?" he asked.

"No, I had an easily twisted ankle," I retorted, crossing my arms over my chest to convey that this conversation was over.

He looked off into the hills—surely pondering leaving me to the coyotes and kidnappers. Then he said, "I know where there's a waterfall not far from here."

My chin rose marginally. "One with clean, running water?"

"Year-round."

"How much water?"

"Enough to wash the entire Sonoran desert out of your hair," he said. "I'll even provide the soap."

My chin rose a little higher. "Throw in conditioner and maybe you've got a deal."

"Done."

I hesitated another minute, suspicious of how much that bag of his could hold. Still, there was no denying he had great hair. Maybe he was telling me the truth.

"Scout's honor," he added with that eerie ability he had to read my mind.

"And I'll bet you were an Eagle."

"Yes."

So here was the deal: if I didn't fall to an agonizing death on the rocks below, I could not only wash my hair, I could find out what products Batguy used to make his so thick and glossy. I reached for an end of the rope and looped it around my waist.

"Let me tie it," he suggested. "You probably twisted your thumb just before they taught knots at camp."

If I'd been willing to waste energy in a glare, he'd have received my best effort.

A few minutes later, I stood at the edge of a cliff, trying not to look down.

"Turn around," Clay instructed.

"You want me to fall down *backward*?"

"I want you to climb down using the footholds and handholds you find along the way," he said. "The rope is for insurance. I won't let you fall."

"I'm not a climber," I said, looking down at my formerly manicured hands. "Can't you lower me? I don't weigh much."

"It's not your weight I'm worried about," he said. "I'm trying to keep you from scraping all the skin off your face."

When it's explained that way, your whole paradigm shifts. Maybe I was a climber after all. Still, there was the fact that we were one hundred feet from the ground to consider. "I hate heights."

"Don't look down."

"But—"

"Go, Jill," he said firmly. "Worrying about something is twice as hard as doing it." Something in his face assured me he knew whereof he spoke.

I knelt at the edge of the cliff facing Clay and wedged one toe gingerly in the crevice. Then I looked up. "Promise me you won't let go of the rope." He'd already used a boulder to brace himself. The muscles in his upper arms flexed comfortingly beneath his cotton shirt. Everything about him inspired trust. Still, I hesitated. I'd been a coward too long to turn into a daredevil without at least a few minutes in the chrysalis stage. "And promise me again you have shampoo and conditioner."

"Yes," he said. "I promise. Now go. You'll be fine."

"I will not panic," I told myself as I crept over the side a few millimeters at a time. "I will not panic," I repeated when at last I was far enough down to stare an expressionless rock wall in the face.

"Good girl," Clay called encouragingly. The rope around my waist was taut. Secure. I pictured Batguy holding it, and my confidence grew. "Keep going," he urged, "but take it slow."

He didn't have to tell me that, when "fast" meant sliding down face-first. I found a foothold and lowered myself onto it, then found another. A silt-covered piece of rock came loose in my hand and I lost my grip. I yelped in fear but, as promised, the rope held me in place and I found another crevice to grab before my face impacted with stone.

"I will not panic," I reminded myself. "Clay caught me once. He'll catch me again." I inched farther, not looking down and not allowing my toes to curl in anxiety. The eye tics didn't bother me since my eyes were squeezed shut. There wasn't much to look at anyway. When you've seen the first five or ten feet of a stone monolith, you've seen it all.

"I will not panic," I chanted, groping for my next hold. "I will keep going." More rocks came loose in my hand, but the rope was always there to hold me steady.

"You're doing great!" Clay called from the top.

I opened my eyes. He was right. I *was* doing great. Climbing down this chimney really *wasn't* as hard as standing at the top dreading doing it.

I reached solid ground sometime before Christmas and let out a yell of triumph loud enough to be heard at the North Pole. (But not, I could only hope after reflection, by kidnappers on this continent.)

"Clay! I did it!" I wanted to mention that Lozen herself couldn't have done any better, but not being absolutely sure of that fact, I didn't.

He looked over the edge of the ledge and I thought I might be willing to do it all again if only to see the smile that split his handsome, dirty face. Then he motioned me back from the cliff, tossed down his parfleche and walking stick—and let go of his end of the rope. It wasn't until I saw it lying in a tangle at my feet that I really panicked. Clay had kept me from falling half a dozen times on my way down, but there was nobody at the top now to hold a rope for *him*.

I wanted to call out for him to stop as his legs extended down over the side—to plead with him to find another way down. But the words were caught behind the terror that constricted my throat. He looked impossibly big to be coming down such a narrow chimney. Even if he could find holds for his hands, how would he ever cram those huge boots of his into the narrow cracks that had scarcely accommodated my size eight tennies? The *real* Batman couldn't descend a wall like that, even with all the Batgear on his utility belt.

As if to confirm my worst fears, Clay's legs swung out from the edge of the cliff when he was still eighty feet or more above the ground. He held on only with his fingertips, and I knew from recent experience how tenuous that grip must be.

In a flash, my imagination showed me what would happen next. Clay Eskiminzin would fall to his death before I could explain to him that I didn't really have a boyfriend, and there was no power on earth to stop it.

chapter 12

Perhaps you've already noticed by this point in my narrative, but I don't handle terror particularly well. When both Clay's feet lost their hold in the narrow chimney, and then one of his hands also came free, I did pretty much what you'd expect. First I screamed, and then I closed my eyes and collapsed on the ground in a heap.

While I was down on my knees, I did the other thing that comes naturally to me—I prayed. Although I petitioned heaven for all I was worth, I was faithless enough to also listen in dread. (I had to listen through the palms of my hands because I had clasped them to my ears to muffle the horrifying, bone-crushing thud I expected at any moment.) Perhaps I muffled my ears too well because I didn't hear anything until the sound of my name.

I opened my eyes to see Clay's big, wonderful boots right in front of me. If I hadn't been startled senseless, I probably would have bathed them in kisses.

"You okay?" he said.

He seemed to be asking me that a lot. You'd think somebody as observant as Clay would see for himself that I was *not* okay and save himself the bother of inquiry. Truly, I hadn't been okay since that morning at the TV station when I was expertly applying my lipstick.

I said, "I'm . . . I'm . . . fine. I . . . I was praying for you."

Clay seemed touched. "Thanks. It was a little trickier than I expected."

I drew in a breath. I think it was the first I'd taken since I saw him hanging by one hand. "How did you—"

"It must have been your prayer." He extended a hand to pull me up. "Shall we untie the rope from around your waist and then go see if we can find that waterfall I promised you?"

"*See* if we can find it?" I replied, looking back toward the cliff with a shudder. "Clay Eskiminzin, if you don't find that waterfall, you are so dead."

As we walked in silence—as usual—I considered all the possible ways I might murder him. With each step the dry terrain beneath my aching feet got rockier. I figured his chances of finding a waterfall in this canyon were about as good as locating a saguaro cactus on a beach in Oahu. The only thing that gave me hope was the fact I couldn't see much more than a stone's throw ahead. (And I throw stones like a girl.) It *was* possible I could have missed a waterfall the size of Niagara in all that gloom.

After a while, I wasn't sure I could stand it any longer. The silence felt as thick and oppressive as the air, and I imagined myself moving slowly, aimlessly, through a giant Etch-a-Sketch. "Do you think it was like this after Zarahemla was destroyed?" I asked.

"I think it was darker then," Clay said. "But ask me again in a couple of hours when the sun goes down."

"I hate the dark."

"I thought you hated helicopters." He slowed. "And spiders and guns and snakes and scorpions." He looked up into the sky, but what he could possibly be seeing was a mystery to me. "And heights."

"And dark," I assured him. (There are more things I hate, of course, but I hesitated to list them at the time.) "Are we almost there?"

"We are there." He pointed up at a rocky outcropping and at last I saw what he did. Birds. Big birds. But not the friendly, fuzzy, yellow variety you find on *Sesame Street*. These were scraggly, gray, *ugly* big birds.

I hung back. "Those aren't vultures, are they?"

"Do you hate vultures?"

"Yes."

"How do you feel about . . ." He seemed to be searching for a word. ". . . condors?"

That didn't sound so bad. In fact, *condor* sounds rather noble, don't you agree? It would have been horrible to think I was in a desert surrounded by vultures, but it was more of an honor to share a habitat with condors.

"Oh, good," I said, and smiled up at the birds. Then I looked back at Clay. The way he stood with his stick in his hand looking so self-congratulatory, you'd think he was Charlton Heston and had just led the Children of Israel into the Promised Land.

But from what I could see of the set, Chuck was all promise and no deliverance. I peered harder into the murk. I listened for the sound of falling water. I even sniffed the air for a whiff of chlorine. (You may recall I'm a city girl. I thought *all* water smelled like chlorine until the know-it-all ranger told me otherwise.) None of my five senses picked up anything promising, but my sixth sense warned me that I'd been hoodwinked.

I placed my hands on my hips. "Unless you can use that rod of yours to smite a rock for water," I told Clay, "you're in big trouble."

He motioned for me to follow him to the base of a sheer cliff. Then he led me along it until we came to an opening not much wider than the door to a linen closet. Intrigued, I stepped through ahead of him.

I'll tell you right off that this wouldn't be the part of the movie where the music swells and the camera pans a lush, tropical oasis—but for the middle of the barren, southern Arizona wilderness, it wasn't bad. The same plants grew here that grew everywhere else in a hundred-mile radius, but there were more of them and they were prettier. There was even fauna of the non-arachnid variety, which was a welcome change. I watched the oddest-looking rabbit race from a boulder to a bush and look back at us accusingly.

"You're probably the first person it's ever seen," Clay said.

"That's the most deformed bunny I've ever seen," I replied. "What happened to its poor little legs and ears?"

He chuckled. "It's a jackrabbit, Jill."

By now I was too busy beholding Clay's miraculous waterfall to be offended by the display of his superior knowledge of fauna. A spout of clear water two or three feet wide gushed out of a crevice fifteen feet or more above our heads. It splashed against the rocks on its way to the desert floor, formed a small pool over the gravel at the base of the cliff, and then disappeared into nowhere.

"Was Moses here?" I asked in awe.

"You'd think so, wouldn't you?"

"Really, where does the water come from, Clay? Where does it go?"

"There's a spring on the other side of this rock formation," he explained. "It's some ten miles from here. The water travels all that way through a fissure in the rock. Then it falls like you see it and slips into another fissure where it runs sixty miles or so underground before it finally comes back to the surface in the San Carlos Valley."

"How do you *know* that?" I asked, as impressed by him as I was by his waterfall.

"I followed it once."

"You—"

Clay interrupted me with a shrug. "It was one of the first things Chee taught me. If you can't find water, and find it fast, you might as well not learn anything else about desert survival, because you won't live long enough to put it into practice." He turned away. "I'll leave you to find out for yourself how cold that water is. I'll be around the corner if you need anything."

"Wait!" I said. "You promised me shampoo and conditioner."

He dropped his bag. "So I did."

I expected him to open the bag. I didn't expect him to leave it on the ground while he pulled a long, wicked-looking knife from a leather sheath on his hip. But that's what he did. Then he knelt next to one of the smaller varieties of a plant with spiky, sword-shaped leaves. I didn't know what it was called, though I'd seen them in landscaping designs all over Tucson.

"It's a yucca," he said as he used the knife to dig at its roots. "The Spaniards called it soap weed. It contains saponin, an all-natural soap."

"You're kidding."

As usual, he wasn't. He'd already cut off a piece of root and peeled away the brown outer skin to expose a white cane inside. This he laid on a broad rock and used another rock to smash it into bits. He stood and handed me a slice about the size of one of the bars of soap they give you in a hotel. "Indians used it for thousands of years," he said. "Get it wet, then rub it. It'll make mounds of lather. You'll love it."

If it was so great, why wasn't it on the shelf at Bath and Body Works? Still, I extended my hand. "I'm afraid to ask about the conditioner."

If this place had anything, it had plenty of spiky plants. Clay chose a large specimen—a succulent this time—and cut off a long spear. Then he sliced it open and brought it to me. "Aloe vera," he said. "You probably have it in your conditioner at home."

"No," I said. (The aloe is in my hand lotion, but I wouldn't admit it and give him the satisfaction.)

"Squeeze it all out," he advised. "It's good for everything. But watch out for the spines along the edges."

I held the plant parts in my hand and regarded him dubiously. "Is there anything else growing out here I might need?"

"Sure. Do you have a headache?"

"Now that you mention it, yes."

"While you wash your hair, I'll find you some twigs to chew." He reached into his bag at last and withdrew a small black comb and something else that he palmed before I could see what it was.

"Ancient Apaches carried pocket combs?" I asked when he extended it.

"They would have if they'd known how many things you can use them for."

My hand froze in mid-reach. "Are any of those uses disgusting?"

"Yes," he said, "but this is a relatively new comb. It's never been used for anything but hair combing."

I held out my palm and he dropped the comb into it along with a small pot that bore actual English words and a genuine U.S. trademark. I was so happy to see it I almost cried. "Shea butter? I love shea butter!"

"My sister gave it to me," he said. "I've never tried it myself. It's unscented, so you can use it all if you want to."

It was the best gift anybody had ever given me. I looked up at Clay in gratitude. "If the three wise men appeared at this moment with gold, frankincense, and myrrh, I wouldn't appreciate it half as much as I appreciate all this."

"You're welcome," he said, picking up his bag and heading for the opening between the cliffs. "Don't worry about the buzzards. They're curious, but they won't get close enough to bother you."

"Buzzards?" I cried after him. "You told me they were condors!"

"Buzzards. Condors. Vultures. Unless you're a biologist, it's mostly a matter of semantics." He kept his face averted—I suspected so I wouldn't see him smile. "The only difference between them is that you hate vultures, but you admire condors."

If I'd had anything in my hands I thought I could spare, I'd have lobbed it at the back of his head. Instead, I let him go and carried my shea butter and desert flora to a flat rock at the side of the waterfall.

First I took off Clay's shirt and shook it vigorously. With so much dust already in the air, it was hard to say if it made any difference. Then I sat down and pulled off my shoes, grateful to discover my feet weren't as swollen as I'd feared. Instead, my shoes were once again filled with sand. I emptied them out and pulled off my socks. As I did, I crinkled my nose and looked hastily up at the birds on the ledge above. The odor of my socks was surely pungent enough to attract the attention of every buzzard in the state. I considered tossing the horrid things up to them, but knew my blisters would get blisters if I didn't put them back on, as distasteful as the thought was.

Next I stood and grasped the lower hem of my T-shirt to pull it over my head. That's when I froze in mortification. While I had no qualms about stripping off a swimsuit in a roomful of female strangers before donning an evening gown, I'd never in my life disrobed outdoors. With my arms still crisscrossed across my tummy, I looked carefully around. Nothing moved but the heaving of my chest as my lungs geared up to hyperventilate. I looked up. Nothing there but the dreary brown sky above the black, encircling cliffs. Except for those darned vultures—I mean *condors*—I was all alone.

I don't like to be alone. And there was way too much *nothing* around to suit me. I'd felt vulnerable enough in baggy sweat pants and a lime green T-shirt. There was no possible way I could take off all my clothes under the open sky right here in the center of the world. *I couldn't.* But I couldn't go another ten seconds looking like the younger, newly homeless sister of the Wicked Witch of the West, either.

Finally, I stripped down to my under things. "Go on and ogle," I told the condors. "You'd see more skin on primetime TV."

I sat on a stone and slipped my sore feet into the pool. Clay wasn't kidding about the water being cold. Apparently the spring was a little farther away than he'd told me. This water was runoff from the polar ice caps. I waited for my feet to adjust to the temperature of the water before I dared to wet my head, but my toes just turned blue. I pulled them out of the pool.

"Remember, Jillanne," I told myself as I shivered. "It's easier to do something than it is to sit and dread doing it." Before I could talk any real sense into myself, I plunged my head under the waterfall. Thankfully, the scream froze in my throat or Clay might have come running to see what the matter was.

At least there was some satisfaction in watching the pool below the falls turn almost as brown as the surrounding desert floor—the water turning my hair back to blond. Before I lost my nerve, or froze into a solid block of ice, I grabbed the yucca root, scooped it down into the water, and massaged it for all I was worth. I could have saved myself a lot of effort. Aladdin's lamp took less rubbing to operate. I couldn't help but wonder if yucca was the secret ingredient in Mr. Bubble. I rubbed it into my hair and onto my exposed skin and hoped it could clean as well as it could foam. At the very least, it *looked* soapy.

The frigid rinse cycle tempted me to skip the conditioner phase, but it didn't take more than a second or two of trying to drag my fingers through my hopelessly knotted tresses for me to reconsider. I reached for the aloe and squeezed the clear, viscous liquid into my palms.

"I can't believe I'm doing this," I muttered to the condors as I massaged cactus juice into my scalp and hair, and then slathered it over my sore, chapped face and neck. "Who does he think I am, Pocahontas?"

The birds didn't know, but they seemed willing to take it to caucus. They huddled together and peered down at me with interest. These were no condors, I decided. They were vultures.

I believe in being up-front and honest with things that want to eat me. "Don't get any ideas," I said. "I'm not washing off all this dirt so I'll be less crunchy for you." I moved closer to the waterfall again. "Besides, I'm going to live through this adventure." I plunged my head back into the freezing water. "Maybe."

It might be the only thing Clay couldn't produce out here, but he hadn't come up with a towel tree, so I reached blindly for his cotton shirt and used the inside to dry my hair, face, and the rest of me as best I could. Then I slipped back into my gym clothes, trying not to think about the dirt in them turning to mud on my damp skin.

I reached then for the comb, and was grateful and amazed in turns when I was able to get it through my long, wavy hair without pulling much more than half of it from my scalp. I started to gather my squeaky-clean locks into a ponytail, then changed my mind and let it fall across my shoulders to dry faster.

Next I did one of the hardest things I'd ever done to that point in my life—I put back on my damp, wrinkled, dirty, smelly socks. In doing so I realized why the contestants on *Survivor* go barefoot. Dirty socks are too disgusting for even the coarsest reality TV show.

But I had something to restore my spirits. I pulled the cap off the little tub of shea butter and reverentially dipped the tip of my little finger into the ointment. Every once in a while, a mere mortal is granted a glimpse into what heaven must be like. Massaging that magical stuff into the tender, swollen skin below my eyes was my glimpse. I wanted to kiss Clay. (More than ever, I mean.)

When I finished with my face and neck, I put the cream everywhere else I could reach until I'd used the whole pot. Only then did I feel guilty, especially since his sister had given it to him. Instinctively, I glanced up at the vultures. "He said to use it all," I pointed out defensively.

Noble condors would have understood, but these birds weren't interested in my explanation. Like so many men I'd dated, they were only interested in the package my conscience came in. I watched in horror as they licked their long, beaky chops at the thought of my newly tenderized flesh.

I gathered up my few possessions as quickly as I could and backed away from the ill-intentioned crew of carrion-seekers. One of the vultures stretched its wrinkly red neck, lowered its head, and gave me a knowing wink. (I swear!) Another displayed an amazingly wide wingspan as if wanting to embrace me. The third merely salivated.

Aghast, I dropped Clay's shirt and my shoes and plants with a shriek, turned on my heels, and ran to find Clay just as fast as my stinky little sock-clad feet could carry me.

chapter 13

I wish I could report that the first look Clay gave the newly rinsed, scrubbed, and moisturized me was one of appreciation, but frankly I think it was more along the lines of amazement. The first thing he said was, "Where are your shoes?" The next thing he said was, "Don't step there!"

I froze, teetering on the tips of five sock-covered toes, afraid to bring the other five back to earth. The prima ballerina in *Swan Princess* didn't have anything on me—except grace and poise and better clothes.

"The rock," he said. "Step onto the rock."

I collapsed onto it instead and drew up both legs. Then I wrapped my arms around my knees as if this rock were the only lifeboat in the Atlantic and I was the sole survivor of the *Titanic*.

"Those were no condors!" I complained when I regained the breath to speak. "They were vultures. They heard there was an all-you-can-eat buffet coming . . . and I . . . I buttered myself up for it!" I lay my chin on my knees and glared through the murk at him. "That was your plan, wasn't it? You wanted them to eat *me* first!"

Clay put down the several parts of radio that were in his hand and stood. "That was stupid."

At first I thought he meant my remark, but he came close and crouched down to look at my feet, so I knew he meant my barefoot gallop away from the buzzards. I tried to hide my stinky socks beneath me, but the rock wasn't wide enough. "Ouch!"

"You're lucky it wasn't a whole prickly pear," he said, tossing aside the thorns he'd pulled from my paw. "Or a cholla. A cholla spine can pierce tanned leather. Think what it could have done to your bare foot."

"I don't want to think about it," I pouted.

"You don't want to think at all."

It was the way Clay said the words that made them sharper than a cholla spine. He wasn't angry or sarcastic. He was calm and matter-of-fact. When he'd finished examining my feet and found no damage to them beyond the few thorn pricks—which still smarted—he said, "You are beyond doubt the luckiest person I've ever seen." Before I could retort, or even reply, he rolled onto his toes and stood. "But dumb luck isn't enough out here," he said. "You have to stop *reacting* to things, Jill. You have to *think* and then *act*."

I wanted to tell Clay that I can't even think before I speak and that reaction is the only way I've learned to live, but for once I didn't have the words. All I could manage was a weak, "I know."

He frowned. "No, you don't. But I hope for both our sakes you're a fast learner. Otherwise, you're going to get us killed." He reached for his parfleche and looped it over his shoulder. "Can you sit there for ten minutes, please?"

I nodded, my eyes fixed on the things of his that remained on the ground. When he picked up the canteen, I prayed he'd leave his walking stick as an indication he planned to return to me. He didn't leave it. All he left was the radio, and it lay in pieces in the dirt.

* * *

Time is relative. If you're talking on the phone and your best friend says, "He thinks you're hot!" ten minutes can seem like ten seconds. If you're standing on stage at the Miss Arizona pageant when the emcee says, "The envelope, please," ten seconds can seem like ten hours. If you're sitting alone in the desert, left behind by a man you've fallen in love with—quickly, completely, and irrevocably—ten minutes can seem like ten years.

Think of this as the voice of experience speaking. Not only have I talked on that phone and stood on that stage, I've loved only one man before Clay. The man was my father, and he left me too.

While Dad proved to be a man of action, he wasn't around long enough to teach me that, or much of anything else. My long experience with *reacting*, then, comes from my mother. As far as I know,

Marty Jackson Caldwell has never taken a single thought-out action in her life. Her childhood was a long series of reactions to her dysfunctional parents. Her first adult sorrow was the result of her reaction to her boyfriend's desires. Leaving school at seventeen was a reaction to her pregnancy. Her wedding was a reaction to her lack of education and/or training. Even her short marriage was one reaction after another to my father's many facets of resentment. And, when he left us, her only reaction was to be sorry for it and wait for him to come back. When we lost the shabby house, she "waited" in a nearby government-subsidized apartment. She's still "waiting" for him to return, I guess, but across town now in a nice condo purchased with my reaction to a lifetime of being poor and almost incapable of making a decision on my own.

It's true. I'm a born-and-bred reactionary, who is incapable of making a move that isn't totally impetuous and/or prompted by somebody else. Ruts are my way of life. I mean, look at the choices. You either stay in your nice, comfortable, made-to-order rut (and maybe call it a groove) or you forge a new path, right? Since forging a new path requires action and choices, the two things I'm most afraid of (what if I choose to go a new direction and it's the wrong way?), I stay in the groove. Mine is a comfortable and tastefully decorated groove, thank you very much. Besides, it's one I'm fortunate to be in, since I'd probably still be selling popcorn at the local Harkins Theater if not for Shar. At seventeen she wanted to enter the Miss Tucson pageant. I wanted to do everything she did. We entered together and one of us won.

I'd played enough Monopoly to believe that winning first place in a beauty contest got you nothing but a blue ten-dollar bill. That might be true in the game, but people who win the pageant *and* attract the attention of Mrs. Leona Funke get more. Much more. A former Miss America herself, Mrs. Funke took me under her boa and finagled that prize all the way up to a "Get Out of Poverty Free" card.

So that's how I got the condo and clothes, but how did I end up in journalism? Mrs. Funke again, of course. We'd devoted almost two years of my life to getting me all the way to the Miss America pageant. And if you think that isn't a full-time job, you've never been in a national pageant. Heck, you probably haven't seen *Miss*

Congeniality. In my case, without the FBI to pay the grooming bills, I resorted to modeling to earn money for manicurists, makeup, and evening gowns. That's when I learned that it's *still* not enough to look good and practice crying prettily for when a tiara is placed on your fluffy blond head. The judges expect you to have something *inside* that head. Specifically, they want to know what you plan to do with all the scholarship money you might happen to receive.

I'd always said "rocket scientist" or "brain surgeon" when people asked me what I was going to be when I grew up, because I figured the money was probably good, and I liked the look it brought to people's faces. But since my aversion to blood is roughly on par with my hatred of math, they were always more conversation stoppers than actual career goals. I had so-so grades and no real gift for anything but looking good, so Mrs. Funke decided I would be a communications major. After announcing it on coast-to-coast TV, what else could I enroll in when I plunked down my scholarship check at ASU?

It proved to be the most fortuitous corner I ever backed myself into. Not only did I love journalism, but when I impetuously threw away my decent six-figure modeling contract—reacting to being dumped on by yet another agent, agency, and/or low-life photographer—I had something to fall back on. I had a degree that got me a lowish five-figure salary at an obscure TV station in Tucson, Arizona. What could be better than that?

Isn't it funny how life's events are so intertwined? A myriad of people and experiences we don't stop to appreciate—or even consider—eventually lead us right to where we sit at each and every moment of our lives. (I don't know how to put this well, despite my degree as a communicator, so try to follow me, okay?) I'm trying to say that I believe my lifelong friendship with Shar led to me being in the pageant, which led to the modeling contract, which led to the money to buy the condo, which led to me being in the same ward with Shar again and teaching Primary and adoring Connor.

Got that? Then consider this. Being in the pageant led to Mrs. Funke, which led to the degree, which led to the job, which led to me being able to get on the helicopter (only because I know Shar) and come out to look for Connor, which led to me being in the middle of the desert, which was the last place on earth I'd ever have expected to meet the only man I've ever thought seriously about taking home from that metaphorical department-store window. But there I was to prove it. Right there in the middle of wherever, sitting on a rock surrounded by dirt I was now afraid to put my socks on, waiting for a man I thought I loved (who probably scorned me) to come back when that was probably the last thing on his agenda.

It was too much philosophy for a communications major. I'd started to lay my fluffy blond head down on my knees to better rest my brain when I was distracted by the sight of the radio.

Why had Clay taken it apart? Was he trying to fix it, or was he looking for a sign of sabotage?

Instead of dismissing the thought of sabotage as too farfetched to consider, I considered it. Clay wanted me to think; I would think. Unfortunately, my thoughts didn't make much sense.

Nobody but the kidnappers would have anything to gain by disabling Clay's radio. But how in the world would they know before they took Connor from the ranch which radio Clay would eventually use, or that he'd be there at all, or even who the heck he was, for that matter?

I hadn't much gift for thinking, I realized. None of this was making sense even to me. My head sank back toward my knees.

Unless . . .

I scrambled over to retrieve the pieces of radio and took them back to my rock. I don't believe in inanimate objects giving off psychic vibes, but I do like to have something to fiddle with while I think. Examining the radio as I tried to fit it back together told me four things: (1) it belonged to the Pinal County Sheriff's Office, (2) it was easy to take apart, (3) it had a battery, and (4) it didn't work. Most likely, the battery was dead.

Unless . . .

What if the kidnappers had an accomplice who was still back at the ranch? What if he'd heard of Clay's extraordinary skills as a tracker and had sabotaged the radio while Clay was in the command center, hoping to slow him down a little? Maybe the *same* somebody had followed us and stolen the jeep.

I gripped the radio and wished Clay would come back so I could share my theory. I just wished he'd come back at all. But the theory *did* make sense. It was the *only* thing that made sense besides a dead battery.

Unless . . .

What if it *wasn't* necessarily Clay they wanted to slow down? What if it was *me* somebody wanted to get rid of? And what if the somebody was United States Senator Alex Teagler?

The radio slipped from my hand as I wondered if I was the only person on earth who has trouble telling paranoia apart from inspiration. (Somebody once said that just because you're paranoid doesn't mean they're not out to get you.) I *had* overheard the sheriff say that Alex asked Clay to take me along with him. Why would he do that? There were easier ways to keep me away from Shar than to try to lose me in the desert. One call to my TV station and I'd have been out of there faster than he could curl that aristocratic upper lip of his.

I bit my own chapped lip as I tried to think it through. I tried to remember every detail of what I'd seen and heard today, but mostly what came back to me were bits and pieces of what I'd *thought*. Ever since I'd sat in the helicopter and heard Alex make his statement to the press, there'd been a nagging little something tugging away at the fringe of my consciousness. I tried to name it. Doubt, maybe. Distrust, probably. But *why*?

All of a sudden a memory of Shar's engagement flashed into my mind. It still stung to remember how I'd seen it on television before I'd heard it in person from my best friend. Alex Teagler had proposed toward the end of his senatorial campaign. He'd not only made headlines in every paper in the state, he'd charmed most of the rest of the nation as well. Now that he was announcing a bid for the presidency, most of the TV sets in America were likely tuned in to the desperate search for a grieving father's only child.

Maybe Connor *wasn't* lost. Maybe he *hadn't* been kidnapped. Maybe he'd been hidden by his own father in one of the most twisted ploys in the long, sordid history of national campaigning. And maybe I was the only one Alex thought might suspect such a thing, so he had concocted a spur-of-the moment plan to get rid of me.

Maybe Batguy was even in on it. He'd been pretty quick to agree to bring me, hadn't he? Those things about taking me back to the ranch or letting me wait in the jeep could have been ploys. Maybe the jeep was right where we left it and he was most of the way back to it by now. Maybe the only part of Alex's plan that didn't work was that Clay didn't have the heart to shoot me or let me fall backward off a cliff. Maybe instead of killing me, Clay had been like the Wicked Queen's huntsman in *Snow White.* Maybe he had brought me here deep into the woods to leave me to find friendly dwarfs or die.

And maybe fatigue, hunger, and mind-numbing fear had made me delusional.

"Here are your shoes," Clay said.

I fell off the rock.

When I determined for certain that I hadn't had a massive coronary, I glared up at him. "Are you always so *quiet*?"

"Yes." He extended the shoes. "Put them on. I checked them for arachnids."

He'd come back! Clay Eskiminzin looked as good wet as he did dry, and only a little better clean than he did dirty. Boundless joy wrestled with inane apprehension at the revolver I saw he now had in a holster strapped to his hip. I had to swallow three or four times, but relief finally won out over fear. "Th-thank you," I managed, extending my hands for the shoes.

"Put them on," he said. "We need to find another place to spend the night."

"I mean, thank you for coming back for me."

His eyebrows drew together and he didn't speak for several moments. At last he said, "I'm sorry about what I said earlier."

I lowered my eyes. "It was true."

"Sometimes it isn't necessary to speak the truth."

"Did Chee teach you that?"

"No." When I looked up he pointed at my shoes and I began to pull one on. "That would be one of my grandfather's pearls of wisdom. But I did think about Chee while I cleaned up. He'd be very disappointed in me."

I paused with one shoe on and one shoe off. "But the canyon . . . and the storm . . . and the waterfall. Clay, you must remember everything you ever learned from him!"

"Everything except what it was like *to* learn." He knelt so close I held my breath and feared I'd have a hard time hearing him over the beating of my heart. "I was raised in the city too," he said. "I know how vast and frightening this place can seem at first. There are only two differences between our experiences, Jill. The biggest one is that I had a better guide."

He looked away. I wanted to take his face in my hands and turn it back to me. I wanted to tell him that he was the only guide I'd ever want and that as irrational as it might sound, I'd rather be in danger here with him than without him anywhere else in the world. I wondered if Snow White had felt this way about her huntsman.

"The other difference," he continued, "is that I always knew I could give up and go home anytime I wanted to."

"Did you ever want to?"

"Not more than six or eight times a day at first," he admitted. "Chee left as much as possible for me to figure out on my own, and I wasn't a fast pupil. Besides that, it seemed like he never slept, never rested, never ate, never hurt. Sometimes I almost hated him."

My second shoe dropped from my fingers. "Why *didn't* you leave?" I asked. "Why didn't you go back to Harvard where you belonged?"

At the word *belonged* Clay smiled, but it was rueful and his eyes were on the mountains. At last he said, "I stayed because I knew if I gave up too soon I'd never learn who I really am."

I looked down at my feet but didn't notice that one still lacked a shoe. I felt more like crying now than I had when I feared Clay might abandon me. I felt like sobbing because I suspected there were more—and bigger—differences between us than he knew. After all, there was somebody strong and brave and good inside Clay for him to find. But I was different. I'd never looked very deep inside myself, because I was afraid that if I ever did I might learn that my heart is as superficial as the artfully maintained body I keep it in. Then I'd have to accept once and for all that my "groove" will always be as flashy—and meaningless—as the fairy tales on the silver screen.

chapter 14

Before I could cry, or confess my shortcomings, or slink away, Clay picked up my other shoe and slipped it on my foot. "Good news, Cinderella," he said as he tied the laces. "It fits."

"Cinderella?" I sniffed happily. "Not Snow White?"

A moment's hesitancy crossed his face. "Do I have the wrong fairy tale?"

"Do I?"

He sat back on his heels. "Tell me this much, Jill. Do *other* people understand you?"

Despite everything, I smiled. "Before you came back I was thinking about this, um, possibly farfetched, er . . . idea . . . I had about Connor's disappearance."

"I'm listening."

That was his mistake. I poured out everything I'd been thinking about the weird and wonderful way the patterns of life come together. Then I explained the even more random idea I had about Alex Teagler being behind his own son's kidnapping. I knew I had Batguy's undivided attention at last, but it was difficult to say what he thought. "It even occurred to me," I confessed in conclusion, "that Alex might have hired you as the huntsman who'd take me deep into the woods to murder me. Like in *Snow White*."

(What I didn't confess is that I've always had a bit of a princess complex. I was ten years old before my mother could convince me to eat red apples, applesauce, or apple pie. Having seen the *Snow White* video ten or fifty times too many, I was highly suspicious of every red apple in the world. No wonder my first thought under these circumstances was of Clay being the huntsman.)

"Lucky for you," Clay said, "the woods around here are pretty thin."

Looking around at the bushes and stunted evergreens, I had to agree. This was no place for a picturesque little cottage. "In the movie remake, you could have abandoned me in the desert," I pointed out.

"Tough break. Your dwarfs are going to be real short on diamond mines. About the only thing they can dig up in this part of the state is copper."

"Any singing animals?"

He shrugged. "The coyotes can set up a pretty fair chorus."

"This version isn't going to go over half as well at the box office."

"Probably not. Especially with princes being as scarce as they are in the Galiuros."

Now there he was wrong. Apache chiefs might not exactly be nobility, but this descendent of Eskiminzin didn't need a title to catch the eye of any princess.

The fine lines around Clay's eyes crinkled, but I couldn't determine whether he smiled or frowned. "Now tell me which parts of this tale you believe."

I wondered if he'd read my mind again. He looked into my eyes—for once—as if the answer was important. "I—I don't believe you'd kill me," I stammered. "Or leave me behind on purpose."

"I'm glad to hear that."

"But I don't trust Alex." When I said it out loud, it felt right.

"How well do you know him?" Clay asked. "I'm under the impression that your relationship with the Teaglers is tenuous."

"I see him at church sometimes," I confessed. "He and Shar have been married six years now and . . . and Shar hasn't talked to me much in that time." I lowered my eyes. "She hasn't talked to me at all before today," I admitted.

"Because Senator Teagler won't let her?"

I nodded miserably.

"You're sure?"

"Who else could keep her on a leash like that?"

He didn't answer. Instead he said, "You don't really know Alex Teagler then, do you? For instance, you don't know Eliot Fuller, his chief advisor."

"I know *of* him," I said, not sure why Clay asked, but unwilling to be thought ignorant yet again. Eliot Fuller was one of the richest and most powerful financiers in the state. The nation. Maybe even the world. "Everybody in America with a TV set knows about Eliot Fuller." I smiled. "I guess that leaves you out."

"You might be surprised," Clay said cryptically. He reached for the useless radio as he rose. "Pack it in, pack it out." When it was back in his bag, he added, "Believe me when I say I'm sorry, Jill. About everything. If it weren't for my stupidity, you wouldn't be in this mess."

"I don't—"

"We need to go," he said, extending a hand to help me up. "The animals will come in for water at dusk." He turned and took a few long strides away, pausing when he realized I hadn't followed.

I wasn't sure I *could* follow. Sometime between the time I sat down and the time I tried to walk again my legs had turned from flesh and bone to rubber and lead. "I'm coming," I called to him. "Maybe."

He waited patiently. "I don't want you more than three feet away from me at any time tonight, okay?"

Was it *okay*? I'd hoped and prayed and wished on every star in the galaxy that a guy like him would say words like that to me. Under other circumstances I would have swooned. Under these particular circumstances I was apprehensive. "What's out there?"

He didn't respond.

I moved as quickly to his side as my wobbly little legs could carry me, still mindful of the gun on his hip. "Is it the kidnappers?"

"No," he said. "It's a couple of puma." Remembering he was talking to me, he added, "Cougar. Mountain lion. Wildcat. Take your pick."

"Um, cougar," I decided. "I've seen BYU's mascot. How bad can they be?"

"They can be plenty bad." He took hold of my elbow to move me along. "Especially under certain circumstances."

Under certain *particular* circumstances, no doubt. I moved closer.

"Pumas are strongly territorial," he continued, "and they don't like interlopers at their water holes. Plus, it's late summer, so the big one still considers her offspring a kitten. But the kitten is a male, so he's not sticking as close to mama as she'd like." Clay talked and walked and pulled me over the rough ground simultaneously. "There's no suicide much quicker than getting between a mother cat and her young."

"But how do you know—?"

"They don't call this canyon Del Gato for nothing."

So it *wasn't* Bell Grotto or Del Monte. I should have figured it out before. Even my limited high-school Spanish could have told me that *del gato* means "belonging to a cat." A very big cat, in this case.

"I picked up the tracks early," Clay said, "but knew she wasn't close because of the abundance of wildlife at the falls. Watch it." He steered me around a prickly pear I might have seen there on the ground if I hadn't been searching the cliffs for non-mascot-like cougars. "Pumas are nocturnal. They'll head down for water later tonight. It's better if we're upwind when they come and at least a mile or more away."

That was too much information to have come from a few measly prints in the sand. "I can see how you might know there's more than one of them," I said, "and even their sizes, but don't tell me you can tell if an animal's male or female by its footprints."

"I know the cub's a male by the way he's marking his territory."

"Oh." I'd had cats (albeit considerably smaller, tamer cats) so I didn't need to ask what he meant. He released my elbow, but I followed along closely, looking over my shoulder every nanosecond or so and trying not to sniff the air. Every shadowy ledge looked ominous; every stunted evergreen seemed capable of concealing a hundred-pound feline. After a while—a very long while—I started to remind myself of Piglet and had to stifle a giggle. (I have a tendency to get silly when I get tired, and this was about as tired as I'd ever been in my life.)

"Do you know *Winnie the Pooh*?" I asked Clay.

He missed a half step. If nothing else, I could usually surprise him. He said, "Not personally. Does this look like the Hundred Acre Woods to you?"

"I mean, do you know the stories?"

He kept walking. "I wasn't raised by wolves."

"Right. So, anyway, I've been thinking of the movie where Pooh and Piglet walk through the woods, scared to death of Jagulars. Doesn't this remind you of that?"

"Except that Jagulars were figments of the imagination of a make-believe character," Clay said. "Whereas we're real people in a real canyon with real pumas."

"Except for that," I conceded with a shudder.

"Does *everything* remind you of a movie?"

I paused, caught between the truth and my desire to conceal at least some of my innate shallowness. I resolved then and there to pretend to be as thoughtful and deep as Clay was until we were attacked by mountain lions or murdered by kidnappers. I figured neither event should be so far distant that I couldn't pull it off if I really tried.

I ignored his question to ask one of my own. "You said you stayed out here in the wilderness so you could learn who you really are. How did you do that?" Although I asked conversationally and with the utmost casualness, I'd never asked a question I more wanted to know the answer to. Even if we were about to die, maybe I could learn enough from him first to get a head start for the post-existence. I mean, if I couldn't take anything with me to heaven but intelligence, I might as well try for that. "What did you do first?"

"I was quiet," he said.

I stopped in my tracks, hoping not to be directly below a puma-bearing ledge. After a second Clay realized I wasn't following and turned. "I didn't mean that as a criticism. I was answering your question as honestly as I can."

"I'm not very good at quiet," I said weakly.

"Most people aren't."

He indicated that we should keep walking, and I put one foot in front of the other.

You had to be there to fully appreciate how much harder that was than it sounds. I knew if I sat down just then, I'd probably never get up again, no matter how many Jagulars and/or pumas appeared on the trail or in the trees or on the cliffs. I didn't know how much time had elapsed from the time we first got into the jeep that morning, but I estimated it at about a century. Maybe a little longer.

"Quiet, huh?" I whispered. Quiet was another item on the long list of things I hate. Alphabetically, it came just after "puma" and right before "rattlesnake." So much for learning how to polish up my spirit before I died.

"Most Americans at any given moment are talking to someone, listening to news, watching TV, or using a computer," Clay said. "Sometimes they do it all at once."

"And you quit watching and listening to *everything*?" It wasn't a question as much as a cry of astonishment. "For how long?"

"About five years now."

I gasped and he spun around to see what had startled me. When he realized it wasn't a rattler that had gotten me but only the thought of not seeing a movie for two hundred and sixty weeks, he smiled. "If it makes you feel any better, I did see all nine or so hours of *The Lord of the Rings* when I was in Maryland last Christmas. I'm a big Tolkien fan." He started walking again. "And I do own a computer. I even turn it on every week or so to file reports for work and let my mother know I'm still alive."

"But what do you *do*?" I walked at his side now, not out of fear but fascination. Sauron got more news and social interaction than this guy.

"You mean to pass the time, or professionally?"

"Both." There wasn't anything about Clay Eskiminzin I didn't want to know. Talk about a time when a Vulcan mind-meld would have come in handy.

"When I'm not working," he said, "I like to read. Meditate. Pray. Hike."

"And when you are working?"

"I mostly hike. Pray. Meditate. On slow days I read." He used his stick to push aside some brush so I could better pass by. "As you can see, I'm not very well-rounded."

That wasn't what I saw at all. "So, you do search-and-rescue work?"

"Sometimes."

We'd been following the cliffs long enough that Clay had apparently decided we were far enough away, or far enough upwind, to look for a place to stop for the night. I was immensely relieved. There wasn't enough rubber left in my legs to bend the lead in them, and I worried that if my stomach growled any louder Clay might mistake it for a wildcat and shoot me.

He continued, "My family tells people I work for the Department of the Interior, but more specifically I'm a forest ranger—with forest being a relative term in this part of the country." He had stopped in front of a gaping black hole in the side of the cliff. He might have thought it looked promising, but to me it looked like it might as well have a flashing neon sign that said *OMINOUS*. "I patrol for poachers, man lookout towers, fight wildfires . . ." Then he added, "And once a month or more there's a prison escape or search-and-rescue they call me out to." He bent to look into the cave as I backed away from it. "So what do you think?"

About him? About the cave? About quiet? About kidnappers? About cougars? I didn't understand the question. The thoughts in my head spun around so fast that I closed my eyes. When I opened them it wasn't just the thoughts—the trees and rocks and cacti and ground and ranger were all rotating too. I felt ill. The next second I didn't feel anything at all.

Jill's Argument for Aerobic Activity

There are better motivations for keeping your body in top condition than the fear you might one day have to hike eighty miles down into a canyon. One of the most obvious reasons to exercise is so you'll look sensational. Exercise stimulates blood to carry oxygen and nutrients to skin, making it firmer and better nourished. It's also a proven fact that exercise slows aging. (Yes, Aunt Sue, I do mean you! All that power walking has really paid off.) In addition to the cosmetic benefits, you'll feel great. You'll be more energized, alert, and self-confident if you lay down the book (after you've finished it, of course!) and get off the couch. You'll be better able to handle stress and less likely to catch cold. In other words, if exercise doesn't top your to-do list, you need to reorganize your priorities.

Five things can help you stick to a regular exercise routine: (1) Choose something you love. Walking, swimming, ballet, dance, kickboxing—whatever! The key is to focus on what you can do, not what you can't. (2) Set realistic goals and start at a comfortable level. Whoever told you "no pain, no gain" lied. You should never be too sore to move the next day. Exercise isn't a race (unless you're training for a marathon), and it's not a contest (unless you hope to make the U.S. Olympic team), it's a way of life. (3) Plan ahead. Be sure you have the right equipment and attire. You don't have to look good while you exercise (unless you do it at a country club), but you do have to feel good. (4) Find a partner or team to make you stick with it. Just as you're a lot more likely to go to the gym if you know your trainer's there waiting for you, you're a lot more likely to walk if you have someone to walk with. Make exercise a team sport. (5) Always warm up and cool down. Most injuries are caused by setting out to walk a mile before stretching muscles that aren't used to walking farther than the refrigerator. Again, start slowly and carefully, then build up.

When you've put in your time on your feet, here's something to perk them right up again. Take two cans of soda from the fridge. (You're not going to drink them, so it doesn't matter if they're diet.) Place them on the floor in front of a chair and roll your hot, tired tootsies back and forth over them. Ahhh. Now, lay down for that power nap, but this time prop your feet up. Any swelling will disappear as the trapped fluids circulate back down your legs toward your heart.

chapter 15

"No!" I said firmly, if indistinctly. "I don't want to wake up. I'll miss the end of the movie. Go away!"

"Jill?"

At the sound of the leading man's voice, I opened my eyes the merest crack. Clay Eskiminzin was approximately as close to me as I wanted him to be for the rest of forever. "No!" I said again, grabbing for him as if the ground beneath me had turned to quicksand. "Don't go away!"

"Shh. You're okay." He disentangled my arms from around his neck and leaned me back against the trunk of an evergreen. Then he shined the beam of a small flashlight into my unfocused eyeballs.

I lay back and considered the tree trunk between my shoulder blades. Even in near-consciousness I knew I had been standing in a clearing when I fainted, well away from cougar-concealing trees. Clay must have carried me here. In other words, it was in all probability the one and only time he would ever hold me in his arms and I had *missed it!* Of all the really rotten things that could have happened to me, that was the worst. I closed my eyes. "Just let me die."

"You're not going to die," he said, returning the flashlight to a pocket in his pants. "But you went down too fast for me to catch you, so you've got a nasty bump on your head."

The way my luck was running, it would be in the most unattractive place possible. I raised my fingers to a prominent cheekbone, but it seemed to be intact. That's when I realized Clay was holding a cold, wet cloth above my right ear. It was another remnant of the all-purpose shirt he'd loaned me early in the day, but the cold water didn't help much. My head hurt like heck. I looked up into the tree for buzzards. "Are you sure I'm not going to die?"

He smiled. "Yes."

While I was looking up, I noticed that the sky had changed again. Blue in the morning and brown in the afternoon, in evening the vast expanse had turned a drab near-green with only a hard yellow glow near the western horizon to indicate there had ever been a sun. I frowned. "I saw *Cast Away*. What happened to those spectacular sunsets you're supposed to see when you're marooned in the great outdoors?"

He followed my gaze. "It's early. Watch the mountains. In another ten minutes those purple shadows will run together and turn gray. The sky will look metallic then. Five minutes after that, the shadows will have deepened to black and all this dust will glow into the Arizona-sunset-orange you've grown to expect. Watch. I guarantee a spectacular show."

I didn't need a guarantee. I didn't even need to watch. If Clay said it would happen, it would. Surely Clay was as much an expert on sunsets as he was on everything else out here. Of course, what else did he have to do in the evening besides watch the sun set? I felt obliged to point out, "They make portable DVD players that are smaller than a canteen. You could watch movies right in the discomfort of your own desert."

"I haven't seen all there is to see in a sunset yet." Then he sang, "Have you heard the whisper of the desert wind? From the mountains, from the valley it comes to my ears. The desert whispers, 'Listen.' It whispers, 'Understand.' It whispers, 'Stay in peace.'" Clay was still holding the cool cloth to my head, but with his free hand he pulled his bag closer, reaching in it. "Chee says those are the words of Eskiminzin." He found what he was looking for, managed to open the small bottle one-handed, and extended two small tablets. "Ibuprofen."

I looked down at the pills. "I didn't think you were kidding about giving me twigs to chew for a headache."

"I could find you some bark that would help a little," he said, "but this is faster." He held the canteen to my parched lips. "More," he urged when I swallowed only enough water to wash down the pain reliever.

My throat felt raw, but I obliged. It tasted too good to have come out of a faucet in Tucson. Clay must have refilled the canteen at the waterfall. Grateful, I drank about a quart of unbottled spring water.

"Good," he said at last. "Now you need to eat and then you need to rest. Eight miles was way too much to expect of you today, Jill. Again, I'm sorry."

Forget the heartfelt apology; I was stuck on the clearly inaccurate mileage. I sat up. "*Eight miles*?" I cried. "Don't you mean *eighty*? We must have walked eight miles just from the waterfall!"

"It only seemed farther because . . ." His words trailed into silence.

Let me tell you something. Men—even well-trained men—don't survive long in the desert without good instincts. Batguy's were the best. (Either that or he'd seen the look on my face before—maybe he'd once run across a rabid, hunger-crazed raccoon.)

Whatever the explanation, his eyebrows rose and he said, "You're right. We walked eighty miles today. Maybe a hundred."

"That's what I thought." I leaned back against the tree, content now to sit for the rest of my life with my head cradled in his hand. Longer if I could work it out.

Gently, he removed his hand from my aching head and stuck it in his parfleche.

"Mary Poppins had a bag like that," I observed. "Do you have a spoonful of sugar to help the medicine go down?"

"No, but I have a leftover turkey sandwich to help keep it down."

"Anything else?" I asked hopefully.

"Dried fruit," he said. "Seeds. Nuts. Elk jerky."

"I'll take the sandwich." It was not only smashed, it was stale—and a little gritty from the dust storm. All in all, it looked delicious. Still, I lifted a corner of the bread in disappointment. "No mayonnaise?"

"No food poisoning," he pointed out. "Eat."

Ravenous wolverines have been known to eat more slowly and with better manners than I used devouring that sandwich. "What kind of fruit?" I asked, still chewing the last bite of dry bread.

"Apricot." Clay extended a pouch. "But don't eat more than a handful, or when it reconstitutes in all that water you drank, your stomach will feel worse than your head."

Mammy's counsel from *Gone with the Wind* flashed into my mind. "*Men likes their womenfolk to eat like birds*," she'd told Scarlett before the Wilkes's barbeque. I'd eaten like a bird, all right. A seagull. But I took the dried fruit anyway, and to make up for the sandwich-scarfing, daintily tried to eat it and the nuts he gave me next. While I ate I watched the sunset. Unlike most movies, it was every bit as spectacular as advertised.

"Feel better?" he asked when supper was over.

"Yes," I said, and it was true. The pain reliever had lived up to its name, and the food had not only tamed the beast in my stomach, it had stilled the wooziness that had made me faint.

"Good." He returned the pouches of food to his bag.

Clay, I'd noted, ate only a couple of pieces of shriveled meat and a handful each of fruit and nuts. While he chewed in silence, he'd taken a few sunflower seeds out of one of the many pockets in his cargo pants, but he didn't eat them. He turned them over in his hand, added a few more, and then seemed to count them as he returned them to the zippered pocket. I remembered he'd done something similar this morning when he talked to Shar.

And he thought *I* was strange.

Clay looked up at the almost-dark sky, pivoted his crouch until he was beside me, and pointed toward the hole in the side of the cliff. "Watch this," he said as if *Star Wars* was about to begin. I wished I had a tub of popcorn.

It was a good thing I didn't, or in the next few seconds I would have strewn it from there to Colorado. Something came out of the hole. Something small and black and shaped kind of like a flying mouse. It took three or four blinked frames of consciousness for me to realize it wasn't Mickey dressed for Halloween. It was a bat. A real bat. A bat with its fangs bared and its talons fully extended. (Clay insists that bats have toes, not talons, but if you'd have been there, you'd have thought "talons" too. As for vegetarian bats having fangs, I'm gonna have to side with the makers of *Dracula* on that one, too.)

Too horrified too scream, I let out a tiny little "eek."

Apparently "eek" is a universal bat call, because more bats followed the first intrepid little rodent into the purple-blue sky. Dozens of bats. Hundreds of bats. Very possibly thousands and millions of bats poured from that hole before my very eyes. (Very wide eyes. Wider surely than they ever had been before or ever would be again.)

"Isn't that incredible?" Clay asked.

He wasn't referring to the fact that I was practically in his lap by now. He scooted away as if he assumed I needed a little more space in the middle of a million acres of barren dirt, but he didn't take his eyes from the sky.

Incredible wasn't the word for it, but I was too dumbstruck to know what was. It looked like a tornado of bats at first, spiraling up into the sky and then widening into a thundercloud of flapping and twittering. The miracle was that they didn't bash into each other and litter the countryside with their unconscious little carcasses.

"Look at them!" Clay said as if there was anyplace else *to* look that wasn't full of acrobatic winged rats. "I can't think of anything I like more."

"Than *bats?"* I scooted away from him. Then I scooted a little farther. The man was gorgeous. He was smart. He was kind. He was strong and brave and reverent and . . . obviously insane. *Batguy* took on a whole new connotation in my mind.

"Call me 'Batguy,'" he said. I think he laughed, but I was too stunned to swear to it. I even forgot about the bats for a second.

"Where did you ever . . . ?" I began. "I mean, how . . . ? I mean, I never—"

"Yes," he said. "You did. Several times." I shook my head, but he nodded and prompted, "You called me 'Batguy' back at the ranch when you were talking on the porch with Mrs. Teagler."

That was before I had known how well he could hear. I bit my bottom lip.

"And up at the top of the cliff," he continued. "I believe it was right at the beginning of your discourse on how movie actresses never become unattractively disheveled."

Who else but him would remember all the ravings of a wild woman? "You should have finished law school," I mumbled. "You missed your calling."

"Plus," he concluded, "you have an amazing ability to talk even while unconscious."

"You're making that one up!"

He rose and reached into one of his many pockets for a small black flashlight different from the one he'd shone in my eyes. "That's about as likely as you walking eighty miles today," he said. I could scarcely believe that I'd survived a helicopter ride, Alex's goons, a careening jeep, a dust storm, and a climb down a sheer cliff only to be done in by mortification. I slumped forward. *Somebody call the buzzards.*

"The only thing I can't figure out," Batfink said, "is what you mean by it."

My head rose along with my spirits. He was clueless. (See where missing a couple decades of movie classics will get you?) "It means I think you're batty," I said loftily. Then I added, "Crazy," to make sure he got the point.

I think that gave him pause, but because he was always so deliberate about the way he did everything, it was hard to tell for sure. At any rate, he walked toward the bat cave, leaving me alone . . . in the dark.

Scrambling to my feet made my head throb again, but I ignored it. I followed Clay to the entrance. "You're not going in there, I hope."

"We're going to sleep in there," he said. "There's too much going on out in the open. Besides, in a few hours the temperature will drop sixty degrees. Without concrete to hold the heat, the desert gets as cold at night as it does hot during the day. We'll need shelter."

I stared into the hole and shuddered. "Are all the bats gone?"

"Yes."

"Won't they come back?"

"Yes."

"Then—"

"We won't be here then."

I took a step back, thinking I'd rather freeze to death on my feet than crawl into that cave on my knees. "Is there anything *else* in there?"

He held up the tiny flashlight. "That's what I'm going to find out."

I could have sworn I saw him press the switch, but there was no light. "Your flashlight works about as well as your radio," I observed.

"You're half right," he said. "This *is* my flashlight, but like the rest of *my* stuff, it works fine. It's an ultraviolet light."

A black light? Interesting, but not very helpful unless you have psychedelic posters left over from the '70s that you want to hang in your cave.

"It's used to look for scorpions at night."

Or that. Despite myself, I peered over his shoulder.

"Scorpions phosphoresce," he explained.

"You mean they glow in the dark?"

"In a manner of speaking." He swung the beam of purple light across the walls, then focused it on the ceiling. "See there?"

How could I miss it? I'd eaten lobster smaller than the scorpion plastered to the side of that rock. Worse, it looked as though it was being worshiped by half a dozen small, glowing minions.

"It's the little ones you have to watch out for," Clay said. "Their poison is more concentrated. Without medical attention, a few stings can kill you."

"That's okay," I whispered. "I'm going to die of fright and save them the trouble."

He withdrew his head from the cave opening and said, "A quote from the book of Ezekiel: 'And thou, son of man, . . . though briers and thorns be with thee, and thou dost dwell among scorpions: be not afraid.'"

"I'm not a son of man," I said. "I'm a daughter of God."

He almost smiled. "Then maybe you'd better step back a little."

I'd have backed all the way to Florida if I hadn't feared mountain lions as much as scorpions. Having backed a prudent distance, I turned around. Then I squeezed my eyes closed and covered my ears for good measure. (Don't tell me it was a little much until *you've* seen a very large scorpion and its entourage Day-Glo for yourself.) Several minutes later when Clay touched my shoulder, I almost jumped out of my skin.

"You can go in now," he said.

I turned. He'd left a light on—a yellow-beamed flashlight this time. Still, it was no Motel 6. It wasn't even a Motel 1. It was a dark, distasteful *cave*. "Please tell me you have a Plan B."

"Sorry yet again."

I looked around, considering my options. It was as dark now as the inside of a movie theater just before they roll the film. Plus, somebody had turned up the surround sound. Something in the mountains above yipped, and I cringed. Something else rustled through the nearby bushes, and I jumped. Overhead, yet a third something—larger than a bat—whooshed, and I shrieked.

"Mexican spotted owl," Clay observed with his Batvision. "They're endangered."

"That one would be extinct if I'd had your stick."

He ignored my empty threat on a protected species and said, "So, what's it going to be? You either hang in the bat cave with me or you take your chances out here alone."

In the distance, a woman's scream reverberated against the canyon walls.

"That would be the mother puma," Clay said calmly as I wrapped myself around his arm like a boa constrictor. "She sounds almost human, doesn't she?"

"I like bats," I lied fervently. "They are at the very top of the list of things I like very, very much." I practically pushed him back toward the cave. "Just so you know."

Jill's Tips for Being Beautiful from the Inside Out

Aside from being lost in the desert without food, the best motivation I know for starting a diet and sticking to it is to schedule yourself to appear in a swimsuit before 15 million of your closest friends. You won't have to buy an expensive diet book or join a group to have someplace to weigh in because you will be too busy wondering what possessed you to enter the Miss America pageant to think about food, and too mortified at the thought of what you've done to be able to swallow it.

Seriously, though, if you are a real person in the real world with real concerns about diet and nutrition, you can't go wrong reading Section 89 of the Doctrine and Covenants. (Again, who can give you better advice about what to put in your body than its Creator?) My favorite line in the scripture is in verse three, where it says, "Given for a principle with promise, adapted to the capacity of the weak and the weakest of all Saints, who are or can be called Saints." (Even though I know it was written just for me, I've always been grateful that the Lord didn't inspire Joseph to mention me by name.)

Anyway, what the Word of Wisdom does is command us to eat sensibly. If we do that—and drink gallons of water—we won't need to count carbs, calories, fat grams, or the pounds creeping up on the bathroom scale. Here are some of my favorite beauty foods: **Apple cider vinegar**—besides its incredible healing properties, it makes your skin supple and breaks down fat. I eat it on fresh and cooked spinach. Yum! **Carrots**—forget the old "apple a day" motto and eat a carrot instead to prevent premature aging. **Sweet potatoes**—my great-grandmother swears that sweet potatoes are the key to clearer, smoother skin, fewer wrinkles, and longer life. At 97, I figure she ought to know. **Nonfat yogurt**—whiter smile, fewer cavities, stronger bones, and no more yeast infections. Who could ask more from a food? **Citrus**—Another great immunity booster, citrus fruit also helps the body form collagen, which holds skin cells together for fresher, younger-looking faces. **Garlic**—if there is an all-around wonder food, garlic is it. Just be careful when and how you use it because, believe me, it can repel more than vampires!

chapter 16

"Connor!" I screamed. It was the middle of the night and only Clay's arm around my shoulder kept me from bolting up from my nightmare and sustaining yet another concussion.

"I heard him!" I cried, struggling to get away from Clay, to get out of this cave, to find the clearly terrified child. If only I could tell which way was out. With the moon and stars obscured by clouds—or dust—or both, every direction seemed equally black. Even Clay was only a dim outline.

Another haunted cry echoed across the universe and I wondered how God could fail to respond to such a supplication.

"Jill!" Clay had to shout to get my attention. "It isn't Connor. It's only a coyote."

I stopped struggling, but every muscle in my body remained taut. "Only a . . . ?"

"A coyote," he repeated. "Listen." The horrifying cry was echoed by a mournful dirge that gave me goose bumps of trepidation—or perhaps sympathy.

"What's wrong with them?"

"They're complaining about the dark," he said. "Or they're celebrating a kill. Or having a sing-a-long. It's hard to say with coyotes."

"It sounded like a child crying." I shuddered and Clay's arm tightened around my shoulder for just a moment before he removed it and moved away. "It sounded like . . ." Words failed me.

"They can sound like everything but the Mormon Tabernacle Choir," he said.

"I—"

"Let me guess," he interrupted. "You hate coyotes."

It was too dark for him to see me frown. "Can we just say I like Roadrunner better than Wile E. and leave it at that?"

"Cartoons gave coyotes a bad rap," Clay said. "They're terrific creatures."

"Better than bats?"

"Different," he said. "Did you know coyotes have been known to follow hunters, dig up their traps, turn the traps over and urinate on them before retreating to the hills?"

I didn't know, nor did I particularly want to.

"According to an old Indian saying," he continued, "a feather fell from the sky. The eagle saw it fall, the deer heard it fall, the bear smelled it as it fell, but the coyote did all three at once."

If Clay was waiting for me to join his Wile E. Coyote fan club—remarkable as the inspirations for the cartoon character may be—he'd have a long wait. "Are you *sure* it wasn't Connor?"

"Yes."

I tried to look around, but finally understood the cliché "too dark to see your hand in front of your face." I leaned back against the cave wall. "What time is it?"

"Almost midnight."

I hadn't heard Big Ben chime, and Clay didn't wear a Batwatch, so I wondered how he knew. I stretched, only to find that every muscle I possessed hurt. I curled back into the fetal position my body seemed to prefer. If sleep had tightened my muscles, at least it had also loosened the ache from my head and I could think. "Did I make it all the way into the cave before I fell asleep?" I wondered out loud.

"Barely."

"Narcolepsy can be acquired," I told him. "I can sleep anytime, anywhere. And I sleep best when I'm terrified. It's one of many skills I picked up training for the Miss America pageant."

"You were Miss America?"

The fact that he didn't sound sarcastic, or even surprised, might not have been an outright compliment, but I chose to take it as one and filed it away to relish later. "First runner-up," I confessed.

"I'm impressed."

Again, he wasn't being ironic, but I found it hard to believe that placing second in a beauty pageant was something that would impress him. And why should it? In Atlantic City, where it really counted, I'd *lost.*

"Nobody remembers the runners-up," I admitted. "All I have to show for the years of agony is an old VHS recording of the telecast that nobody I know has a machine to even play it on anymore, and a few dried roses from my consolation bouquet."

"No college scholarship?"

I was surprised at his insight, to say the least. The only thing most men know about the Miss America pageant is that approximately fifteen of the one hundred and twenty minutes of airtime feature swimsuits. "Well, yes," I replied. "I graduated from ASU on the scholarship they gave me."

"The scholarship you *won,*" he pointed out. "Besides which, you developed the poise and confidence to appear professionally on TV, and . . ." He trailed off. I suspected it was because he'd run out of positive things to list, but he sounded almost shy. "Anyway," he picked up, "Aren't you the one who told me everything we do is important because it leads in one way or another to who we are at the moment?"

Again I was astonished. Clay Eskiminzin had *listened* to me ramble? *And* remembered what I said? Wow. As I said earlier, I'm used to men looking at me, but I'm not used to them listening to me. My so-called boyfriend hadn't responded to a word I'd said besides "no" in the last two months. (And he didn't respond favorably to that one.)

I resolved again to think before I speak. Then I said a quick prayer of gratitude—one of thankfulness to be exactly where I was at that given moment. (I'm sure God was a little surprised, if not baffled. He knows me better than anyone, and had never before known me to want to be anywhere dirty, smelly and/or dangerous.) "You listened to me," I sighed, meaning both Heavenly Father and Clay.

Clay was quiet for a while as if he were thinking, and then he said, "Let me tell you another coyote story, one about the sacred Coyote of legend."

Not being able to see Clay's face as he talked was another reason—and a better one—to hate the dark. I squinted in his direction, but it was no use. Post-destruction Zarahemla *must* have been like this, I decided.

"One day Coyote saw some lizards playing a game he didn't know," Clay began. "They held onto flat, round stones and used them to slide down a steep rock. It looked like great fun to Coyote, so he grabbed a stone of his own and lined up to take his turn. The lizards warned him that what was sport for them was dangerous for a coyote, but he wouldn't listen. Instead, he pushed off and slid halfway down the rock before he hit a fissure, flipped his stone, and landed on his back with the stone on top of him."

"Sounds like Wile E. Coyote to me," I giggled.

"But there's a point to this story," Clay said patiently. "Coyote learned that coyotes shouldn't want to be lizards, let alone try to be."

There was a reason he told me this story, I knew. I also knew that unlike Aesop, Clay wasn't going to tell me what the moral was. I wasn't going to ask either. I'd figure it out for myself. Eventually.

A coyote—a real one this time—yelped not fifty feet from our cave and I scooted into Clay's warm, reassuring side. He didn't put his arm around me again as I'd hoped, but he didn't move away, either.

"Where do you think Connor is right now?" I asked.

"If your theory is right, he's someplace safe."

I nodded and prayed that my suspicions were correct. I might suspect Alex Teagler of hiding his son away on purpose, but I didn't believe he'd put him in real danger. Unless he didn't know how dangerous it was. "Why *here*?" I asked Clay. "Why wouldn't Alex have taken Connor to the city?"

Batguy didn't have to resolve to think before he spoke. It came naturally. At last he said, "Whoever took Connor chose this time and place very carefully. At this point, there's probably no federal involvement, just local search-and-rescue. Anson's going to handle it as a lost child as long as he thinks he can get away with it. With the senator's support, that could be days. By the time the focus shifts, if it ever does, even the best forensics experts will have one heck of a time coming up with a trail."

He made it sound like the perfect kidnapping. "But *might* they have taken Connor back to Tucson?" I asked hopefully. Even though I'd seen the tracks and the ATV and the little boot print in the dirt, the thought of a child in this danger-filled canyon was horrifying enough to convert me to cockeyed optimism in a heartbeat.

Clay remained a realist. His failure to respond at once was all the answer I needed. I hugged my knees tighter.

"Remember," Clay said at last, "how carefully planned this was. The cave where they've taken Connor is about as safe as any you can find in this canyon."

At least that was something to hold on to. I imagined a well-fed Connor in his pajamas with blankets and pillows and surrounded by black light to ward off scorpions. Lost in my dream, it was several minutes before I realized the implication of Clay's words. I sat upright. "You *know* where Connor is?"

"I think I do. The tracks were leading toward a cave I know of, and there's been every indication that somebody has been down here before this morning. Several times. They probably started setting up last week."

And brought in food, pillows, and blankets! I thought. Connor *was* safe. Surely by morning his father would have milked the disappearance for all it was worth and the little boy would turn up safe and sound in time for breakfast. I felt better.

"I'll know if I'm right in a few more hours," Clay said.

I felt worse again. "What do you mean you'll know if you're right? *How* will you know?" I turned toward him, even if I couldn't see his face. "Surely you're not planning to confront the kidnappers!"

I didn't expect an answer, and I didn't get one.

"Clay," I said reasonably, "all we have to do is wait for the sun to come up. Alex has all the publicity he needs by now and—"

"It's not that simple. You think Connor can walk back to the ranch, no questions asked?"

"Alex will handle it," I said stubbornly. "He always does."

"I'm not so sure."

Whatever *that* meant.

"And what about us?" he continued.

"Well, the sheriff will find us," I said, missing his point entirely. "There'll be helicopters and dogs and—"

"Not very soon, there won't be," Clay interrupted. "The storm wiped out every trace of us being here and, as I told you before, our jeep will be found six canyons over." I felt rather than saw him lean back into the wall of the cave as he waited for me to figure it out for myself. When I didn't, he gave me another hint. "The bad guys have most of the advantages, Jill. They know we're here, whereas nobody else does."

"What does that mean?"

"It means that unlike us, they have nothing to lose."

I still didn't understand. I especially didn't understand why Clay thought he had to confront Alex's henchmen. "Everything will be fine," I said again. "You'll see."

My confidence in my "all is well" speech faltered as, at last, the "truth reflected on my senses." A man desperate enough to try to win an election by staging the disappearance of his own son was surely desperate enough to ensure that his ploy remained a secret. I gasped. "You think he'll murder us!"

"I'm sure they'd rather we die a convenient, natural death out here in the desert," Clay said. "But that isn't going to happen."

As relieved as I was to hear that last part, I was terrified to think what *would* happen when the new day dawned. "Clay!" I said. "What are we going to do?"

He folded his arms behind his head. "We're going to go back to sleep."

chapter 17

Although trepidation usually activates my automatic sleep mechanism, I'm not used to sleeping in the dark. (I like there to be a difference between what I see with my eyes open and what I see with them closed. Streetlights, nightlights, and those cool little battery-operated globes you activate with a touch of your finger were invented for people like me.) Besides, the apprehension I felt in that cave now went beyond simple terror. It was more like complex near-hysteria. Thank goodness Clay couldn't see me vibrate and/or tic in the dark. I wondered if the Apaches had come up with an herbal remedy for anxiety attacks. At that point, I'd have swallowed a cactus whole if it could have calmed my jangled nerves.

"Tell me another story," I entreated in the absence of tranquilizers, natural or otherwise.

"I don't know—"

"Tell me about your ancestor," I suggested before Clay could finish demurring. "Tell me about Eskiminzin."

"What do you want to know?"

"Everything."

"I don't know everything," he said. "I only know what I've read and what I've been told."

"Then tell me that." My reaction to a sudden howl from above our cave was to knock a formerly uninjured piece of my head against the hard rock wall. "Ouch!"

Clay squeezed my hand. "A coyote," he reminded me gently. "Lean your head against my shoulder and try to go back to sleep."

Although his shoulder wasn't much softer than the cave wall, it was infinitely more comforting. But I might as well have tried to see in the dark as to sleep in it. Both were impossible. "Please, Clay," I begged. "Talk to me. Tell me about the Apache chief and why you admire him."

The answering call of another coyote punctuated my plea and Clay cleared his throat. "Apaches didn't have chiefs," he said. "At least not the way you probably think of them. Apache warriors elected their leaders by common consent, not right of birth. That's how Eskiminzin came to lead the Aravaipa, his first wife's tribe, even though he was born a Pinal Apache. Eskiminzin was a name he acquired as an adult. It means Angry Men Stand in Line for Him."

"Did he know Geronimo and Cochise?" I asked. I wasn't exactly breathless, but even to my own ears I sounded like a child seeking the most exciting part of a story first.

But I wasn't going to get sensationalism first, because Clay didn't tell stories that way. "Everybody who lived in this area knew Geronimo and Cochise," he said. "One way or another. But Eskiminzin was a different kind of Apache than the ones you've seen in the movies. Unlike most of his contemporaries, he recognized the futility of trying to hold on to the land. Eskiminzin is said to have told Geronimo that stopping the white men coming would be like trying to halt the thunderclouds that move across the open sky."

Already I sensed that this story might be sensational only in its sadness.

"Eskiminzin believed that the Apaches' best chance for survival was through peace," Clay said. "So he took his people back to the Little Running Water and asked the United States Cavalry at Fort Grant for 'permission' to live again on the land their people had farmed for centuries. It was the last thing anybody expected of an Apache chief, because it required not only courage but humility."

"And faith," I observed.

"Yes," Clay said. "Faith. And maybe desperation. Although he was still a relatively young man at the time, Eskiminzin was tired and sick. He was tired of running and sick at heart from watching the women and children of his tribe suffer and die." Clay shifted position, but I didn't move my head from his shoulder. "But I think even worse was the weight of decision he bore. Every day that Eskiminzin awoke he had to decide if it would be the day he would kill or be killed. He echoed the sentiment of the war chief who said, *If my warriors are to fight they are too few; if they are to die they are too many.* That's why, after prayer and fasting, he petitioned a man by the name of Royal Whitman for peace like a stone."

"Like a stone?" I asked, intrigued.

"Lieutenant Whitman recorded that Eskiminzin's words were, "*May peace between our people be like this stone. May it be hard and lasting and endure the test of time. May we return to our peace as to this stone and say, 'Enju—it is well. It continues forever.'*"

"Did the peace last?" I asked.

"It could have," Clay said. "Whitman was a good man. The days passed into weeks and then months, until there were more than five hundred Apaches living along the creek up the canyon from the fort. They planted corn and vegetables and lived almost as they had before the soldiers came."

Again Clay moved on the hard stone floor, and again I moved with him. (It would have taken an act of heaven to move me away.)

"Whitman wrote several letters describing what he called his 'family in the desert,'" Clay continued. "He told everyone from San Francisco to Washington D.C. that while the Aravaipa men were poorly clothed and 'ignorant,' they refused to lie or steal, and that the women worked like slaves to clothe their children and themselves. He pointed out, too, that while the natives were 'unschooled in the word of God,' they held their virtue and honor above price."

Despite this story being about good people, it wasn't going to end with "happily ever after." I could tell that much from Clay's long, reflective pause. Something had happened to that peace like a stone. I waited for him to tell me what it was.

"The thing was," Clay said, "that it wasn't profitable for a few of the folks in Tucson to have the Aravaipas settle down to their farming. It was about 1870, remember, and ambitious Tucsonans were anxious to establish their businesses and thereby assure their rightful place in society and government before the territory applied for statehood."

I didn't understand and said so.

"Without Apaches to fight," Clay explained, "there would be no need to keep the forts around the town open. A whole lot of the money that passed through Tucson was from the military. Most of the money, in fact. Without the U.S. government stationed there, Tucson stood to lose not only a big chunk of its economy, but also its prospect for becoming the capital of a new state."

"You're kidding," I said, anticipating what was to come in the story. "Settlers would kill innocent people for—"

"Most Anglos didn't consider Apaches people," he pointed out. "They were *Indians*, which put them roughly on par with coyotes on the socioeconomic spectrum of the period."

I remembered Shar telling us about the cowboys and Indians game she had played with Connor this morning, and cringed. It was more than a cultural faux pas, I realized. It was a way of looking at people that I didn't think she'd learned growing up. Like the rest of her current beliefs, it had been fashioned by her aristocratic husband, whose roots lay deep in Old Tucson.

I wasn't sure now that I wanted to know the rest of Eskiminzin's story, but Clay had taken it up again. "There was a group in town called the Tucson Committee of Public Safety," he said. "Ironically, Alex Teagler's family was prominent in it. These stalwart community leaders left the saloons and gambling halls empty one night long enough to get together at Bennett's to discuss a recent Apache raid. A young couple had been killed by one of Geronimo's war parties and somebody had to pay for it. Vengeful Chiricahuas . . . peaceful Aravaipas . . . what's the difference?" Under my cheek, Clay's shoulder moved in a disdainful shrug. "If you've seen one Apache, you've seen them all, right?"

I drew in a breath as he continued.

"A mob met at the mouth of Rillito Canyon a few days later. The Anglos were the organizers, but only a handful showed up. The people with the most to lose from peaceful Indians were also the ones with money enough to pay Mexicans and Papagos Indians to kill for them."

Now I *knew* I didn't want to hear the rest of the story, but it was too late.

"The group of one hundred and fifty or so traveled to within a mile of the village on Saturday night, April 29, 1871," Clay said as if reciting a history lesson. Then his voice changed. It wasn't history anymore. It was *his* story again. Eskiminzin's story. "They waited another four hours to attack. It was easy then. Too easy. There were only two aged lookouts because a people who believed they were protected had little to fear. Besides, night is sacred to the Apache because it is the time the dead can return to their homes. The mob knew nobody in the rancheria would stir before the dawn."

"But they *were* protected," I interrupted. "The soldiers at Fort Grant! Surely *they* had guards. Didn't you say the village was near the fort?"

"Not near enough," Clay said. "Five miles was too far for the military sentries to hear the screams of the women and children, let alone the sound of the Papago skull-smashers." Clay cleared his throat again, but I think all he had to dislodge from it was the memory of his family's fate. "The men went from wikiup to wikiup—family to family—with a speed and proficiency that was as incredible as it was horrific." His voice lowered. "But it wasn't enough for them to murder these people. They violated the women, mutilated the men, and took the children to sell into slavery. Then they burned the rancheria practically to the ground." Clay sounded as sick as if he'd seen it for himself. "They even killed many of the dogs."

"Eskiminzin?" I asked when it seemed he wouldn't continue. "He was murdered?"

"No," Clay said. "He'd heard a cry and was sitting up when two Papagos charged into his home. As he started to stand, they swung one of their cowhide-sheathed stones into the side of his face."

I gasped.

"It was a blessing," Clay said. "Eskiminzin was spared the agony of seeing his wife tortured and his children murdered. As he fell, his body collapsed onto his youngest daughter, Chita. Because the men didn't know who he was, and thought he was dead, both their lives were spared."

"And then?"

"Then it was over. By the time the sun reached the tops of the Galiuros, the killers were rested, breakfasted, and on their way to a hero's welcome back in Tucson." Clay paused. "I doubt a single one of those upstanding citizens ever asked themselves if their 'crusade' was an appropriate way to observe the Sabbath."

After almost a full minute of silence he concluded, "There were one hundred thirty-eight dead, and only eight of them were warriors-turned-farmers—the rest of the men were away on a hunt. Lieutenant Whitman wrote letter after graphic letter about the bodies of babies and elderly women strewn everywhere."

I didn't think I could speak. Even breathing was difficult. "What did Eskiminzin do?"

"He aged a hundred years overnight. He cut off his braids in sorrow—and in guilt for failing the people who had trusted him. After a few days in the canyons, he and his shaman, Santo, went back to the rancheria to properly mourn the dead the soldiers had finally buried in a mass grave. Then," Clay's voice filled with admiration, "believe it or not, Eskiminzin led the few surviving families of his tribe back to the fort."

"He *did?*" I was beginning to think Geronimo was the Apache with the right idea for dealing with the Anglos. At least some Anglos. I wondered how history would be different if Alex's family had appropriated their ranchland from Geronimo instead of Eskiminzin. Chances are that one-hundred-fifty-some years later, the senator from Arizona wouldn't be named Teagler—Alex's family line would probably have ended quite abruptly in 1870.

"Eskiminzin told Lieutenant Whitman that while he no longer wanted to live, he *would* live," Clay continued. "He'd live to show the people who had ordered the massacre that all they had done—and all they could do—would never make him break his word. As long as Whitman and the U.S. government were loyal to him, Eskiminzin said he would remain faithful to the government. They would have their peace like a stone."

Maybe this story would have a happy ending after all, I thought. But I thought it too soon.

"The peace lasted four weeks," Clay said. "Then Eskiminzin and Santo rode back into the canyons to retrieve an old man and his family who had been too frightened to return to Fort Grant. On their way, a group of soldiers from Fort Apache fired on them. Later, the soldiers admitted they did it for sport. Hunting Indians was a great game where no buffalo were available."

So the U.S. Army *hadn't* been loyal, at least not in the chief's eyes. My next question was almost a whisper. "What did Eskiminzin do then?"

"To put it in the modern vernacular," Clay said, "he lost it."

Like you could blame him.

"The Aravaipa Apaches went on the warpath that afternoon," Clay said. "Many—probably most—of his men were glad of it. Since the massacre, they'd felt more like cattle waiting for slaughter than Apache braves." His voice lowered. "But it was a tragic time for Eskiminzin. On what he said was the worst day in a long life filled with sorrow, he killed a white man. In all those years of desperate conflict, it was the only time he took a life. He never got over it and spent the rest of his life trying to make it right with his God. He died before he ever felt he could."

"But with his family brutalized," I breathed, "and losing so many of his people, and being betrayed again and again—"

"One more reason I'm glad I'm the one who stands before the bar," Clay said, "instead of being the One who judges."

I didn't want to think about it anymore. It made me too confused and too sad. But I had to know the end. "How did it turn out?" I asked. "I mean, finally?"

"I should have warned you that I'm not a good storyteller."

"It's not that!" I said. "It's—"

"*The Reader's Digest* version," Clay interrupted, "is that Eskiminzin had no gift, or heart, for war. He wanted to raise cattle and grow melons, so the Aravaipa were the first Apaches to settle the new San Carlos Reservation—or "Hell's Forty Acres" as the army called part of it. After more than a decade, Eskiminzin was successful enough at farming to purchase his own land. Big mistake. About the time he proved to Tucson's inner circle that he was as good at business as they were—or better—he was falsely accused of harboring a criminal and sentenced to work on an Alabama chain gang. He was about sixty at the time. An old man in those days."

"I can't believe—"

"Believe it," Clay said. "If nothing else, those good American citizens knew how to get the land they wanted. And how to further their careers, of course."

Some things hadn't changed over the centuries. Or maybe it was some people that hadn't changed. Was lust for money and power genetic, or a learned behavior passed from father to son? Either way, I worried for Connor.

"In early spring of 1894," Clay concluded, "Eskiminzin was finally pardoned and sent back to Arizona. But being home for him was worse than working on the chain gang. His days were haunted and his nights sleepless. In his old age, he couldn't put aside his guilt over the man he'd killed. The voices of his murdered tribespeople called out to him in his dreams. One night, about a year later, his spirit finally left his body to seek in death the 'peace like a stone' that he had never found in life."

"Wow." It wasn't an eloquent reply, but it was all I could manage. At last I added, "I see why you took his name. Surely your family must be pleased. He is an incredible ancestor to claim."

Clay laughed.

"What?" I asked, confused.

"I never said my family claims him. Acknowledges him as a curiosity, maybe, but *claims* him?" Clay's chuckle died in his throat. "Well, they probably claim the first Eskiminzin about as much as they claim *me*."

I raised my head from Clay's shoulder. I could just make out his face through the gloom. It was too early for the sun to have risen, but maybe the dust had finally settled enough to allow a little moonlight to peek through.

"Clay Eskiminzin," I said, "who *are* you? Who are you *really*?"

chapter 18

Don't you hate it when somebody answers your question with a question of his own? Sitting in that cave in the middle of the night with nothing further from my mind than sleep, I wanted to learn everything there was to know about this latter-day Lamanite. But instead of spilling his guts, Clay wanted to play word games.

"Who are *you* really?" he responded to my attempt to find out his secret identity.

"You know who I am!"

"I do?" He made himself more comfortable. (If that's possible in a bat hole.) "Let's see . . . I know you're a former Miss Arizona. A graduate of ASU. A reporter for some news program in Tucson. A Primary teacher. Somebody's girlfriend. A hater of the great outdoors. And a lover of everything made for the silver screen."

Before I could clarify the girlfriend thing, he continued. "And you know I'm a law-school dropout. A forest ranger. A lover of the great outdoors. And possibly the only person in the country who can cheerfully survive years at a time without seeing a movie. I'd say that makes us even in the information exchange."

I'd say he'd conveniently left out quite a bit—like the part about whether or not he had a girlfriend. But I had ways of making him talk. "Okay, then," I suggested. "Let's find out everything else we ever wanted to know about each other but were afraid to ask."

He shook his head. "I haven't played Truth or Dare since my sister made me climb into Lincoln's lap at the Memorial. You'd be surprised at the lack of humor in the U.S. Marine Corps. If I hadn't been twelve at the time—and had good connections—I'd probably be in Guantanamo right now."

"That's it!" I said in triumph. "That's *exactly* the kind of thing I want to know about you."

"You're kidding."

"But you can go first," I offered magnanimously. "Ask me anything." I crossed my fingers in the hope he would ask me about my boyfriend so I could tell him how meaningless the relationship was—without having to manufacture a way to bring it up myself. "Go ahead."

"Okay," he said. "Here's something I want to know. Do you plan to go back to sleep anytime tonight?"

"No," I said. "My turn." But I had so many questions tumbling around in my brain it was hard to choose one. Plus, there was my pride to consider. (True, I didn't have much pride left, but I still had some.) Even though the only question I really wanted to ask Clay was, *How's your love life?* I determined to be subtle and use leading questions. I decided to start with, "Why did you join the Church?"

"Because the Spirit told me it was true."

Of course, but unless he was a latter-day Saul or Alma the Younger, the Spirit probably hadn't stopped him by surprise one day in the middle of a road. "There wasn't a pretty girl involved?" (I believe I might have mentioned that subtlety's name has never been Jillanne.)

"Isn't that two questions?"

"No," I said. "The second part is a follow-up question. I learned that in the Walter Cronkite School of Journalism."

How could Batguy not concede the point?

"A pretty girl gave me the Book of Mormon," he admitted. "But she didn't read it to me. And while she may have prayed for me, she didn't get the answer for me."

"What happened to that girl?"

"She married in the DC temple while I was on my mission."

"Did she break your heart?"

"No." I heard him unzip one of the pockets in his cargo pants. "She merely bruised it a little. Just how many follow-up questions are allowed, anyway?"

"It depends on their relevance," I said. I congratulated myself—that was such a good answer it almost made up for my dumb question.

I crossed my arms over my chest in an attempt to ward off the ever-increasing cold. "Your turn."

"Okay. Here's my next question: Do you think you're suffering from a concussion?"

"No!" I said quickly.

"Follow-up," he said, turning on the small flashlight he'd used earlier. "Can I check your pupils to see for myself?"

I would have scowled except for the fear my face would freeze that way. I widened my eyes alluringly and wished Clay would gaze into them instead of examining them for signs of brain damage. "Am I okay?" I asked sarcastically.

"I think so," he said. "Do you have a follow-up question?"

"Hey! That's not fair."

"That's not a question. It's a statement. My turn." He swung the beam of light toward the corner of the cave. He chose the very corner I'd been steadfastly telling myself was *not* emitting little skittering noises. "How do you feel about kangaroo rats?"

I screeched and plowed into him at the sight of two equally startled rodents.

"That's what I thought you'd answer," Clay observed. "But watch this." He pulled a sunflower seed from a pocket and tossed it a few inches from my feet. One of the two fuzzy little furballs hopped after it. I tucked my feet securely under my rear and screwed my eyes closed.

"Cutest little critters you'll ever see," Clay said.

In spite of my best intentions, I opened one eye. The little guy seemed to be sitting on his long tail, earnestly examining the unfamiliar seed. In the next second he'd cracked it, eaten it, and moved over to Clay as if to ask for more. He was soon joined by his curious companion. As much as I hated to admit it, they were cute.

"Fearless and Fearlesser," Clay dubbed them, tossing out a half dozen more seeds.

The kangaroo rats filled their elastic little cheeks and darted back into the darkness. I was almost disappointed when Clay turned off the flashlight and let them go.

"I guess I don't hate kangaroo rats," I admitted, stretching my legs—cautiously, in case there was something more ominous than wild gerbils lurking out there in the darkness. "Just so you know."

It was my turn to ask a question. *Will you tell me everything there is to know about you?* seemed a little too broad, so I settled on, "Do you have only the one sister you've mentioned?"

"Yes."

"Older or younger?"

"Older."

"What does she do?"

"She's a high-powered corporate attorney," he said.

"Like your father?"

"No, like my mother."

"What does your father do?" I pressed.

"Are you sure these are all follow-up questions?"

"Yes," I said. "You should have finished law school and then you'd know when to object. Answer the question."

"My father worked as an intern for the senate while he attended Georgetown," Clay said.

That sounded like the start of a story. Maybe I was wearing him down.

"He met my mother at the capitol rotunda and has spent his entire career—since his internship—in my grandfather's office." Clay put his arms behind his neck and leaned back. End of story. "Is that enough truth for you for one night?"

Not by a long shot. I could practically feel myself closing in on a revelation. But it *was* Clay's turn. "No more trick questions," I warned him.

"I haven't asked you anything I didn't want to know."

Meaning he already knew enough about me to last him a lifetime? I hugged myself, but it wasn't much consolation.

"Are you cold?"

"Yes," I sniffed. "Freezing."

"I can fix that."

For a minute I thought he would take me in his arms. It was a wonderful minute, but delusional. While I dreamed, he produced from his bag one of those space-age blanket thingies that fold up to practically nothing and have a softness rating roughly on par with aluminum foil.

"Better?" he asked when the plastic was wrapped around me like packing tape.

Better than becoming a Jillsicle? Yes. Better than what I had hoped for? Not even. "Aren't you cold?" I asked, hoping to at least sit close enough to him to share the blanket.

"No," he said. "I'm used to being out here at night."

"That wasn't my question!" I cried. "My question is what does your grandfather do?"

As the silence grew, I knew he wasn't going to answer. If it had been daylight, I would have seen Clay staring into the mountains. Since it was too dark to see more than half a foot, he probably stared at nothing at all.

"I can't talk to you about my grandfather, Jillanne," he said at last. "It's the family's cardinal law. I may have broken most of their rules by joining the Church and dropping out of law school and changing my name, but even *I* can't talk to the press about Grandfather."

"Huh?"

"Game's over," he said. "Go to sleep."

I struggled out of my crinkly cocoon and reached for his arm. "I don't care if your grandfather's an ax murderer," I assured him. As soon as the words were out I realized they didn't make sense. Ax murderers don't have offices for their sons-in-law to work in. "Who *is* your grandfather?"

"Jill, please."

"But I'm not a member of the press!" I blurted out. "Clay, I cover dog shows and ostrich races and kiss-ins!" When the words were out I realized how true they were, and how much of a joke it was. How much of a joke I was. I hadn't meant for my career to turn out this way. I *wanted* to be a real journalist. I wanted to be a real *anything*. But all I'd turned out to be was a pretty shell—the type of girl that men like Clay Eskiminzin thought were too empty to even ask questions of. Then the full truth sank in. Out here I wasn't even pretty.

I let go of his arm and pulled the blanket back up under my chin. When you're sore and cold and frightened and ugly, insecurities have a way of magnifying themselves a million times over. In another minute or two I was going to have a good cry. I turned away from him before I did it.

"I'd *never* use you," I managed to gulp out before the first sob. "I'd never use *anybody*. Even if I *were* a real reporter." The sniffles were coming and my brain was going. "Besides," I cried, "just who do you think I'd tell? We're going to die out here you know, and the buzzards don't care *who* they eat!"

The only sound for the next few minutes was me crying. Even the coyotes were quiet. Then Batguy laid a hand on my shoulder. "I believe you."

He shocked the sniffles right out of me. "About the buzzards?" I gasped. "You really *do* think we're going to die?"

"No," he said. "I believe you wouldn't use anybody. And I know you won't use anything I tell you for your news show. Your honesty is one of the things I most admire about you, Jill."

I committed that sentence to my very narrow mental folder of all the possibly-complimentary things Clay had said to me. Then I highlighted the "things I *most* admire" phrase. After all, "things" is plural. Maybe he also admired my . . . I was at a loss. He'd held my shoe for quite some time, I finally decided. Maybe he admired my taste in footwear. (Hey, it was something. I'd take whatever I could come up with.)

"My grandfather is a United States senator," Clay said as if he were admitting to having an ax murderer on the family tree only a limb or so over from Eskiminzin. Or maybe it was like he was admitting to *being* the ax murderer in an otherwise impressive arbor. "My grandfather is Henry Hamil Clayton. My mother is his youngest daughter."

Every one of my body functions ceased.

"Breathe," Clay suggested.

I gasped in a ragged breath.

"Now exhale," he said. "Then repeat. That's how breathing works."

"But—" But what? Henry Hamil Clayton had been a senator since . . . I didn't know . . . probably Abraham Lincoln. (Richer than Midas, he had probably funded the marble memorial of Mr. Lincoln as a magnanimous gesture to a lesser-known friend. No wonder Clay was allowed to climb on it.) One of the august senator's sons was in the House; another was a governor—or maybe the ruler of a small third-world country. And wasn't Senator Clayton's brother the guy I saw routinely on the monitors at the news station standing just behind the president? In short (or is it too late for that?), the Clayton dynasty made the Kennedys look like wannabes from the Vineyard.

"So, your real name is Clayton?" I said when I could speak.

"Henry Clayton Montgomery," he said. "Don't tell the buzzards." He stretched out his legs. "And never call me Henry."

"But you must be related to Cynthia Clayton!" I gushed. (Naturally I named the movie star in the clan first.)

"My cousin," Clay said.

"And the ambassador to—"

"My great aunt."

"The governor of—"

"My uncle."

"The guy who was indicted for—"

"Another cousin," Clay sighed. "If they're on Court TV, CNN, or the cover of *People*, I probably sit down with them at Thanksgiving dinner."

"What in the world are *you* doing *here*?" (I hadn't forgotten my resolution to think before I spoke, but the exclamation kinda slipped out while I was still working on the "keep breathing" thing.)

"I'm trying to sleep," Clay said. He refolded his arms behind his head and leaned back against the wall.

"I mean—"

"I know what you mean, Jill. Believe me, it was the most frequently asked question on talk radio for a while. And it's one of the reasons I changed my name."

"But—"

"I think it's my turn for a question," he said and pretended to consider. "Okay, I have one. Why did you start calling me Batguy before you knew anything about me? The truth this time."

Fortunately, it was still too dark for him to see my eye tic. "I'll take the dare," I mumbled.

"Good," he said. "I dare you to go to sleep."

Like *that* was going to happen when there were so many noises all around, and so many questions still swirling through my head. But squinting over at Clay, I decided that maybe I could talk to myself for a change—silently—and let him sleep.

If the sound of his deep breathing was any indication, Clay could fall asleep as quickly as I could. Or as quickly as I usually could.

Tonight I rolled myself up in the space blanket and then sat awake for hours more, with only the kangaroo rats for company. I thought things like *What's a nice girl like me doing in a cave like this?* and *What is Henry Clayton Montgomery doing in the Arizona desert when he could be anywhere else in the whole wide world?* Underlying my sleeplessness, of course, were the two questions I didn't dare ask: *What will Clay do when the sun rises?* and *Will either of us come out of it alive?*

chapter 19

I should have known Clay would rise before the sun. The moon was still the main attraction when he nudged my cocoon and said, "Jill, wake up."

"No, thanks," I mumbled.

Besides being dark, it was cold. Besides being cold I was sleepy. Since I hadn't been able to fall back asleep for hours after we'd talked, I'd probably been dozing only twenty minutes or so, not even long enough to dream.

When Clay nudged me again I told him what I tell my pesky alarm clock: "Another twenty minutes." I tried to snuggle more securely into the cave wall. It was difficult, but not impossible given my advanced state of exhaustion.

"Okay," he said. "Excuse me. I assumed you'd want to leave the cave before the bats return."

My eyes flew open and I fought against the plastic wrap to no avail. I was wrapped up tighter than an Egyptian mummy.

There was enough moonlight coming in the cave opening for me to see Clay conceal a grin as he grasped an edge of my space blanket and unwound me. "Good morning."

"You're being ironic, I assume."

"By that you mean, it's not 'good' or it's not 'morning'?"

"Both."

"Oh, it's morning," he said.

I squinted out into the near-dark. "When is the sun going to find out?"

He pointed over my head toward the east. "The sun is right on time. It rises today at 5:34." Before I could ask how he *knew* that, he added, "But bats don't need almanacs or watches to know when it's daybreak."

As if Clay were the director of a horror flick who had just cued special effects, I felt a swish of leathery wing brush my cheek and heard a startled "eek!" The latter was me. The former was the lead bat. It flapped wildly around the cave entrance while I flailed away at it with my bare hands. It would have been difficult to say which of us was more terrorized by the other.

Ever calm, Clay grasped me by the ankles and slid me out of the cave on my rear. It was an ignominious exit, but a welcome one. When he released my feet, I used them to push myself backward into the overgrowth where I tried to concentrate on the copper-tinged horizon rather than the winged rodents fleeing by it.

It would have been easier to look away from a train wreck. Clay had been right about the sun. It was somewhere there in the east, lighting the vast bowl of sky to pewter and tin. But it wasn't the colors of the sky that interested me, it was the simile it brought to mind. It was like this sky was a huge bat-filled basin and the cave its recently unplugged drain. Bats funneled into the small opening with a fury. At first they came by ones and twos and threes and then sixes. Then they came by the dozens and hundreds. I marveled again that there could be so many bats in the whole world, let alone this one little part of it.

"How big *is* that cave?" I asked Clay. The opening where we had huddled wasn't large enough to accommodate a fraction of these bats. Besides, it had seemed like it would be too open by day to please the little shadow-lovers. "Where do they all go?"

"Hard to say how big the cave is," he responded. "There could be a whole labyrinth under that cliff. Eskiminzin used interconnecting caves in these canyons to hide his people for years."

"You mean Apaches might have lived right here?"

"It's more likely they were closer to the spring." As usual, he was more into reason than romanticism.

"But they were in this canyon."

"Certainly."

"Wow." I sat silently for several minutes, keeping an eye on the bats, but mostly pondering the lives of Clay's Lamanite ancestors and thanking God that I had been sent to mortality to dwell in a condo in one of the multistoried "cliff houses" that made up modern-day Tucson.

The copper on the eastern edge of the world brightened to bronzed gold before the last caped crusader of the desert returned to its bat cave. With the dust settled, it was light enough now to see quite well. Naturally, I looked at Clay. Then I stared at him. He was watching the tardiest of the bats return home. (I don't know what the little critter had been doing all night, but whatever it had eaten must have been fermented, because this guy was clearly intoxicated.) I might have enjoyed watching the bat-antics myself if not for my interest in Clay. He was as transfixed as if he were in the Kennedy Center watching a performance of the Bolshoi Ballet.

Remembering what he'd revealed to me during the night, I couldn't help but ask, "You've seen the Bolshoi Ballet perform at the Kennedy Center, haven't you?"

With his trance broken, he cast me a quizzical look before reaching for his parfleche. "Yes."

"And you like bats better."

"Yes."

I leaned forward with a sigh, wanting so much to understand how this man could have walked away from everything in life I'd always wanted. "What are you doing out here, Clay?"

He removed the pouches of nuts and dried meat from his bag and set them on a flat rock. "I'm making breakfast."

I knew he knew I knew he knew what I meant. (At least I *think* we knew it. You know?) At any rate, I couldn't help but imagine how different his breakfasts must be in Maryland—and I have a great imagination when it comes to sterling silver and eggs benedict. "I mean, why do you live here?" I pressed.

I was certain that a great tragedy or lost love was responsible for his self-exile to Oblivion, Arizona. If I could help heal it, maybe he could return home at last—and take me with him. It was such a romantic notion that I caught my breath and began to fantasize about my trousseau.

"It's beautiful here," he said. "I can't imagine living anywhere else."

I shoved the fantasy trousseau back in the fictional hope chest. "You don't *need* imagination!" I said. "You just need a better *memory.*"

I opened my empty hands as if presenting his life on the East Coast back to him. "Ballets are beautiful, Clay. Bone china is beautiful. Chandeliers and designer clothes and mansions are beautiful!"

"My family would love you," he said.

The way he said it made it ineligible for the possibly-complimentary-things-Clay-has-said-to-me folder in my brain. Still, I wouldn't give up. I scooped up a handful of sand and let it run through my fingers. "You had *everything* back East, and here all you have are bats and rocks and sun and *dirt.*"

He pulled the knife from the sheath on his hip and approached a cactus. "I guess that depends on how you look at it."

"*Is* there another way to look at it?" I asked. I sincerely wanted to know. "Is there really?"

Clay knelt beside the plant. While he worked to remove the cactus's prickly purple fruit, he said, "For the Apache, the desert and its plants and creatures were more than beautiful. They were a whole universe of wonder in and of themselves, one that defied the comprehension of man."

And of woman. The only reason I could see for the Apaches to appreciate the life they led was because they never knew anything better. What I couldn't see was Clay's reason for loving it since he *had* known another world. The real world.

"Have you ever stopped to look at the world, Jill?" he asked. "The real world."

I didn't know how he did that mind-reading thing. Probably the same way he told time without a watch. And I didn't know whether to nod my head or shake it, since I didn't know what he meant by "real world," either.

Clay had removed several cactus pods by now. I watched as he deftly peeled and split them. There was yet another thing I didn't understand—how he did that without ending up with fingers that looked like miniature porcupines from all the cactus needles. He extended a piece of fruit and I accepted it tentatively. The flesh looked juicy and good—rather like a pomegranate. I licked at the juice that ran between my fingers. Aside from needing about a tablespoon of sugar, it was pretty good. I put the fruit in my mouth and held out the cleaner of my two hands for another piece.

Clay gave me all he'd prepared, then added the canteen to the breakfast buffet. While we ate he said, "Haven't you ever watched a spider spin a web and marveled at its industry and ingenuity? Or lay on your back and watched the stars come out in the sky?"

Grateful that my mouth was too full to reply, I lowered my eyes. I didn't want Clay to know that a glimpse of a spider sent me running for a can of Raid, and that I'd missed the stars, too—probably because I was inside talking on the phone or watching DVDs every night when the stars made their appearance.

When I looked back up, Clay had rolled forward on his toes and was resecuring the strip of red flannel across his forehead. I tried to imagine him dressed for a night at the ballet, but I couldn't get the tuxedo to fit. He looked too much at home here; too darn good against the backdrop of the desert. I tried to reassure myself that he was as much a product of modern society as I was (albeit high society in his case), but it was difficult to believe. Of all the metaphorical windows I'd shopped at for the perfect husband, it had never even occurred to me to loiter in front of the ritzy Tiffany's or the outdoorsy L.L. Bean.

"My ancestors believed that everything has a personality," he said. "They believed the animals and plants and even the mountains themselves differ from us only in form. To them the world was a living scripture and its books were the stones and storms and inhabitants of the earth."

I stopped chewing to listen.

"Nothing was casual or commonplace," he continued. "Not even the dirt. Especially not the dirt. The Apache loved the earth and all things of the earth, and their attachment grew with their age and wisdom. The old people often removed their moccasins to take the sacredness of the earth into themselves before their journey to the eternal home."

He picked up his own handful of dirt but didn't allow it to run through his fingers as I had. He held it tight. "The Apache wikiups were built on this dirt and their altars were made of it. They knew that the birds that fly in the air come at last to light upon the earth and that it is the final resting place of all things that live and grow." Clay still held the dirt, but he looked up into the blue-brushed sky.

"To sit upon the ground is to be able to feel more keenly and think more deeply, to . . ."

His words trailed off. While I was still considering what he had said, awed by the spirit in which he had said it, he whispered to himself, "The birds."

I followed his line of sight. Where once there had been bats, there were now birds. Or I assumed they were birds because Clay said they were. To me they looked like black dots caught up in a very slow-spinning whirlwind. (Here in Arizona we call them dust devils, but I don't know why.)

I watched the distant concentric circles drift lower and grow tighter as Clay released the soil from slack fingers and rose slowly to his feet. The look on his face told me there was something going on there I should recognize.

In the next second I knew what it was. He'd said yesterday that birds could tell him everything—where there were people, where there was water, where there was—

I swallowed. Or I tried to swallow, but there was nothing but fear in my throat. These birds were messengers all right, but I didn't want to hear what they had to say. They weren't the kind of little birds that whisper in your ear, and they weren't bluebirds of happiness, either. They were another kind of bird. An awful kind. Doesn't everybody who lives in the Southwest—or who has ever seen a western—know what birds circling a desert cliff mean?

"Clay!" I cried. "What does it mean?" (I don't like westerns.)

He must have spared me enough of a glance to see the apprehension on my face, because he said, "It could mean anything. Or nothing. Most likely the buzzards have found part of a dead animal the coyotes left behind."

His words might have carried more assurance if he hadn't been quickly gathering up our few supplies as he said them. The thought of Connor hurt—or worse—flashed into my mind, but I dismissed it. Clay didn't lie. It *could* be anything. *It* is *anything*, I told myself. *Anything but Connor.*

"Drink some more water," he said, offering me the canteen before flinging it over his shoulder. "And take a couple of ibuprofen if you need them. We have another eight . . . eighty . . . miles ahead of us today."

I scrambled to my feet, grateful that my legs held me. Although I did swallow a pain reliever with the water, I already felt remarkably better than I'd expected. (But since I'd expected dead, it wasn't a terribly difficult expectation to exceed.) "I'm ready," I said. I was scared to death, but anxious not to hold Clay back from whatever rescue mission he had in mind.

He was deliberately looking up at the sky as he said, "There's no hurry. Whatever it is will wait." He paused. "I've been up long enough to have prayer and . . . everything, but you haven't. I'm going to walk over that bluff to get a better view of the far cliffs. I'll be well out of sight, but I can still hear you if you need me."

At first I didn't understand what he was saying, and then in a rush I did and was grateful. "I'll only be a few minutes," I assured him.

Since being alone in the wilderness was the very last thing on my to-do list—and since I didn't have a mirror, makeup case, wardrobe, or even a comb—I was as good as my word. Minutes later I found Clay standing with his stick in hand, gazing off into the mountains.

"If you ever do that mesmerized-thingie of yours in the city, somebody will have you committed," I told him helpfully.

Although I'd come up from behind, he wasn't startled. He'd undoubtedly heard something coming and knew it was me, not by my signature cologne this time, but probably by my morning breath. I pressed my lips together just in case. If only I knew which way was downwind, I'd be sure to stay there when I spoke.

"What 'mesmerized-thingie'?" he asked.

"You know, the way you stare into the mountains as if there's something there to see."

"There isn't?"

"There *is*?"

"Moses went to the mountains," he pointed out. "The Brother of Jared. Nephi." He turned toward me. "Don't you suppose there was a reason Christ took Peter, James, and John to a mountain instead of a city before the Transfiguration?"

"Because people in Jerusalem would have had them committed too?"

He nodded. Then he held out the shirt he'd given me to wear the day before. Even new it wouldn't have met L.L. Bean standards. In its current state it was dirty and torn and stained and smelly and—

"Put it on," Clay said.

"Thanks, but—"

"Jill," he interrupted, "that green T-shirt of yours could be seen by a space shuttle."

"Don't we *want* to be seen?" I said reasonably. "What if there's a rescue helicopter?"

"What if there's a sniper?"

At a loss for a snappy comeback in the face of mind-numbing reality, I snatched the shirt from his hand. "Your shirt stinks," I said as I pulled it over my bare arms. I tried to sound sanctimonious, but really I was just hoping to at least lay the blame for my body "fragrance" at his feet.

Ever the gentleman, he accepted it. "Sorry." Then he picked up his pack. "How's your head?"

"It hurts every time I move my face." I couldn't keep the surprise or annoyance out of my voice.

He tried not to smile. "Go figure."

"Well, it's not like that in the movies," I explained as he started off toward the eastern cliffs with me following. "In the movies they can get hit by a truck in one scene and go dancing in the next. I've seen it happen over and over."

"Anytime now you're going to start picking up on the distinctions between real life and reel life."

It took me a few beats just to pick up on the pun. When I did, I groaned. Then the real-life angle started to sink in. This *wasn't* a movie, I realized anew as we hiked across the bottom of the canyon. The stuff on my skin wasn't makeup artfully applied for attractive dishevelment; it was dirt. When I walked eighty miles (or even eight), I got sore feet and painful blisters. When I didn't eat, I got hungry and faint. When I hit my head on a rock, it hurt and kept on hurting. *Ergo*, my thoughts continued, *if I fall down a cliff or am bitten by a snake or shot by a sniper . . . well . . . I might find out I'm an expendable extra instead of the star of the show as I've always imagined.*

"Clay," I panted as I struggled to keep up with his long strides, "I think I understand."

He didn't reply. He was too engrossed in that looking/listening/smelling/thinking/praying thing he did while he walked.

But he must have at least noted my breathlessness because he slowed down a little. For my part, I gave up exploring my frightening revelation and concentrated instead on keeping up, avoiding further injury to my too un-fictitious body, and praying to that great Screenwriter in the Sky for our script to have a happy ending.

We continued to hike for miles and miles and miles and miles across that canyon. (If you need to know how far it actually was, you'll have to wait for Batguy, the human pedometer, to write his own technically accurate account of our adventure. But I wouldn't hold my breath if I were you.) I was so focused on putting one foot in front of the other—and putting neither foot on a tarantula, scorpion, or rattlesnake—that it was some time before I realized we had begun to climb again. It was only when I recognized a rock formation that looked rather like the *Dauntless* from *Pirates of the Caribbean* that I realized we must have made a large loop on the valley floor and returned another way. We were almost back to the place where we'd weathered the dust storm the day before. That meant we weren't very far now from where Clay had pointed out Connor's boot print.

With "not very far" being a relative term. Clay kept walking. About the time I thought I'd just sit down and wait for the buzzards to join me, he stopped. Repeating the pattern of the day before, I ran into him. Fortunately, he again turned and caught me before I fell backward.

This time Clay didn't ask if I was okay as he lowered me onto a boulder. Either the answer was finally self-evident, or he had more important things on his mind. It wasn't long before I realized it was the latter.

"Buzzards!" I gasped. With my eyes on the ground, I hadn't realized we'd come so close to the circling carrion-seekers. Whatever they were so interested in was still some way distant, mercifully obscured from view by a series of dirt-and-stone sentinels.

Several big, ugly birds perched on the outcroppings turned at the sound of my voice. They seemed uncertain of their next course of action. Clay hurried their decision along by picking up a stone and hurling it in their direction. The buzzards, with numerous of their partners-in-crime on the ground, took off in a loud flapping of wing and beak.

"Thank goodness they're gone," I said.

"They're not all gone," Clay said grimly. "And the ones that flew off will be back."

The expression on his face frightened me. "What is it?"

He shook his head. It didn't mean *no* or *I don't know*. It meant *you don't want to know*. He dropped his stick, parfleche, and canteen on the ground and rolled up his sleeves.

My heart had started to beat faster, but when he reached for the holster at his waist and undid the leather strap that secured the gun, my pulse pounded in my ears. "Clay—"

Hearing his name must have reminded him I was there. He looked at me, looked around us, then grasped my elbow to pull me up. We moved about fifty yards back along the trail to a small opening between two stone formations. He pushed me between the rocks without taking time to check for scorpions, gave me the canteen and the leather bag, and rearranged the creosote bushes to cover my lair.

"I don't think there's anything alive up there but scavengers," he said. (If he meant to reassure me, it didn't work.) "But if I'm wrong, you might need this and the snake-shot revolver. It's in the parfleche. Get it out now." He moved away. "I'll come back for you." After another step he paused and added, "But remember, Jill: act, don't react. No matter what."

"No matter *what* what?"

Clay didn't answer. He was already on his way toward whatever lay beyond those rocks.

I reached for his bag, but instead of opening it to retrieve the gun, I clutched it to my chest and prayed. I prayed that I could be a warrior princess, that like Lozen I would have the wisdom and courage to know when to act and how to do it. I prayed that Clay would be protected from every "no matter what" in the world. And I prayed that the dead thing up ahead was something—anything—but a four-year-old little boy.

chapter 20

I have no greater gift for measuring time than I do distance. If you'd asked me how long I crouched in the stone crevice alternating prayer with worry and indecision, I would have told you it was forever. But the sun didn't set and rise enough times to make that possible, so it was in all probability much longer than an hour but slightly shorter than a lifetime. In all that time, there were no gunshots or screams or cries of exultation. There were no sounds at all except for the breeze and the birds and my own rapid breathing. It was so dang quiet that after a while I could hear myself obsess.

I should wait here patiently like Clay said, I told myself.

But he also said to act, another voice in my head pointed out. *You're not acting; you're hiding. What if Clay needs you? What if Connor needs you?*

It was like my brain was holding a panel discussion with itself.

Needs you for what? a sarcastic little panelist pointed out. *What could YOU do? Scream? Faint? Babble on endlessly so Clay couldn't think?*

"Stop!" I commanded the voices. "I can decide for myself."

I don't know if it was a decision to act so much as it was a reaction to incipient insanity, but I crawled out of my hidey-hole and turned in the direction Clay had gone. The sky was true-blue now and mostly free of buzzards, although a few of the most stubborn—or hungry—birds still floated lazily above as if hoping the buffet would reopen for a noontime rush.

"Clay?" I called out softly. Even with his developed senses it was a long shot that he could hear me. "Clay!" I called again.

There was no answer, so I slung the bag and canteen over my shoulder and set out along the path. Before I passed each of the sentrylike boulders, I paused and called Clay's name again. (The last thing I wanted to do was to round a corner, be mistaken for a poorly dressed mountain lion, and shot dead. After all, my hide was too scrawny to make a good rug and I certainly wouldn't want my head to be mounted above a fireplace with my hair looking like it did at that moment.)

On about the fifteenth call, my diligence was rewarded. Clay appeared, coming toward me at a dead run. When he was still fifty yards away or so, he must have realized I was okay because he slid to a stop. It might have occurred to me to be flattered by his obvious concern if something else about him hadn't been more obvious. He was covered in blood.

My hand flew to my throat. "Oh my heck! I . . . you . . . Clay, I . . . oh!"

That nasty little voice in my head knew me too well. I *was* going to babble, then I was going to scream, and then I was going to faint. If I ever revived and saw Clay hurt, I'd just do it all over again.

"Jillanne!" he called before I could keel over. "It isn't *my* blood."

I couldn't reply. For one thing, the hand I had clasped to my throat was constricting my windpipe.

"Breathe," he suggested from afar.

My first efforts were more like hiccups, but they sufficed to keep me upright for another moment or two. "You're . . . you're okay? You're really okay, Clay?"

"I'm fine." He held his hands out sheepishly. "I was going to wash this off before I went back for you."

"Then who?" I gasped. "What?" I felt myself sway again. "Not Connor!"

"No!" he said quickly.

"An animal?"

This time Clay's response was slower. "No."

"Where's Connor?" I cried.

He took a couple of steps toward me, then paused, probably at the look of horror on my face. It wasn't something I could hide. He looked like the guy from *The Temple of Doom* who had just ripped out a beating human heart. Or maybe an extra from *Pearl Harbor* after the bombing. Or Mel Gibson in—

I shook my head. *Real life,* I reminded myself. *This is real life, Jillanne. In real life this is real blood.* It was a terrible thought. I replaced it quickly with an affirmation. *I am okay and Clay is okay and Connor—* "Where is Connor?" I pleaded, moving forward.

Clay held up a hand to stop me. "Jill, don't. Connor isn't there."

I didn't stop walking. I couldn't. I might have been enacting a scene from *King of the Zombies.* "*Was* he there, Clay?"

"Yes."

"Then where—?"

"I don't know. I need more time to figure things out." He took a step back. "Wait for me back there. Please."

I shook my head. "I need to see. I need to know. Clay, *somehow* I need to help."

"There's nothing you can do," he said. "And it's . . . Jill, you *don't* want to see."

But I did. Something stubborn and desperate and possibly perverse in me insisted that I see. Clay backed up and I moved forward, and finally he stopped and waited for me to join him. When I refused again to turn back, he finally led me where he'd been—the place the kidnappers had held Connor.

The sight of the blood that smeared the rocks and stained the soil was too obscene to explain in mere words. But worse was the smell of it—sharp and pungent and animal-wild. I coughed and retched and finally collapsed near a thatch of dry desert grass, my stomach empty, my sides sore from heaving, and my head as light as the clouds that drifted overhead.

It's not supposed to be like this, a voice in my head insisted. *You've seen death in the movies. You've seen it on the TV monitors at the news station. It's not* like *this!*

But real life had finally caught up to me. Death *was* like this, I knew. Sometimes—some violent, horrific times—it was. I'd never again be able to glance at a horribly hurt human being on TV and then walk away to exchange small talk with a co-worker. I knew, too, that there was a whole genre of movies I could never again watch.

Clay crouched at my side, silently, compassionately, protectively. When he saw I was almost conscious again he explained, "It looks so bad because the predators were here before us. I think the death itself was painless. The guy's neck was broken. He died before he ever knew what happened."

There was so much I wanted to know, but I couldn't yet form the questions.

"It was the puma," Clay said. "Early this morning. Well before daybreak. The kidnapper must have come out of the cave to investigate a noise. She jumped him from the ledge above."

Because he came between her and her cub.

"Cats don't eat human flesh except as a last resort," Clay continued. "It was the coyotes and buzzards that made the mess."

"Who was he?" I managed.

"If he had ID on him, I haven't found it yet," Clay said. "I put the body—what was left of it—in a crevice and rocked it in. It's the only thing we can do right now."

I closed my eyes, but it made the picture of what Clay must have had to face more vivid. And it brought another picture to mind. I choked on the bile that rose again in my throat. *Connor.*

"Connor isn't here," Clay reminded me as if I'd spoken.

"But where—"

"I don't know." He rolled forward onto his toes, preparing to stand. "That's what I'm trying to find out now."

"The puma—"

"No," he interrupted firmly before I could scream it to the mountains. "There's no sign of that at all."

"All that blood—"

"Came from one body," he said. "One adult body. Not Connor's."

"Maybe she carried him off!"

"No," Clay said. "Connor was asleep in the cave when it happened. The puma's only interest was in protecting her cub. She accomplished her objective with one well-placed lunge and moved on. I'm sure of it."

"Then the coyotes—"

"The coyotes wouldn't have come within a half mile of here if a living human were still present. They're intelligent and they're cowards."

Despite everything, my worry for Connor was returning my senses to me and I could almost think. I marveled at the resiliency of the human spirit. And I empathized with the mother puma. The threat to one's young had to be a powerful stimulant. I looked up at Clay, and even with the blood still on him, my stomach held. I wanted to help him find Connor. Now that I knew how unpredictable and wild and absolutely terrifying real life was, I wanted to help more than ever. I tried to nudge my brain from its disconnected thoughts into deductive reasoning. "Then there *was* another kidnapper here?"

Clay hesitated. "I don't think so. Not since yesterday afternoon, at least." He let out a long breath. "The more I've thought about it, the more I've doubted they followed us out here. The distance was too far to have trailed us without me seeing them. But I think they knew when we left the ranch and when we talked to Anson. They were working with somebody with good connections." He frowned. "I think one of them must have gone up the canyon while we came down. He took our jeep, but he hasn't been back since the storm."

Logical reasoning was apparently beyond me. "If Connor isn't here and he isn't dead and he wasn't taken away by wild animals or another kidnapper, *where is he*?"

"I don't know."

"He didn't disappear into thin air!"

"No," Clay agreed, but he didn't sound as though he believed the assertion with all his heart. He stood. "I need to take a better look around, but first I need to wash this blood off. We don't want to attract every scavenger in the canyon."

I didn't buy his excuse about the scavengers. Rather, I didn't accept as true that it was his whole reason for wanting to scrub clean his hands and arms. Clay Eskiminzin might appear as solid as a stone on the outside, but his blue eyes reflected the awfulness of all he had seen and done this morning. And they mirrored my defeat and discouragement over not being able to find Connor. I nodded and rose to follow.

"Wait here," he said. "The less done to disturb the scene the better."

He should have told the coyotes that, I thought with revulsion. *What kind of damage could I do compared with them?* Still, I sat back down and stared steadfastly away from the scene of carnage as he returned to the cave where Connor had spent the night. Part of the night, at least.

My mind began to spin scenarios of what had happened. Maybe Clay was wrong. Maybe Connor had awakened when the mountain lion attacked and crept to the edge of the cave. The puma had grabbed him and dragged him farther into the canyon where we'd eventually stumble upon his broken and bloody little corpse.

That was the worst scenario.

Or maybe Clay was right. Maybe Connor had slept through the attack, but woke when the coyotes came. Maybe he had seen them rip into his kidnapper's flesh. Maybe he'd run terrified into the desert night and—

That scenario was the worst.

They were all the worst.

I sat for almost an hour in the sun, but didn't feel the heat. I didn't see the sky. I didn't hear the birds or insects. Instead, movie after movie of what might have become of Connor played on the silver screen behind my eyes. Never in my life had I dreamed I had such a gift for concocting horror. (If I ever get really serious about writing, Stephen King might want to consider another line of work.) Not only could I see the daymares vividly, I could hear the soundtrack replay the terrifying cries I'd heard throughout the night.

Suddenly the "crawling flesh" cliché sprang to mind and I appreciated how apt it really was. It felt as if a thousand maggots had infested my back and were migrating up my neck into my scalp. I rubbed my head vigorously and bit the insides of my cheeks, desperate not to be sick again. When I couldn't stand it another second, I sprang up and called out to Clay.

"Over here," he called from the base of the cliff. "Come over if you want to."

I wanted to. There was nothing I wanted more than to be close to Clay, unless it was to have Connor close to me.

By taking a wide enough circle, I managed to avoid the worst of the heat-baked, bloodstained earth. I glanced at the impromptu mausoleum Clay had constructed of loose stone, but I didn't really look at it because I couldn't think about it. I couldn't think about anything but Clay if I wanted to remain upright.

He stood at the entrance to a cave much larger than the one we had stayed in.

His hands and arms were mostly clean now and he wore a borrowed shirt. The light knit fabric strained across his chest and around his upper arms, but it covered his garments and it wasn't soaked with blood. A definite improvement.

"This is where they brought Connor," he said, motioning into the cavern. When I hesitated he added, "You can go in if you want to."

Because the mouth of the cave was so wide, it didn't lack sunlight. The first thing I saw was a small puddle of mud on the floor beneath a five-gallon metal canister of water that Clay must have used to clean himself up. Nearby was a small sterno stove with two discarded cans of Spaghettios lying nearby. I thought of the dead man and pitied him for having such a sorry last meal.

Then I saw the sleeping bags.

"Connor slept in the one on the right," Clay told me.

My eyes filled with tears. He *had* had a pillow. Not only that, but he'd slept with a foam pad beneath him and a scruffy-looking Woody doll at his side. I knelt, picked up the little stuffed cowboy and held it to my cheek. "Where is he, Clay?" I whispered.

It was a long time before he answered. "I don't know. Nobody was here last night except the two of them, and it doesn't look like Connor left the cavern."

I peered through the saltwater in my eyes into the dark corners. There was nothing in this cave except camping gear and a couple of large boulders against the walls. Narrow crevasses split the rock, floor to ceiling; otherwise, the walls were smooth. There was nowhere for even a small boy to hide.

"You might have missed his tracks going out of the cave," I said, desperation making me as eager now to challenge Clay's tracking skill as the sheriff had been the day before.

"I might have," Clay responded doubtfully. Then he shook his head. "I must have."

"The ice chest?" I suggested.

"I checked it, Jill," he said. "I've checked everything. Twice." But the determination in his voice told me he'd do it three times if I asked him—or a hundred and three if he thought it would give him a clue to Connor's whereabouts.

"A radio!" I exclaimed in another flash of inspiration. "They must have had a radio, Clay! We can call for help."

Obviously sorry to disappoint me, he shook his head again. "The guy had a cell phone in his pocket when he was attacked. It was shattered, chewed on, soaked in . . ."

His words trailed off, but I got the picture and it was as vivid as all the rest. I rose, still clutching Connor's favorite plaything, and wondering what Woody and Buzz Lightyear would have done if Andy had been kidnapped and then gone missing in the desert. (I was through with real life. I liked *Toy Story* much better.)

"What are we going to do, Clay?" I asked.

"We're going to keep looking," he said. "I haven't moved those rocks yet."

Nor walked on water. Looking at the boulders I thought the two acts seemed equally reasonable. "Move them? Why?"

"There may be tunnels behind them," he said. "There's something behind that one for sure."

In the next moment I was on my knees beside the rock he had indicated. There *was* a tunnel back there, or at least a deep hole, but the space between it and the boulder was unbelievably narrow. I doubted an emaciated coyote could squeeze through, let alone Connor. Nor was there any way in the world a four-year-old could have moved a rock that Clay probably couldn't budge. The only explanation then for falling to my stomach and pressing my face to the crack was that desperate people really *will* do desperate things.

"Connor!" I hollered into the darkness. "Connor!"

"I called," Clay said as if it had felt insane when he did it too, "but—"

"You told me that sometimes children won't answer," I pointed out. "It's me, Connor!" I cried. "Sister Caldwell! Connor, please!" The last was a sob.

Clay took my shoulders and pulled me gently back. "I shouldn't have mentioned the tunnel," he said. "He couldn't have fit in there. He couldn't have moved the rock."

"Then it's hopeless?" I asked, slumping into him. "We'll never find Connor? No matter what we've done? No matter what we do?"

Clay let out a long breath. He was so different now from the confident "I'll-find-him" Batguy of the day before.

I pulled away from him. I didn't think I could bear it if the greatest tracker in the Southwest came right out and admitted that not only could he not find Connor alive, he couldn't find him dead. Couldn't find him at all.

"Scoot over a little," he said. "I'm going to move that stone."

Not without another strong man—one who drove a bulldozer—he wasn't. After a full minute of both of us straining, futility sunk through Clay's resolve and he gave up.

Or so I thought.

"I need something for leverage," he said.

I rose when he did, trying to review the few laws of physics I understood. Clay quickly catalogued the room with his eyes, then walked outside to survey the nearby landscape for something strong enough to use as a lever.

It's simply amazing how barren the desert is. No heavy machinery or crowbars or oak trees as far as the eye can see. "Your stick?" I suggested.

"It's made of a saguaro spine," he said. "Strong, but not strong enough to move a rock that size." He went back into the cave and came out dragging the ice chest. "Aluminum-coated plastic," he reported unhappily.

I walked over to see for myself. (Also I hoped it might be full of ice-cold Diet Coke. Or even the regular kind since I could have used a sugar/caffeine rush right about then.) What it was mostly full of was beer. I closed it in disgust and kicked it for good measure.

It was as if the kick ricocheted off my toe and into the wall of the cliff just behind where we stood. Fragments of stone flew into the back of my neck like a swarm of angry bees.

I froze in shock and confusion. No law of physics I'd ever heard could explain what had just happened. Nothing could explain what happened next, either. Before I could gasp or think or raise my hand to my stinging flesh, Clay pushed me to the ground and fell on top of me. Just then, another piece of stone disintegrated with a snap, crackle, and pop.

It made no sense. Rocks don't spontaneously combust.

Clay rolled us twice over the hard, hot ground until we were behind one of the stone monoliths at the cave's entrance. He practically pushed my face into the dirt as he crouched over me.

I sputtered incoherencies into the pebbles.

"Don't move," he said.

He should have saved his breath. I *couldn't* move—at least I couldn't move more than enough to turn my face out of the dirt. As I did I saw Clay draw his gun.

Only then did it occur to me what was happening. It was the sniper Clay had feared. The other kidnapper had come back and maybe brought friends. We hadn't heard the shots because—as Clay had also feared—their guns had silencers on them.

In this case, silence wasn't golden. I'd have preferred the warning of an explosion, but silent or not, I'd seen what the bullets could do to a rock wall. It didn't take an imagination as good as mine to know what they'd do to our flesh and bones.

I'd like to say I was heroic in this moment of crisis, but the truth is I don't remember *what* I was. I probably lay obediently still. I think I clutched Woody out of harm's way. The only thing I remember for sure is that I prayed—prayed, and wondered if God had been forced to have another line installed in the last twenty-four hours just to handle everything He kept hearing from me.

chapter 21

"Get ready to move," Clay said when the first barrage of bullets let up.

I managed to push myself up to my hands and knees. "Are they gone?" It wasn't so much a stupid question as a hopeful one.

"No."

"Can you see them?"

"No, but I know where he is."

"He?"

"Okay," he said levelly, "she. Does that make you happy?"

"I was asking for a number," I informed him. "Not a gender."

"I think there are two of them," Clay said. "But only one is shooting at us. At the moment." He raised his revolver. "Ready?"

I turned toward the cave and said that I was. It was a lie.

"Not that way," Clay said.

"But shouldn't we hide in the cave?"

"Have you ever heard the expression 'like shooting fish in a barrel'?"

I swallowed. "Where, then?"

"We're going to stay behind these boulders as best we can for about a mile. Then we'll slip into a narrow ravine that circles back behind these cliffs. It's a fair bet nobody knows it's there but me."

"But—"

"If you have a better plan, Jill, tell me now."

I shook my head.

"Then we go on my call. Try to stay down, keep behind the rocks, and for gosh sakes move quick."

I nodded and he raised the revolver to his shoulder and fired off three shots angled into the air.

"Shouldn't you be shooting at *them*?" I said. "What kind of time is this to hunt buzzards?"

"I can't shoot at them," Clay said, "because what I shoot at, I hit." I couldn't see anything wrong with that plan until he added, "And I don't know for sure that they don't have Connor with them."

"Then why did you waste the bullets?"

"It was a distress signal," he said. "Since the bad guys know exactly where we are at this moment, we don't have anything to gain from being quiet."

My spirits lifted. "Do you think somebody heard it?"

"Honestly?"

"No!" I said. "Just this one time, Clay Eskiminzin, please *lie* to me."

"I think somebody heard it." He returned his pistol to its holster and put a strong arm around my shoulder. Clearly, he intended to stay between me and the shooter the whole way. "Ready?"

With my mouth finally glued shut by fear, I nodded.

You've probably seen people dodge bullets in the movies. (For my money, there's nobody finer to watch do it than Ben Affleck or Harrison Ford.) But nobody on screen or off does it any better than Clay Eskiminzin. It was like he had a sixth sense about when the guy would fire and where the bullet would hit. He wasn't wrong once. (If he had been, you'd be reading somebody else's book right now.) Long before we reached the narrow pass, the gunfire had stopped.

"Did we lose them?" I gasped.

Safely to the spot he'd sought, Clay leaned back against the rock wall with his eyes closed, the strain on his face the only indication that death-defying heroics aren't nearly as easy as they look in reel life. "Yes," he said.

"Are you still lying to me?"

Despite everything, he grinned. "I hope not."

I managed a wan smile of my own.

"Catch your breath," he advised, trying to do the same. "We've got to keep moving."

In another few minutes, Clay was pushing our way through the dense mesquite trees and shoulder-high thorn bushes that crowded the narrow gap between the canyons.

"Where did all this flora come from?" I complained among the "ouches" and "oh my hecks" that punctuated almost every painful step of the trek into the ravine.

"Water runoff from the cliffs," he replied, turning at last to see why my voice had come from so far behind. When he saw me in the clutches of yet another woman-eating plant from Hades, he came back. "Let me," he said, disentangling my hair from the thorns. "They call this stuff 'catclaw' for a reason."

"They ought to call it . . ." My words trailed off. I couldn't think of anything bad enough for them to call it.

"You're getting a nasty sunburn." He must have noticed the two or three square inches of exposed skin that hadn't yet been clawed away. "I wish I at least had mud to give you."

"Mud? You don't have sunblock?" As soon as the words were out I wished for them back. He didn't have anything and I knew it. His parfleche, his canteen, and even his stick had been left back at the cave. All we had now to ensure our continued survival were Clay's wits, the knife, rope, and gun on his belt, and whatever he had stowed in those Batpockets of his. "I mean . . ."

"I know what you mean." As if my pessimism were contagious, he seemed to deflate. "Let's take a break," he suggested. He fought our way toward a broad rock at the base of the cliff so we could do so.

Prince Philip hadn't done a better job with the briars in *Sleeping Beauty*. It wouldn't surprise me to learn that Clay had "dragon defeating" on his résumé.

As he lowered himself onto the one island in the sea of catclaw and leaned back against the cliff, I said confidently, "You've been in worse situations than this, haven't you?"

"No."

Maybe I was wrong about the dragon. "You're through lying to me, huh?"

"Yes."

"Are you just going to sit there?"

"No." He pulled a small paperback book from one of the upper pockets of his cargo pants. "I'm going to read."

"You're kidding! We're lost in the desert at the end of summer with no water and no food and people trying to kill us!"

"That's why I'm reading."

My hopes rose. "You have a survival manual!" Of course he did. He had *everything*. Undoubtedly he was looking up *How to Avoid Being Shot by Desperados* even as we spoke.

Clay opened the well-creased book. It was scarcely bigger than a deck of cards. He said, "You could call it a survival manual, I guess."

I leaned over to peer down at the pages. The type was incredibly small, but I could make out a few familiar words as he flipped through. *And it came to pass,* I read upside down. "What kind of a survival manual is that?"

"The best kind."

"Where did you get it?" Never in my life had I seen a Book of Mormon so small.

"It's designed for military use," he explained. "Sized to take everywhere you need the scriptures most."

"But—"

(Dear Reader, please don't get me wrong here. I *believe* in reading the scriptures. When I'm at home I read them every day—*almost* every day. Honest. But when I'm huddled in a canyon that belongs to a corpse-creating cougar, without food or water or sunblock or a cell phone, being shot at by desperate criminals . . . well . . . frankly . . . feasting upon the words of Isaiah doesn't tend to enter my mind.)

"There are people who have been in worse situations than ours," Clay pointed out. "Here in the eighth chapter of Mormon, Moroni writes . . . 'and I even remain alone to write the sad tale of the destruction of my people. But behold, they are gone, and I fulfil the commandment of my father . . . for I am alone. My father hath been slain in battle, and all my kinsfolk, and I have not friends nor whither to go; and how long the Lord will suffer that I may live I know not.'"

He looked up at me. "Moroni didn't think he had a chance of survival, but *he* lived to fulfill the Lord's mission. His odds were a lot worse than ours."

I sat down and scooted back to lean against the cliff. The ibuprofen must have worn off. I hurt all over. Even my eyelids ached from all their anxious twitching. (It's amazing how painful it is to run for your life. Poor Moroni.) "I don't suppose you have any other books."

"A Doctrine and Covenants," he said, reaching for another pocket.

"Never mind," I sighed. "It'd probably just fall open to the part about all these things being for our experience and doing us good."

Clay nodded. "That's the attitude."

Either he was a truly rotten judge of sarcasm or too good to judge me for my rotten attitude. I felt ashamed. "I'm sorry," I said. "I'm not used to being shot at."

"I don't think it's something you get used to." After a few minutes of silence he said, "Shall I read to you?"

Although I feared that it might be like hearing last rites, I nodded.

Of all the things for him to choose, Clay read me the first sixteen verses of the third chapter of Ether. (You know, where the Brother of Jared needs a way to light their vessels for the voyage across the sea, so he makes sixteen stones and goes up on a mountain to ask the Lord to make them into lanterns, and the Lord touches them, then shows Himself to the prophet and reveals that He is Jesus Christ.) When Clay finished, the deep lines were gone from his face, and he smiled.

"That's the pattern to solve any problem," he said. "Temporal. Spiritual. Emotional. Anything at all."

"It is?" I said. "I mean, what is it?"

"You do like the Brother of Jared," he explained. "First, you figure out a solution for yourself and then you give it all you've got in working your plan, remembering while you're doing it to be humble and patient and constantly repentant. While you do everything you can for yourself, you pray for help in accomplishing the rest." He paused to let that much sink in. "Then," he said, "comes the place where we falter. You have to have absolute faith that the Lord can, and will, help you. Finally, you receive a confirmation. In the case of the Brother of Jared, it was the confirmation of all things, but usually it's affirmation that what you've done is acceptable. The Lord blesses you with what you really need, according to His will."

I looked down at the little cowboy doll that I still had in my hand. (It would have taken more than a couple of gunmen—or a well-equipped army—to part me from Connor's toy.) "Does it always work, Clay?" I asked softly.

"Yes," he said. "It does."

"Can I see your book?"

When he passed it to me, I squinted down at the pages and the tiny numbers—one through six—that he'd put beside the verses to mark the steps he'd just explained. At the top he'd penned "Blueprint for Blessings."

I thought about the time, and especially the contemplation, that he'd put into that account of what to me had always been a quaint story. It occurred to me then that Moroni hadn't painstakingly recorded them on his plates as literary fiction. Nor had Clay read them to fulfill a quota or to "be good" before he went to bed. He'd read them in his conscious hours; studied them while he was alert. And he hadn't dismissed it as "just a story." He'd read it looking for real answers to real problems.

How many times had I sung "Search, Ponder, and Pray" with my Primary children? How many times had I listened to the words? Most importantly, how many times had I followed them? I frowned. My nightly devotional was more like "Pray, Read Fast, and Get to Sleep." No wonder I spent so much time wondering who I was and what my Heavenly Father wanted me to make of my life.

I read through the verses again and committed both the scripture reference and the blueprint to memory.

In the meantime, Clay had removed a small handful of sunflower seeds from another pocket. I watched him take them from his hand one at a time and lay them on a rock. Once they were arranged, he considered the formation of seeds as he might a chess board in the final round of the Grand Masters.

"What are you doing?" I asked. (This is why I'm never assigned to cover chess tournaments.)

He started. "What?"

It was not flattering that another human being—let alone the man I was in love with—could forget I existed while I sat less than twelve inches away.

"I asked what you're doing. If you're contemplating our last meal, I want to know it."

"No," he said. "I'm thinking about Connor."

"It looks like you're playing chess with sunflower seeds."

"Uh-huh," he murmured absently.

I knew when I'd been tuned out. I watched him pick up one of the seeds and move it to a different cluster. Then he considered a minute more and moved it back.

"Clay!" (I may not be hard to tune out, but I am almost impossible to turn off.)

When he turned toward me I was relieved to see he wasn't nearly as annoyed as I'd have been in his situation.

"It's an old Indian trick," he said, "taught to me by an old Indian." He picked up a sunflower seed. "You may recall me telling you that the Apaches had no written language—no way to record the things they needed to remember."

I nodded.

"Chee says that when important principles were taught or facts were given, an Apache would take a seed or a kernel of hard corn or even a small pebble to mark each item. Later, reviewing the tokens would remind him of everything he had heard or seen or learned. Sometimes, he would then swallow the seeds or stones to internalize the information forever."

I deduced that the ancients didn't know much biology, but I kept the insight to myself. "So that's what you're doing," I said. "That's why you were fiddling with sunflower seeds while you talked to Shar yesterday."

"Yes."

"And again yesterday when I told you my theory about Alex."

"Yes."

I couldn't suppress a sigh. "Have you considered a PDA? A Personal Digital Assistant," I clarified for a man who avoided all things convenient and had probably never heard of one. "They're smaller than your scriptures and can hold everything—including the standard works, an encyclopedia, the complete works of Tolkien, and everything anybody ever tells you."

"Yes," he said, "I know. I have one. I may have a dozen. I think everyone in Maryland gave me one last Christmas."

"But you don't use them."

"Not often."

I slumped back against the rock. "Clayton Eskiminzin, I don't understand you!"

"I know."

When I was quiet for almost a full minute, he went back to rearranging his sunflower seeds. "Why did you leave Maryland?" I asked when I couldn't stand the silence another second. "Why would you *ever* leave?"

"I was called on a mission."

"You go *home* from missions," I pointed out. "That's the way it works. You go on a mission. Then you go home."

"I went home."

"But you didn't stay home! You exiled yourself to the farthest reaches of outer desolation. *Why*?" I was going to learn his deep dark secret if it was the last thing I ever did. (Under our current circumstances, that looked rather likely.)

"There's no big secret, Jill," he said quietly.

"How do you *do* that?" I exclaimed. When he looked baffled, I added, "You read my mind."

"No," he said, holding up a hand in protest. "That's the last thing I can do."

I didn't believe it, but was willing to wait to prove his psychic abilities sometime after I got him to bare his soul. "Tell me why you're here, Clay."

"Aren't you the one with the theory that all the little coincidences in one's life make up a glorious plan that leads one to be in the right time at the right place for the right reasons?" He smiled down at my frown and said, "I hope I'm here to find Connor, and . . ." His eyes seemed to glow before he turned them away from me to look up at the mountains instead. ". . . And get you out of the mess I got you into."

Was there a secret tragedy in Clay's life or wasn't there? I couldn't decide. Maybe his meeting with Chee had been like my meeting with Mrs. Funke—a life-altering twist of fate. Or maybe it was a gift of God for *me*, Heavenly Father's slightly screwball but ever-devoted daughter who had been begging to meet a man like this since I was old enough to lisp a prayer. Surely Clay's mission and years of apprenticeship to a hermit were all that had kept him from marrying a socialite in the Washington DC Temple and becoming . . . becoming . . . I couldn't imagine what he might have become if not for Chee, because I couldn't picture Clay as anything but what he was any easier than I could think of him married to anybody but me.

At that moment it was all I could do not to throw myself into his arms and babble out my newest, most dearly held theory: the universe had orchestrated our union and we were destined to be together forever. If ever Clay would consider me as something other than a chattering liability, that is. And then only if we managed to live all the way through the afternoon.

I didn't realize how long I'd been fantasizing until I felt Clay's gaze. He said, "Did I answer your question?"

"No," I said stubbornly. "I still want to know if there was a person *(I meant as in a female person)* or an event that made you turn your back on everything a sane man could ever want."

A rueful smile crossed his face. "Several events, maybe." He picked up his scriptures from the rock where I'd laid them and secured them in his pocket. "You read *People* magazine. Look at my family, and then remember that I'm the youngest of all the Clayton cousins. Everything that can be done in modern American culture—good, bad, or indifferent—has already been tried by *somebody* I'm related to. I've had the benefit of a whole lot of experience, none of which was personal. Thank goodness." He began to gather up his sunflower seeds. "I've figured out by now that I don't want to be self-destructive and I probably can't save the whole world. Is there anything so wrong, then, in spending my life trying to help who I can, where I can?"

I hadn't yet processed all that before he rolled the last sunflower seed between his fingers and added, "As for the sanity thing, obviously you don't know much about Washington. Sanity doesn't coexist well with ego or power lust—or even fear."

He wasn't talking about his family now, I sensed. I looked from his face to the sunflower seed and knew what he meant. "You *believe* me about the posed kidnapping!" I said. "You think Alex Teagler is insane!"

"Oh, I think he may be losing it all right," Clay agreed, "but—"

A sight or a sound or a sudden psychic vibration interrupted his words, and he rolled from sitting into the familiar crouch, ready for anything.

"What is it?" I asked in alarm.

He looked toward the mouth of the chasm.

Was there a rustling in the trees there or had I imagined it? "You said nobody but you knew about this place," I began. "You—"

Clay pushed me off the boulder into the catclaw, following with his hand over my mouth to keep me from crying out.

"I was wrong," he whispered as I hyperventilated into his palm. When he was sure I would be quiet, he removed his hand from my mouth and used it to reach for his gun. "Let's hope that's all I was wrong about."

chapter 22

Every primal instinct in my body screamed *Run!* but it was the last thing I could do. My back was pressed into a corner formed by the boulder and cliff, and Clay was crouched solidly in front of me, his gun drawn and ready. I wished I knew what he was ready *for*. I wished there was someplace to run to or something to hide in or behind or even under. Most of all, I wished I knew what was coming toward us down that gorge.

Or maybe I didn't.

What if it was the mountain lion? With the sight and smell of the blood from its morning kill so fresh in my mind, it was my greatest fear—though perhaps the most irrational. Pumas didn't hunt by day, Clay had insisted, so it probably wasn't a big cat. There was little doubt that whatever moved so doggedly, if erratically, through the dense growth hunted *something*. And it was definitely day. Although a few dark clouds had moved in, it was still mostly bright and hot, especially now with the sun directly overhead. I felt the heat leach the precious moisture from my skin. Rivulets of sweat ran into my eyes and down my back. With nature's effort to cool my body working overtime, I felt downright chilled. Clammy, even.

"Try to calm down," Clay whispered. "Breathe."

At first I thought he had sensed my fear. Then I wondered if maybe the terror was so strong he could smell it. At last I came to my senses enough to realize that he *felt* it. Reflexively, I had grasped at the back of his shirt, but my fingers clenched flesh and muscle instead of fabric. In what I considered a very impressive act of willpower, I let go of Clay's back and dug my nails into my own palm. If nothing else, it assured me that I was still conscious enough to feel pain.

You're okay, I told myself desperately. *Clay's okay. You probably won't be for long, but you're both okay right this second.* (As affirmations go, it was a little weak. On the other hand, it did help me to keep breathing.)

"Any minute," Clay whispered and took a silent step toward whatever approached through the briars.

It must be a man, I reasoned, albeit a stupid and/or well-armed one. Since he wasn't making the slightest pretext toward stealth, he must either not know we were there or be very confident he could kill us without the element of surprise.

While I rolled myself into the smallest possible target, Clay rose, his finger on the trigger of his gun and both hands wrapped around the stock. My panic lessened a little as I recalled what he'd said earlier when we'd been under fire. He'd said he would hit what he aimed for. If he'd felt so sure he could nail a distant target, could he possibly miss something this close up?

In another minute I'd know. A mesquite tree shook and dropped a long, brown seed pod onto the boulder we'd just evacuated. A branch of creosote snapped under somebody's foot.

Then a wild man appeared. Blood oozed from dozens of tiny scratches on his neck and hands. His clothes were torn, stained—and incongruous for a place like this. But the thing that convinced me he was insane was his face. It was paler than his once-white shirt and completely taken over by wide, crazed eyes.

He turned toward us when he heard Clay stand and I saw a silver revolver clenched in his fist.

The madman was Alex Teagler.

"Shoot him!" I screamed when Clay hesitated. "Shoot him now!"

Inexplicably, Clay lowered his gun, then dropped it. At the same moment, Teagler's gun rose. It pointed at Clay's chest, and then at his face. I couldn't stifle my scream. But I didn't scream loud enough that I would have muffled the "pop" of a silencer. Alex didn't fire. Instead, the gun continued to rise toward the sky as he fell forward.

Clay was at Alex's side in an instant, but I was frozen to the spot, sure I would never move again.

"Jillanne!" Clay called. "I need help." He had lifted the unconscious man into his arms, but Alex's suit coat was too tangled in catclaw to allow much movement. "Pull his clothes free," Clay told me. "Jill, move!"

Somehow I managed to salvage everything my brain's neuropathways once knew about large motor skills and fought my way to Clay's side. I kicked at the shrub and pulled at the clothes until I had managed to add new scratches to my hands and tear the surely expensive fabric of Alex's coat. Then I turned to follow as Clay carried Alex to the rock and laid him down.

"Should I get his gun?' I asked. After all, that would have been the first thing the beautiful-if-useless sidekick would do in the movies. I went back to look for the weapon Alex had dropped. Or the one Clay had dropped, for that matter.

"Leave it," Clay said. He put Alex in the shade of the high cliff and bent over him, checking for vital signs. When he was sure Teagler was breathing, he rolled him gently onto his stomach. "Help me get his coat off."

When we managed to get him out of his jacket, Clay tilted Alex's head well back and then moved both his arms and left leg until the three limbs were at right angles to his torso. I'd been in yoga classes where the instructor had done something similar to me, and I said so.

"It's called the recovery position," Clay explained as he continued to work, now gently bending the elbows and left knee of the unconscious man. "It assures that any fluids will drain from the mouth, and that the shock victim will have better circulation to his heart and brain."

I nodded, all the while thinking that Alex might not be the only one present who was in shock. I couldn't pull my eyes away from a ragged black-and-red hole that was just to the side of his shoulder blade. Although the hole wasn't very big, enough blood had seeped from it to soak his shirt and run down to stain the waistband of his suit pants. I turned and walked several steps away, certain I was going to be sick again.

"Give me your shirt," Clay said.

First I froze, and then I raised shaking fingers and fumbled with the top button.

"Not that one," he said, "your T-shirt. It's a little cleaner."

I nodded as he turned away. Fortunately, the shirt of Clay's that I wore over the top of my own was almost as big as a beach house. I pulled both my arms inside it and managed to wriggle out of the T-shirt underneath with no real difficulty. Not that Clay ever turned back around to watch me do it.

I took the shirt to him and watched him use his knife to slice it to pieces. He used part of a former sleeve, wadding it up and sticking it securely into Alex's wound. The injured man didn't move, but I flinched in his behalf. The next piece Clay folded and used in lieu of a gauze pad as he applied steady pressure. For the second time that day, I noted, his hands were covered in another man's blood. When the bleeding was finally staunched, he used the bottom third of my shirt as a bandage to hold the other two in place.

I'd watched all this silently, willing myself not to scream, faint, or vomit—the three courses of action I knew for sure I could do. When the first (and only possible) aid was complete and Clay had again covered Teagler with the jacket, I said weakly, "He was shot." (Sometimes my keen powers of observation are overshadowed only by my penchant for stating the obvious.)

Clay nodded.

"By who?"

"I don't know."

"The guy who shot at us?"

"I don't know."

"Is he going to be okay?"

"I don't know that, either."

"Did he have a cell phone?"

"I'm sorry, Jill, but no." I marveled at how patient Clay was, even in the worst of times. (The guy I was currently dating was inclined to snap at me for asking him to pass the popcorn during a movie in my own living room.)

Clay said, "The bullet went into muscle and bone. It didn't hit any organs or major arteries, but even so he's lost a lot of blood."

"He won't die, will he?" I tried to forget that minutes before I had yelled "Shoot him!" I hoped Clay had forgotten it too. (It's intimidating enough to feel like you're hanging out with the Good Samaritan without playing the part of a bloodthirsty Gadianton. Or is that mixing my scriptural similes?) "Is there anything more you can do for him?"

Clay wiped the blood from his hands onto his pants as best he could, then reached for yet another pocket. "Yes." From it he removed a small silver vial that I recognized immediately as containing consecrated oil. "I can administer to him."

Suddenly, I wasn't half as frightened—for Alex Teagler or for myself.

* * *

"Eat this," Clay said.

I looked up. For the last couple of hours I had sat by Alex's side, willing him to live. I believed with all my heart that he was a low-down scheming weasel who had orchestrated his own son's kidnapping, but he was my best friend's low-down scheming weasel and I wanted him to live long enough for her to find out the truth and kill him herself.

While I sat and alternated glaring at Alex with worrying about him, Clay had been up and down our narrow gorge twice and had brought back the scars to prove it. He looked rather like he'd been processed by a Cuisinart—but he was *still* the best-looking man I'd ever seen.

"What is it?" I asked suspiciously. The slice of something Clay offered me was slimy, green, and about as appetizing as the slugs I once saw consumed on *Survivor*. No way was I eating slugs. I would starve to death first and do it cheerfully, thank you very much. Not only was I smarter than those scantily clad TV contestants, I had no chance whatsoever of winning a million dollars even if I did survive this.

"It's prickly pear," he said. "You had it for breakfast."

"Breakfast was purple."

"This piece is from the pad. It has more water and nutrients. Besides, there's more of it." When I still hesitated he said, "Eat it, Jillanne," in that tone of voice he used when it was the last thing he was going to say on a subject.

I put a tiny piece of cactus in my mouth in case I had to swallow it whole. It tasted kind of like bitter, slimy celery—possible to eat if you had to, but not something you'd choose from the buffet at Souper Salad.

"Eat it all," Clay said, adding more to my hand. "You're dehydrated."

While I tried to eat the miserable noonday "meal," Clay slit open an aloe vera. Gently, he dabbed cool fluid onto my face.

My skin's reaction to his touch was instant and electric and spread throughout my entire neurological system. I couldn't swallow. I couldn't breathe. I couldn't even think. I scooted back a little before I choked.

Uncertainty flickered across his face and was replaced by . . . what? "Sorry," he said and handed me the spike of aloe before moving away to see to Alex.

"Clay . . ." I said, but I couldn't think of any words to come after his name that weren't likely to send him running from our ravine. If ever there would be a time and place to tell him I loved him madly, this wasn't it.

"We don't have to worry about sunburn anymore," I finally managed a while later, after a few high banks of clouds had rolled in to mercifully obscure the sun. (Arizona's monsoon season had been declared over by our station's meteorologist the week before, but the news had apparently not yet filtered all the way up to these thunderheads.)

Clay didn't look up from the man lying on the rock, but his face was as dark as the clouds.

"Another jeggo?" I worried aloud.

"I wish."

"You mean it's going to rain?" I guessed. Why wasn't he pleased? A little summer shower beat a dust storm any day. "Then we won't have to worry about water. We—"

"Water is exactly what we have to worry about," he interrupted. "This is Arizona, Jill. Even a light rain in the mountains a mile away can send a wall of water down this gully faster than you can say 'oh my heck.'" He looked from me to Alex and squared his shoulders as if to better distribute the weight he must have felt on them.

"You think there could be a flash flood?" I looked up at the sky. It didn't look too bad to me. There were still patches of blue among the blackness. "Maybe the storm will blow over."

"The locals don't seem to think so," Clay said. "The jackrabbits are moving out and their neighbors are moving up." He gestured with his chin toward the cliff wall about eight feet distant.

I stifled a scream at the sight of a tarantula fully as big as the one that had terrified me the day before. Defying the laws of gravity—and decency—the spider made its way up the sheer rock face and squeezed itself into a crevice. Though it wasn't close, and it probably wasn't coming back, I cowered all the same.

"Don't look around," Clay said. "The insects are all seeking higher ground."

When somebody says "Don't look around," that's all you want to do, right? Not me. Not then. Not there. I was too sure of what I'd see: troops of tarantulas, columns of centipedes, and legions of scorpions. If they were going up, I was staying down here and taking my chances in the flash flood. (I grew up in Tucson, remember. I can do more than model a swimsuit; I have a very strong backstroke.)

"We have to get to higher ground," Clay said. "We can't risk leaving the arroyo and being seen by the shooter. There're some switchbacks not far from here that lead up to a cave in the side of the cliffs. They're narrow, but I think we can make it." He looked up toward the mountains above and the clouds above that, and his face set in grim, determined lines. "We have to make it."

Jill's Guide to Two Incredible, Edible, and Otherwise Remarkable Desert Flora

Like the aloe vera, the yucca plant I mentioned earlier in my story is a member of the lily family, but it looks like a stunted palm tree with a long stalk growing up the middle. These stalks have lots of pretty white flowers on them in the spring and early summer. You'll see them in the southwestern United States and much of Mexico, not only in the wild, but as decorative border plants in the city. (There are two outside my condo, in fact.) Whether you harvest the root yourself or get it in a nursery or the mail, get it wet. Now rub it like a bar of soap. You'll get mounds of lather. Use it to wash whatever you want, but be sure to rinse very well afterwards. Having pieces of root left on you would be just . . . well . . . yucca.)

The prickly pear cactus might be the most underrated plant on earth. You can sew with it, grow your own livestock-proof fences, drink from it, make toothpicks, and construct furniture and even houses with its skeleton. Not only that, you can live off it if you have to. (Perhaps "survive" is a better word, because you probably wouldn't want to live if prickly pear was all you ever had to eat.) Although both the pads and fruit are edible and used many ways, my personal favorite is prickly pear jelly. (Don't try this in the desert; it requires the use of a modern kitchen.)

Prickly pear jelly: Harvest the "pears" in late summer/early fall when they turn dark red or purple. Boil or sear thoroughly to remove spines. (Be very careful. These things aren't called prickly for nothing!) Peel fruit. Cover with water and boil until soft. Strain through cheesecloth until you have 2 cups of juice. Bring to boil. Add one box pectin, 3 tablespoons lemon juice, and 3 cups sugar. Boil for three minutes. Check jell. Ladle into jars and process as you would any fruit jelly. Yum! I guarantee you won't even be able to tell you're eating cactus!

chapter 23

"Sorry, Senator," Clay said when Alex groaned. He lowered him as carefully as he could onto the ledge and leaned the man's back against the cliff. With his legs extended, the heels of Teagler's shoes dangled over the edge of the switchback.

How Clay had managed to carry the semiconscious man this far on his shoulders was beyond me. It had been all I could do to get myself across the briar-choked ravine and keep my balance on the series of narrow, rocky ledges that Clay assured me led up to yet another cave. (It was a regular bat apartment complex in that canyon.)

In many places the ledges we'd traversed were just broken, ragged chunks of rock, but in others they seemed too smooth to be natural, almost as if they'd been hewn out of the side of the cliff by human hands. I couldn't ask Clay about them at the time, of course. His breathing was labored as it was. But when I wasn't too preoccupied watching for scorpions and/or rattlesnakes, I marveled at the workmanship. Who could have done it? Who would *want* to live up there besides the Three Mountain Goats Gruff?

"Clayton!" Alex gasped.

I turned to look as Clay crouched at his side. The wounded man had been mumbling incoherently for some time, but now Teagler's eyes were open—full of pain, but clearly focused on Clay's face.

"Clayton—" He tried to raise his hand, but the effort was too great. "I have to tell you . . . you have to know—"

"Quiet," Clay said, putting a hand on Alex's shoulder to calm him. "Rest for a few minutes. As hard as this is for you, we have to go on."

I looked up at the sky. The patches of blue were gone. The parts of sky that weren't obscured by clouds were tinged dull pewter. I smelled the ozone in the approaching storm. What had always been so welcome and invigorating in the ever-parched city was ominous here. The fauna had the right idea. I only wished I could skitter away and hide as fast as they could.

"It's Eliot," Alex continued. It was hard for him to speak, but apparently harder to be still now that he was fully conscious.

"I know," Clay said. "Lie still. I've already figured it out."

Figured what out?

"But he knows who you are!" Alex said. He was able to raise his uninjured arm enough to grasp Clay's shirt. "Clayton, I *told* him, God forgive me." His eyes closed. "They think you're dead, and Eliot's determined to make it so."

I'm sure my mouth hung open far enough to accommodate a whole skyful of bats as it finally sunk in that Alex was calling Clay *Clayton*. It was all I could do not to grasp Clay myself—by the neck. "You *know* Alexander Teagler?" I demanded.

"We've met," Clay said briefly, all his attention focused on the injured senator. "I didn't think he'd remember, though—or recognize me out of context."

"But where . . . ?" I sputtered. "When . . . ?"

If Clay Eskiminzin had learned nothing else in the last twenty-four hours, he'd apparently learned that like a bad itch, I'm lots easier to scratch than to ignore.

"My grandfather liked Senator Teagler when he first arrived in Washington," Clay explained. There was a subtle emphasis on the word *first.* Just enough to make Alex cringe. "He admired him, in fact. When I got the notion to leave law school for a mission, Grandfather invited me to lunch with him and the new senator. He knew Mr. Teagler was a Mormon—a very ambitious one who'd passed up a mission himself—and he hoped he'd talk some 'sense' into me."

Alex's eyes had reopened, but it was impossible for me to read what was in them.

"Senator Teagler advised me to accept the call from the Lord," Clay concluded. "It was a particularly courageous thing to do in front of Henry Hamil Clayton."

Now I knew how it felt to be flabbergasted. I also knew why Clay had dropped his gun when he'd realized our assailant was Alex.

"It was the last courageous thing I ever did," Alex murmured.

Clay turned back to him. "I don't think so, Senator, or Fuller wouldn't have taken Connor and you wouldn't be here now."

"I was sent to kill you," Alex said before I could figure out what Clay meant. The man looked steadfastly down at the ground. I hoped he could see all the way to Hades, because that was where I thought he belonged.

"Elliot said they'd kill Connor if I didn't find you and kill you," Alex continued. "He knew I could do it if anybody could." The words came faster. "I know this canyon, Clayton. I grew up here. And I'm a crack shot. My dad and I used to hunt mountain lion. Later, I used to come here often with a college friend—Kent—who is now my most trusted aide. We'd do overnighters, looking for arrowheads and taking target practice. It's how he knows I can shoot, and how he knew about the cave where they took Connor." Teagler's voice broke. "Of everyone in the world, I thought I could trust Kent."

"And Connor and Shar thought they could trust you!" I blurted out.

Alex Teagler began to sob.

"Quiet," Clay told him gently. "You can't afford to lose any more blood." He cast me a reproving glance. "We all want the same thing, Jill. We want to find Connor and we want to get out of here. Right?"

I nodded contritely.

"Then first we've got to make it to that cave," Clay said. It's probably already raining in the mountains. The flash flood could be a half hour away—or less." He stood. "These ledges will be too slick to navigate if the rain hits here before we make it."

Over the older man's weak protests, Clay raised the senator back onto his shoulders.

I didn't comment, but this was pushing the parable a little too far if you asked me. Hadn't Clay been *listening* to the man? Would even the Good Samaritan have picked up a guy who wanted to kill him?

As we climbed, Alex mumbled.

"Quiet, sir," Clay repeated. "Save your strength."

But Alex seemed to feel compelled to speak—to me this time. "I'm sorry, Jillanne," he said.

I bet he was. I bet Alex was sorry he'd been caught. Sorry he'd been shot. Sorry he was probably going to die in this canyon and have to drag his sorry soul before the Judgment Bar later that afternoon.

"I love Shar," he said, his voice breaking. "I love Connor. They're *all* I love anymore. I was trying to get out. Please believe that. I was trying." The last words dissolved again into sobs.

"Get out of what—fatherhood?"

"Jill!" Clay said as if *I* were the bad guy.

"I'm sorry," I told Alex, figuring that if that Law of Something I said I believed in is true, then a lie told to mollify Clay would come back to bite him and not me.

As the path grew steeper, every step was just a little bit harder to take than the one before. I didn't think Clay could keep it up much longer—he was Batguy, not Superman.

"Let me help," I said in concern, knowing even as I offered how unreasonable the request was. I was scarcely able to keep myself from slipping off the ledge. How could I help carry Alex?

"I'm fine," Clay panted.

"Put me down," Alex said. "Leave me."

I was sure it was the only inspired thing Alexander Teagler had said since encouraging Clay to serve a mission, but this time Clay wouldn't listen.

"Put me down," Alex repeated a few minutes later. "I can walk."

Again Clay wouldn't consider it. But when Alex struggled and almost knocked Clay off his balance, which would have sent them both tumbling into the ravine, he slowed, then stopped and swung Teagler onto the ledge. Clay's normally bronzed face was red with exertion, and his shoulders sagged, even with the weight removed.

"Sit down," I begged him. "Just for a minute."

He looked up at the sky as if gauging whether a minute would be too long. With a single spot of open sky still visible, and the cave only one long switchback away, he dropped down beside Alex.

"I'm sorry," Teagler began again.

"Forget it," Clay panted. He leaned the back of his head against the wall and closed his eyes. "Tell me something I can use. Who knows you're here?"

"Nobody," Teagler said. To his credit, he sounded sorry. Agonized, even. "Nobody who will help."

"How did you get away from all the people at the ranch?"

"I'm not news anymore," the senator said. "You are."

Clay's head rolled toward Alex and his eyes opened. "How's that?"

"I told Eliot who you are," he said again. "I would have told him anything to keep Connor safe."

"And?"

"And Eliot used it. He used you like he uses everybody." He coughed painfully, and I thought Clay would tell him to stop talking, but he didn't. "He had your jeep left at the lip of El Rico," Alex continued. "Near the ranch. After the dust storm they found it—missing enough climbing gear to convince them you'd gone into the canyon."

"Nobody in their right mind would go down those cliffs before a jeggo," Clay said.

"Your colleagues in search-and-rescue don't seem to think you're in your right mind when it comes to looking for lost children."

Even I could have guessed that.

"That's where everybody's looking today," Alex continued. "But they assume you fell. That you're dead. Both of you."

"There are a million fissures down El Rico," Clay said. "Searching for a corpse is a waste of time when—"

"Not if you're looking for Henry Clayton Montgomery," Alex interrupted. "Your family's representative is holding hourly press conferences. The media is having a heyday, especially with the secret identity Apache-rescue-ranger thing." He coughed, but managed, "Your death is bigger news than Princess Di and JFK, Jr. combined."

"Let's hope the obituary is premature," Clay muttered.

I gaped at the celebrity-cum-ranger and for once was speechless, trying to take it all in. Obviously, I didn't know more than the *Reader's Digest* version of Clay's life. My eyes traveled back to Shar's distraught, possibly dying husband. Might I have also missed part of the story when it came to Alex Teagler?

Alex coughed yet again and this time Clay laid a comforting hand on his shoulder. "It's okay," he said.

"You don't know it all yet," Teagler argued, determined to continue at any cost in effort and pain. "I told everyone I was going into Tucson to meet with the FBI. Somebody back there in the press corral might have called it in to their stations, but they were too focused on the search for you to follow me to check it out."

"In other words, you came alone," Clay supplied, trying to help him out, to spare him agonized words.

"Me and Kent," Alex corrected. "Eliot promised that after I killed you, Kent would take me to Connor. I didn't want to do it, Clayton. As God is my witness, I didn't fire those shots at you. But when we got to the cave—" The coughs became sobs. "All that blood! I didn't know if it was you or Connor or what. I went crazy. I turned on Kent and . . . I shot him. Then I just ran away blindly. To look for you . . . to look for Connor . . . I don't know." Before Clay could try to silence him again, he concluded, "Kent must not have been dead, though. He shot me in the back as I ran. I . . ."

The physical and mental torture must have been too much, because Alex couldn't go on. I felt my own eyes fill with tears. In another minute I'd be sobbing with him. I knelt beside my best friend's husband. Had I walked into the theater of Alex's life a few scenes too late to really understand what was going on in it? Had I cast him as the antagonist in my mind when that part had already been assigned to Eliot Fuller—financier and political puppeteer? Had *he* been the driving force behind Alex's ambition—and Shar's virtual imprisonment—all these years?

Condemnation fought with compassion in my psyche. Clay seemed to believe that Alex Teagler's biggest sin was that he was weak—that he had allowed himself to be as controlled as he was controlling of Shar. Maybe that was true. And maybe there was another truth. Maybe Alex had finally seen the light and tried to change himself and save his family. Maybe he had tried to dig his way back out of the pit and this was Fuller's retaliation. Maybe the kidnapping *hadn't* been a bid for publicity—at least not on Alex's part. It might have been part of a bid for ultimate power on the part of Eliot Fuller. What could be more attractive to an aspiring despot than to pin a potential president of the United States under his odious thumb?

I didn't know real life from reel life anymore, or fact from romantic fiction. I only knew I *was* sorry for this clearly contrite, brokenhearted man. (If the Lord doesn't ask any more than that, how could I?) "It's okay," I wept, throwing my arms around his neck. "It's okay, Alex."

But it wasn't okay. Somebody was messing with the lights and it was getting darker by the minute.

About the time I realized this and leaned back in surprise, there was a flash of lightning atop the far cliff and a dry mesquite tree broke into flames. I didn't need to count *one one-thousand, two one-thousand, three one-thousand* to judge the distance, because the accompanying thunder was instantaneous. The ground shook hard enough to loosen my porcelain fillings.

"Move!" Clay said, jumping to his feet. "Jill! Run!"

How could I run? The path was almost vertical and the ground still moved from thunder that didn't end. But that was impossible. Thunder *did* end. What, then, was the noise?

As Clay pulled Alex up I looked up the long ravine and knew. A churning wave of water and rock, cactus and mud, rushed down from the mountains above and roared into the gully. In the widest places it rose ten or fifteen feet up the canyon walls and looked like an angry, swollen river. But in the narrowest places it rose as much as twenty or thirty feet higher and looked more like what it really was—an appalling way to die.

We were in one of those narrow places. Within the next few minutes we'd be caught up in the muddy tide and tossed into the jagged boulders like Connor's little rag doll. I tucked Woody securely into my waistband and reminded myself of the one and only consolation fate had to offer me. When it was finally over, there probably wouldn't be enough left of my body to interest a buzzard.

chapter 24

Clay shoved me from behind. "Go, Jill!"

I'd only taken a single step before he yelled, "There's no time for the trail. Climb to the next ledge. It's your only chance."

In the next instant I knew Clay had released his hold on Alex, because I felt his hands circle my waist. I leaned back into him, content to die if I could do it in his arms. (Surely if we entered paradise together I could haunt somebody here on earth long enough and hard enough to convince them to do my temple work and have me sealed to Clay vicariously. I was considering who in my ward I might work on first when he lifted me off my feet.)

"Grab hold, Jill," he said, pushing me into the rock wall. "Do it!"

Startled, but used to following his commands by now, I dug my fingers into a crevice. They held.

"Climb!" he said, moving his hands to my thighs and then my knees and ankles as he lifted me higher. "You can do it."

It's like the chimney, I thought. *Only this is up*. As strange as it sounds, up was easier. I made it to the next ledge very quickly and collapsed on my tummy. Feeling Connor's doll beneath me, I pulled it from my waistband as I rolled over and tossed it into a cave, just in from the ledge. *Save yourself, Woody!*

"Good girl!" Clay called from below. "Roll back onto your stomach and brace yourself. You'll need to help the senator." He bent down. "Your turn," he said to Alex. "Use your legs and your good arm. You can do it. You *have* to do it."

I didn't know what kind of weights Clay was used to lifting, but I figured it must be sports cars. He raised Alex most of the way above his head. "Stand on my shoulders, Senator," he commanded. "You can do it. From there you only have another foot to climb."

Alex somehow made it to the perch, but swayed. "I can't," he said. "Save yourself."

I knew Clay wouldn't. I glanced into the gully and realized we'd be measuring Clay's time to safety in seconds by the time Teagler was on this ledge. If he ever was.

"Alex!" I screamed. "Shar needs you! Connor needs you! Reach for my hand!"

It was enough. His hand came up and I caught it in both of mine. Although I feared most of my support was of the moral variety, I pulled with all my might and it too was enough. Somehow Alex used his uninjured legs to push himself upwards and I dragged him the last few inches onto the ledge before he passed out.

I leaned over him. "Clay!"

He was already climbing, but I feared he didn't have enough strength—or time—left. The sound of the water rang in my ears. Or maybe it was a scream—mine. Either way, I knew I would go deaf. The tips of Clay's fingers scratched into the ledge at Alex's feet and I scrambled toward them.

"No!" he yelled. "Move back. I don't want to take you with me." With what was left of his strength and willpower, Clay swung himself out and up. One boot—one leg—came over the lip of the rock shelf, but the rest of him dangled below.

There was no tone of voice Clay could have used, no command he could have given, that would have kept me from grabbing his leg and holding onto it for all I was worth.

But too much of him was still below the ledge. He needed to be another foot higher—or maybe only six inches—but there was no way to gain a centimeter. We didn't have the strength and we didn't have the time. In another few seconds he'd be swept away.

At that moment time slowed to a crawl. I felt the first drops of muddy spray from the approaching flash flood hit my face. I raised my eyes to the heavens. "No!" I cried. "No! It's not right! It's not fair!"

Although time was moving impossibly slow, my thoughts moved too fast for me to analyze. The best I can explain is that it suddenly seemed to me that if God could light sixteen little stones for the

Brother of Jared . . . if He could stop the sun in the sky for Joshua . . . if He could help Nephi build a boat . . . and do a thousand other miracles for a thousand other men—then He could widen this gully for Clay Eskiminzin. If the latter was any less faithful, any less deserving, I hadn't seen it. As for my own faith, it was absolute. I knew God *could* widen that gully if only He *would*.

"Please!" I called into the heavens. "Please!"

The really annoying thing about miracles is that you can never be absolutely certain you've received one. Was what happened next an answer to prayer or the very thing that the laws of nature would have caused to happen anyway? All I can tell you is that sometime between the first and second *please*, the incredible force of the deluge dislodged a boulder from the canyon wall a few hundred yards up stream from where Clay clung so precariously to mortality. Behind the huge rock was yet another of the many caverns a long-forgotten river had gouged into those cliffs a millennia before. This particular cavern was wide behind its entrance, and deep. Most importantly, it slanted downhill. Since water always obeys natural laws (except for that one time Moses commanded it not to), it rushed in to fill the opening and beyond. Not all the water funneled away, of course. Not even a lot of it, but enough water poured underground to lower the level aboveground by the eight or ten inches we so desperately needed.

Though drenched to the bone and battered by debris, Clay managed to hold onto the ledge when the water hit. I held onto him. Although it seemed like forty days and forty nights—at least—in reality our flood passed as quickly as it had come. When it was over, Clay hadn't lost his life after all. All he'd lost was one of his boots.

He clawed his way up onto the ledge and lay on his stomach, motionless.

I crawled to his side hoping he didn't need CPR, because I didn't know how to administer it. (I was, however, more than willing to give the mouth-to-mouth resuscitation part a try.)

But Clay breathed on his own. He opened his eyes. I think he might have even smiled. "Let me guess," he said. "You prayed for me."

"I did, Clay!"

"Thank you." He coughed out a lungful of muddy water. "Again."

As if we weren't wet enough, the first raindrops splattered onto the ledge.

"We've got to get Senator Teagler into the cave," Clay said. But he didn't move after he said it. I wondered if he could.

"I'm okay," he reassured me (doing that mind-reading thing he had said he couldn't do). To prove he was telling the truth, he managed to sit up. Still, in the closest he might come to admitting weakness he added, "Help me with him, will you?"

Together we dragged Alex well into the mouth of the cave. As Clay eradicated the scorpions and then checked to see that Teagler hadn't started to bleed again, the senator came around.

"Connor!" he cried.

"Quiet, Alex," I said. I wanted to save Clay any effort I could, even the effort of speaking. "Rest."

He shook his head and tried to rise. He couldn't. Clay and I leaned him gently back against a cavern wall. "Where's Connor?" he asked plaintively.

Neither of us answered. Now that we were safe once again—at least for the moment—that was the question on all our minds.

* * *

I don't know how long it rained, since I don't have Clay's gift for telling Battime without a watch. I only know I sat at the entrance to the cavern and watched the drops fall until they were heavy enough to extinguish the small brush fire that had been started by the lightning. There was more lightning—and thunder, of course—but Clay dozed through it while Alex raved about Connor.

Teagler didn't seem feverish to me, but I worried. In the movies when people had been shot, they soon went out of their minds with pain and fever. At that point, they were either tended by attractive strangers or else they died. Not only was I not exactly a stranger to Alex, I didn't know how to tend a raving man. To add insult to injury, as they say, I probably didn't even qualify as attractive anymore.

I hoped God wasn't tired of hearing me pray because that's what I did. I didn't want Alex to die—and for a righteous reason this time.

"How long did I sleep?" Clay asked, joining me in the front of the cave. Too tired and sore to crouch, he sat beside me.

"Not long," I said. "Not long enough, that's for sure."

He stared into the drizzle. "Yeah, well, I didn't want to miss anything."

"Like what?" I asked apprehensively.

"I don't know." He stretched out his legs and frowned at his sock. Relief that he was okay erased my apprehension and even made me smile. He seemed to like that, because he said, "Well, we haven't been chased by a rabid grizzly bear. Or caught in an avalanche. Or—" he smiled down at me. "You're the one who sees all the disaster movies. What else have we missed?"

I pointed upward. "Alien invasions."

He chuckled. "It wouldn't surprise me at this point."

From his spot in the darkened corner, Alex called out again for Connor. Clay turned.

"He's been doing that all along," I reported sadly. "He thinks he hears Connor crying."

Clay started to shake his head and turn back to me, but seemed to freeze in the process. He turned all the way around toward Alex. "Senator?"

"I hear him, Clayton!"

That was impossible, of course. Why then, I wondered, did Clay move so quickly to his side? To check his pupils for signs of brain damage? My heart lightened a little. If anybody could qualify as attractive, it would be Clay. And they were almost strangers. Maybe Alex would live after all.

But Clay didn't feel for a fever or check for a pulse. He knelt at Alex's side and pressed his ear to the cave wall beside the older man's head.

I rushed to join them. "You don't think—"

Clay held up a hand for silence. After a minute he said, "When did you hear it last?"

"A little while ago," Alex said. He struggled upright, newly invigorated by the thought that Clay might believe him—must believe him, by the looks of things.

I pressed my ear to the wall as well. Since I could never even hear the sound of the ocean in a seashell, it shouldn't have surprised me that I couldn't hear a little boy in a solid rock wall.

After another couple of minutes, Clay sat back.

"You think I'm delirious?" Alex asked. It was apparent from his tone that an affirmative response would devastate—but not surprise—him.

"No," Clay said, surprising me. "I think you heard something." Before either of us could respond he added a caution. "But probably not Connor."

I shook my head. "Then—"

"Maybe bats," Clay said. "Or an animal."

"It's Connor," Alex insisted. "I know my own son!"

Clay's eyes focused on the entrance of the cave. I knew he wished for a mountain to gaze at.

"Is it possible?" I asked, grasping his arm. "Not probable or even very likely, Clay, but *possible*?" The thought gave me goose bumps.

They doubled in size when Clay said, "It's possible." He looked back at the two of us, clearly reluctant to raise our hopes any further. "Most of the cliffs in this area are honeycombed with caves. The one you're familiar with, Senator—the one where they held your son—was a favorite of the Aravaipas when they were hiding in the canyons. They used it because it had several ways out. One of the exits could be here where we are now."

So I had been right about part of the pathway up the cliff being manmade. I wondered how long it had taken the Indian braves, or their wives, to hew those steps out of solid stone. I wondered how they had done it at all, without the gift of wings to keep them airborne as they worked. We often say that modern technology is amazing, but what tends to humble *me* is what our forebears managed to accomplish with stone tools and a whole lot of determination.

"Where is he?" Alex cried, looking desperately around the cave. "Where's Connor?"

Clay shook his head. "I don't think—"

"There he is again!" Alex interrupted. "Don't you hear him, man?"

Again Clay pressed his ear to the wall. I watched his eyes widen and then take on a glow that stopped my heart. "Yes," Clay said. "Yes, Senator. I hear Connor."

chapter 25

Within seconds of identifying the little boy's cries, Clay had pulled a small flashlight from one of the zippered pockets of his cargo pants. Fortunately, unlike his poor waterlogged scriptures, this tool of survival was watertight.

He shined the beam into the far corners of the cave. No grizzly bears. No UFOs. No signs of Connor.

"The opening must have been over there," he mused, exploring a pile of rubble not far from where we'd placed Alex. In no time Clay was on his knees with the flashlight in his mouth, moving rocks. I moved close, but before I could help much he had already cleared a hole about the size of a mailbox. He dropped to his stomach. "Connor!" he yelled into the hole. Then he rose to his knees and moved aside. "Senator," he said. "You call to him."

Alex crawled to Clay's side with amazing alacrity. "Connor!" he cried. "Connor! It's Dad!"

"Daddy?" The distant voice wavered.

Tears filled my eyes and I fell to my knees.

"Connor!" Alex clawed at the stones himself, but was too weak to do much more than bruise his hands.

"Let us," Clay said.

Side by side we tossed stones away from the hole.

"Daddy?"

The voice was close enough to make the hair on the back of my neck stand on end. It was also far enough away to drop my heart into my toes. "Where is he, Clay?" I breathed.

Clay shook his head. "It's hard to say. Connor's voice is echoing off the walls. He could be a few hundred yards in, or he could be a lot farther, back toward the other cave."

"Daddy? It's dark now!"

I couldn't imagine how dark it must be so far underground. Darker than midnight. Darker than I had ever seen. Darker than I could ever bear. "We're coming, Connor!" I called. "Just a few more minutes. We're coming!"

"Mommy?"

"We'll take you to Mommy!" Alex assured his little son, having cleared the raw emotion from his throat.

"Mommy!" Connor screamed. "It's dark!"

Clay had cleared away the rest of the loose rocks. I watched his fists clench, unclench, and clench again. Then he rolled back on his heels and ran his fingers through his hair. When he finally spoke, his voice was flat. "Some of the passage has collapsed. It wasn't very big to start with."

My eyes flew to the entryway as Connor cried out again in fear. Clay was right. The opening was impossibly small, especially for a man his size. It would take a jackhammer to open a gap big enough to accommodate those shoulders. We didn't have a jackhammer. We didn't have anything at all that we could use to—

"Mommy?" Connor screamed. "I want Mommy!"

In a revelation that was simultaneously thrilling and sickening, it hit me. I was a size six who'd been almost fasting for two days. *I could fit through that hole.*

It was a few more minutes before I could say it out loud.

"No," Clay said when finally I did. "I'll hike back around and find a way to move the boulder."

"Barefoot?" I asked. "Besides, the switchbacks are too slick to go down in the rain. You said so yourself." He wasn't convinced, but I pressed on. "And even if you *don't* kill yourself and there *aren't* ten men waiting outside this ravine to kill you, how are you going to move that rock?"

"There's another way in," he said stubbornly.

"Yes." I grasped his arm and pulled him back toward where Alex lay on his stomach, reassuring Connor. "There's *that* way."

He turned away. “Jill, you don’t know what you’re suggesting. You don’t know what’s in there.”

I swallowed. “Connor’s in there. That’s all I need to know.”

“It isn’t,” he said quietly. “These caves aren’t carpeted and they aren’t vacant. The stones are sharp and there could be animals in there. Or snakes. Or scorpions. Or worse.”

I doubted the “worse” part. Nothing was worse than what he’d already named—unless it was the darkness itself.

“And we don’t know where Connor is,” he continued, “or how to get to him. It might be a maze, Jill, and there might be a shaft between here and where Connor is that drops who-knows-how-far. A person shouldn’t go somewhere like that alone even if they’re trained. You’re not trained. You’re . . .”

I waited to hear what I was, but he didn’t finish the sentence. He didn’t even meet my eyes while he didn’t finish it.

“We still have the rope on your belt,” I said. “I’ll tie it around my waist and you’ll hold onto me the whole time. You won’t let me get lost and you won’t let me fall.”

“Jill—”

“You’ve been willing all along to die for Connor . . . for Alex . . . for me,” I said. “I’m not willing to die, Clay. I’m just willing to go in and bring Connor out.” I took his arm again and this time I wouldn’t let him move away from me. “I *felt* I should come here, remember? I felt I should help look for Connor. Maybe this is the whole reason I’m here.”

“No,” he said, his voice deep.

“I have to try,” I insisted. “I can’t live with myself if I don’t try.”

It was almost a minute before he responded. At last his free hand rose to cover the one I had placed on his arm. “I know,” he said at last. “I know.”

chapter 26

"Hold the flashlight in your mouth," Clay instructed as he knelt beside me. "You'll need both hands free. Keep that rope on at all times. No matter what, Jill. Understand?"

I wrapped the fingers of one hand around the nylon rope he had tied securely around my waist and nodded. But I *didn't* understand. I didn't understand anything. Was going after Connor the first real *action* I'd ever taken in my life, or was it an insane *reaction* to too many hours of stress and fatigue? Who did I think I was, Lozen? And what did I think I was doing on my knees about to shimmy into a dirty, long, black tunnel?

"I'll keep the rope taut," Clay continued, "so I'll know how far in you are. If we run out of rope you come back out. No argument."

Again, I nodded.

He hesitated another moment, then held out the small flashlight.

I saw that the hand I extended shook, but that was nothing. My eyes were twitching and my toes had curled into little balls in my shoes.

In a surge of determination, I grabbed the flashlight. Let my body have a grand-mal panic attack if it wanted to. No matter how weak my flesh, my spirit and I were willing to go after Connor.

I looked up at Clay for what I hoped wasn't the last time. Miraculously, his eyes weren't focused on something nobody else could see. This time those blue eyes looked right at me. Through me. I flung my arms around his neck and kissed him full on the mouth.

"Just so you know," I breathed. Then I put the flashlight between my wonderfully smashed, still-tingling lips, fell to my stomach, and slithered into the opening with almost as much ease as a rattlesnake.

A rattlesnake?

I knew at once that I'd be better at this rescue mission if I didn't think so much—and if I hadn't seen so many movies. A dozen flicks came instantly to mind as I wriggled my way down the first few feet of the narrow shaft. It was probably too much to hope that I was John Nash experiencing this horror only in my own beautiful mind. So, was I tunneling my way to Atlantis (or the earth's core) sans digging machine and supporting cast? Was I lost in the tunnels below Hogwarts being ware the basilisk? Wandering ancient catacombs in search of the Holy Grail? Soon to enter Shelob's lair? Something skittered away from the light and I settled on my movie scene. I was Luke Skywalker entering the Jedi-testing cave on Dagoba. Here I would face all *my* greatest fears and conquer them. Or else I would be destroyed.

Conquer, I told myself quickly. But Luke had at least had a lightsaber. All I had was a flashlight that was only as long as a mascara wand and about as big around as a tube of lipstick. *May the Force be with me.*

The tunnel was littered with rocks from the cave-in. I wondered how long ago it had begun to collapse—and especially how long it might be before it finished doing it. I tried to make myself smaller, as if that would make any difference if tons of soil and rock suddenly crashed down on me.

Sharp stones dug into my hands and knees, impeding my progress and causing me to bite my lips to keep from crying out. Connor had ceased to call for his Mommy, but I could hear him whimpering somewhere up ahead. *Somewhere.* I tried to move faster toward the sound.

"Take your time," Clay counseled from the mouth of the tunnel. "Be careful, Jill."

The voice I heard was full of concern but, admittedly, given the fact that I hadn't stopped vibrating since I'd kissed him, my hopeful imagination might have ascribed it.

Miles and miles into the center of the earth (you'll have to take my word for the distance unless you want to measure Clay's rope), the tunnel opened up. Or maybe it opened out. At any rate, it got bigger. I rose to my feet, but I couldn't quite stand upright. If Apaches had used this route often, I now knew why they were so accustomed to crouching.

Going on, I soon discovered that it had been easier to crawl. In no time at all my knees complained as vociferously as the backs of my thighs and fronts of my shins. I could have dropped to my knees and kissed the ground when a few tortuous steps farther down, the tunnel widened again, into a small cavern.

I pulled the flashlight from my mouth and swung it over the walls, searching for Connor. He wasn't there. The underground room had another tunnel to my right, but it was empty.

Or was it?

Something moved above my head. Two somethings. Three somethings. I didn't know *how* many somethings. They moved and they sighed and then the whole ceiling started to come alive.

"Clay!" I screamed. "*Bats!*"

"Turn off the light!" he called. "Do it fast."

I fumbled for the button, found it, and pushed. The room went dark and I screamed again.

"Jill!" Clay called. "Stay still. Be quiet. They won't hurt you. Give them a minute to settle down."

He didn't understand. I wasn't screaming about bats now. I was screaming about dark. This wasn't dark in any manifestation to which surface dwellers are accustomed. This was beyond-dark dark. It filled my eyes and ears and then it crept into my lungs where it threatened to smother me.

"Clay," I whimpered. "Help me."

"Mommy?" It was Connor. "Mommy? I want my Mommy!"

I had to help him.

"What do I do?" I called to Clay. Or to God. Or to anybody else who might be able to tell me the answer.

"Come back," Clay said.

Keep going, a voice seemed to whisper.

My reply was the same to both of them. "In the *dark*?"

"Just for a minute," Clay called. "Just until you're out of that chamber."

The other voice concurred.

I didn't think I could take another step, but I knew I had to. I flicked the flashlight on for a nanosecond—just long enough to reach for the wall that led to the next tunnel. The bats stirred. Having never seen a flashlight—or light of any kind—this far underground, they must have thought the whole world had turned inside out. I was inclined to agree with them.

After a moment's hesitation I edged toward the sound of Connor crying, but it was difficult to move my feet. They seemed stuck to the floor. Once I made a conscious effort to stop hyperventilating and took a breath through my nose, I realized it wasn't just my reluctance to continue in the dark. I was wading in guano—bat droppings. Years and years and years of bat droppings.

I know I would have died an agonized—and extremely stinky—death on that very spot if the sarcastic little voice in my mind hadn't pushed to the front and said, *Just be glad you didn't drop to your knees and kiss the floor like you wanted to.* (Even in the worst of times, there are blessings to appreciate if somebody will just point them out to us.)

I didn't think any more, and I certainly didn't breathe. I just slogged through the dark with my face pressed against the wall until my hand reached the end of it. I was at the other tunnel. I felt my way around the corner. This corridor was a little taller. I could almost stand up.

"I'm coming Connor!" I called into the blackness. "Clay! I'm in the next tunnel." In fact, I was already groping my way down it. Connor couldn't be much farther ahead. He couldn't.

"Jill!" Clay called at the same moment Connor called again for his mother.

"It's all right!" I hollered to both of them. Cautiously, I turned the flashlight back on. No bats. No snakes. No ghosties or ghoulies or long-legged beasties or things that go bump in the dark. But no Connor, either. A few feet ahead, the tunnel turned. Who knew what lay around the next bend?

"Jill!" Clay called again. "You can't go on." To confirm it, the rope around my waist tightened and then pulled me to a stop.

"I'm almost there!" I told Clay. "Just let me go a little farther."

"There's no more rope."

"Connor!" I heard Alex cry in desperation. "Connor!"

"Daddy!"

I stood in the middle, probably no closer to one than I was the other. My mind insisted that I go back to Clay and wait for help. My heart cried out for me to go on to Connor—that help might never come, that Shar's little boy needed me now.

What do I do?

It wasn't a plot twist in a movie and it wasn't a hard interview question in a beauty contest. It was *the* question, and my life—not just my mortal life, but my ability to live with myself from that point forward—depended on how I answered it.

Before I had too much time to think about the twists and turns—and possible bottomless pits—that might lie ahead, my hands flew to the knot at my waist. It was impossibly tight. I took a step back to loosen the tension. I fumbled with one part and then another. I couldn't untie it. And then, suddenly, I did. I dropped the rope to my feet and with the flashlight still between my teeth, stared down at it.

"Jill!" Clay called. "Don't—"

But I already had. I took a step away from the end of the rope—and away from the voice I wanted to run back to.

"I'm okay!" I called to Clay. "I'm going to get Connor. We'll be right out."

I am a very optimistic liar. It is the part of me that sees the truth that tends toward pessimism.

Make it true. Please make it true. It was a prayer to God, and a command to myself. I faced forward. The lifeline was gone. From this point forward, I would walk by faith. If I had to, I would crawl by it.

Funny thing was, after the first few steps it didn't get harder. If anything, each step away from the rope was a little less difficult. Clay's counsel, "It's easier to do something than it is to worry about doing it," came back to me. It was still true.

Nevertheless, I approached the turn with fear and misgivings. Every movie buff knows that this is the part in the script where something horrible jumps out of the shadows. If the actress is the leading lady she's merely carried off screaming to be rescued later. But if she's an extra, she's likely to die a particularly gruesome death. What if I was an extra?

Or, I asked myself, *what if you've just seen too many movies?* Maybe I *was* the drama queen my boyfriends always called me.

It's easier to just do something . . . I reminded myself.

Even if that something is die? myself answered.

Hesitant to form another discussion group, I pulled the flashlight from my mouth, drew a deep breath, and rounded the corner.

The difference between where I was and where I had been is that this part of the tunnel was higher. Also, it was open and dry and the path was as clear as if it had been swept. I could walk now. Heck, I could probably run.

Remembering Clay's caution, I walked. But I did it quickly.

"Connor!" I called.

"Here!" a little voice called out from the darkness. "Here!"

I swung the flashlight in a wide arc. There was another opening ahead. Another cavern. I shuddered. *Another room full of bats?*

But I ran toward it anyway.

"I found him!" I called back to Clay and Alex. "I found him!"

Though premature, the words were soon true. Huddled alone, in the corner of a large cave devoid of bats, was my favorite Primary student, the wish of my heart, little Connor Teagler.

"Sister Caldwell!" he cried when I moved the flashlight beam from his eyes and shone it on myself. "Sister Caldwell!"

In the next moment I had scooped him into my arms. I hugged him and kissed him and cried gallons of cactus-juice tears into his tousled hair—all the while marveling that he wasn't the least bit surprised to see *me*. Probably, after all he'd been through, nothing would ever surprise Connor again.

"Where's Daddy?" he asked. "The white man said Daddy would come to get me. He said I had to be very brave." He wiped at his eyes with grubby fists. "I was brave, Sister Caldwell. I was *very* brave."

"Very brave," I sobbed, scarcely listening to what he said.

"But I was scared when the white man left because he took the light." Connor buried his head in my shoulder. "I wasn't brave then."

"Yes, you were!" I assured him. "You were even braver then."

I felt him shake his head. "I cried. I cried a lot. But then I heard Daddy." He pulled away. "Where's Daddy? I want Daddy! Skimmy *said* he'd come!"

Finally, some of the babble began to register. He'd been talking about a man who was surely not one of the kidnappers. "Skimmy? Who's Skimmy, Connor? What did he look like?"

"He's the man who brought me here. He had on white clothes and had a white light, too. He gave me water."

"You mean the man who took you to the first cave," I said, in case I was wrong about it not being a kidnapper.

"No!" Connor said. "That was a bad man. I thought he was nice, but he wasn't. He . . ."

Connor began to cry and I held him a little closer. "Shh, Connor," I soothed. "You're safe with me now."

As I held him, I shined the light around the large room. Unlike every other cave I'd seen in the last two days, this one wasn't empty. The boulders that lined the walls didn't seem random. They looked like furniture—primitive chairs arranged in advance of a meeting. More remarkable, there were two large clay pots (here on the border with Mexico we call them *ollas*) and several smaller vessels against the walls. One olla lay on its side, broken and empty. The other stood upright, its stone lid still intact. I could only wonder at the contents. Near it—almost where Connor had been sitting—a little stream of water trickled from a crevice, ran down the wall, and disappeared into the floor. A small clay pot lay on its side nearby—still wet from use. Thomas Edison couldn't have designed a better drinking fountain. That must be what Connor meant, but who was the man that had filled the bowl and given it to him?

My mouth opened, but no words came out of it.

"The white man said my Daddy would come," the little boy whimpered. "Where *is* he, Sister Caldwell? Skimmy *promised*!"

"Alex!" I croaked. Clearing the wonderment from my throat, I tried again, louder. "Alex! I have Connor!" The joyful words echoed through the underground, and probably up to heaven itself.

"Connor!" Alex called back.

"See?" I told the little boy. "Daddy is waiting for you a little ways from here. I'll take you back to him." I started to warn him that his daddy was hurt—sick—but thought better of it. He'd see for himself soon enough.

The thought was a sobering one. It reminded me that despite my success and joy in finding Connor alive and well, we weren't quite to the happy ending. If ever there would *be* a happy ending. Even if I could find the rope again and lead Connor out to his father, what then? We still wouldn't have food or water, or much of a chance to get out of this ravine without being hunted down and killed.

I'll think about that later, I decided, rising and taking Connor's hand firmly in my own. *Better yet, I'll let Clay think about it. He and Connor's imaginary friend can work it out together.*

* * *

"What if Connor's friend *isn't* imaginary?" I whispered to Clay so as not to disturb Alex and Connor. The little boy was wrapped in his father's arms while they both slept. Outside, the late afternoon rain had slowed to a steady drizzle and then stopped. Though the flash flood was now only an unpleasant memory, the basin of the gully was still a quagmire of mud. On the one hand, it would be very difficult for anyone to come in after us—which was good. On the other hand, it would be almost impossible for us to get an injured man and a little boy out—which was probably good, too, I decided on further reflection. Alex hadn't killed the gunman, after all. The gunman had a radio. With batteries, presumably. It was hours and hours later. Who knew how many well-armed men Eliot Fuller had dispatched by now to hunt us down?

I watched the water run off a little ledge and fill the small pot I'd tied into Clay's voluminous shirt before I left the interior cave with Connor. Water was no longer a problem. Food was. Apparently, prickly pear was like Chinese takeout—eat a whole meal of it and an hour or two later you're hungry again. I was starved, but I knew how slick the ledge was and how exhausted Clay must still be. Besides, having removed his other boot and both socks, he was barefoot. I wouldn't send him down for more takeout quite yet.

To take my mind off my stomach, I chatted. After all, with his scriptures waterlogged, Clay was only trying to think. (Ignore what yoga practitioners tell you—meditation is not a group activity.) "Suppose there really *was* somebody who helped Connor," I persisted.

Clay stopped staring into space, drew up his knees, and settled himself more comfortably against the wall, probably fearing this could be a long conversation. Or possibly he feared me. Ever since I'd kissed him Clay had seemed a little nervous. I thought he'd acted pleased and relieved when I came back from the tunnel—he didn't even mention the Eau de Batpoop that had permeated my pores when he pulled me through the hole and held me close. But since that brief embrace he'd seemed to be keeping his distance. Maybe he feared that if I kissed him again he'd be carried away by his passion for me. (I didn't *believe* that, of course, but a girl can dream.)

As usual, Clay pulled me back to reality. "That's pretty hard to suppose," he said.

"But you heard what Connor said," I continued. "A bright man in white woke him up in the middle of the night, led him through the tunnel, gave him water, and stayed in the cave with him. When the man left he took the light with him and Connor cried because it was dark. That's when Alex heard him."

"It's common for children to imagine a friend in times of incredible stress and fear," Clay said. "It happens all the time. Some of them have told us they were protected by a big, talking animal."

"But what if it's *true*? What if God sends those children—"

"Smokey the Bear?"

"I'm serious," I said. And suddenly, though I'd only been making conversation at the start, I *was* serious. "How did Connor get *in* there? How could he have possibly found the way by himself?" I leaned forward. "How could he have moved that rock that you and I together couldn't budge?"

"There's a logical explanation, Jill," Clay said. "Either there was another way in—one we didn't see—or Connor moved the rock himself."

I sputtered.

"It happens," he said. "More often than you think. Sudden terror can release an incredible surge of adrenaline. That stimulant makes people, even little people, strong beyond belief. It only lasts a minute, but that could have been long enough for Connor to squeeze past the rock and run blindly down a passage to the place where you found him."

"You should have seen that place," I said. The longing on Clay's face told me it was one point on which we agreed. I remembered the way he'd taken the pot I'd brought to him, and the light in his eyes when he examined it. He told me the room must have been used by the Apaches for refuge, and speculated that the olla contained the remnants of mescal, or perhaps dried corn. If we ever got out of there, I knew Clay would be back to explore it for himself.

"Do you think Eskiminzin was ever in this cave?" I asked impulsively, hugging my knees up under my chin. The thought gave me goose bumps. Good goose bumps. The kind you get sometimes in sacrament meeting.

Then my arms and my knees and my jaw went slack, all at once. I couldn't speak. I could think only one word: *Skimmy*.

Across the cave, Connor woke. He patted his Daddy's arm, grasped his Woody doll, and wriggled out of his father's lap, careful not to disturb the sleeping man. If my arms hadn't been numb, I might have held them out to him. As it was, he padded across the stone floor to Clay. "I'm hungry," he said.

Clay smiled. "I bet you are. Let's see what I have." He rummaged around in those Mary Poppins pockets of his and produced a soggy, broken candy bar.

Hershey's is better than smelling salts for bringing me to my senses. "All this time you've had *chocolate*?" I cried. "And you didn't share it with me?"

"You better split it with Sister Caldwell," Clay warned the child as he unwrapped the candy and gave it to him.

Connor turned obediently toward me with the chocolate pieces in hand.

"No," I said quickly. "You eat it all. I'm saving my appetite for more cactus."

"I want some cactus," Connor said happily. "Can I have some cactus, sir?"

"Sure you can," Clay told the little boy. "In just a little while I'll go get you some."

Connor chewed the first piece of candy thoughtfully as he gazed into Clay's face. "You look like him," he said. "And you're nice like him, too."

"Who?" Clay asked.

"Skimmy."

Clay froze.

"Breathe," I suggested after several seconds. I'd moved to his side by now, astonished and triumphant both at once.

"Did you say—?"

"Skimmy," Connor repeated, his mouth full of chocolate.

Clay turned to me. I saw by his face that he was equally astonished, but twice as skeptical. "The Indian agent at San Carlos . . ." he began, then paused as if his memory were faulty, as if what he'd read in books and letters and knew for a fact could no longer be true. "The agent used to call Eskiminzin 'Skimmy.'"

"Who is Skimmy?" I asked Connor. I knew the answer, but wanted Clay to hear it for himself.

"The white man," Connor said confidently. "Skimmy saved me from the bad man. He stayed with me and kept the lights on until Daddy came." Connor climbed into Clay's lap. "You look like him," he said, touching Clay's face near his eyes. "You look like him there."

"Don't you see?" I whispered. "Eskiminzin saved the life of the son of the son of the son of the son of the man who had his entire family killed."

"Do you know what you're saying?" Clay asked me. His voice was equally low, equally awed.

I thought it through and then I touched Clay's arm. "I'm saying that maybe Eskiminzin was able to make it right, Clay. Maybe now he will finally feel that he can rest in peace."

I watched Connor lay his head against Clay's chest as he finished eating the candy. Clay's hand came up reflexively and stroked Connor's back, but his mind was a million miles—or maybe just a hundred and fifty years—away.

I wondered what Clay would believe once he'd had time to think and pray and work it out in his well-organized mind. Would he write in his journal that Connor had seen a vision induced by stress and fear? Or would he write that Connor encountered a spiritual manifestation of a man who knew the caves in this canyon as well as he knew himself. A man who knew what it was like to lose a child. A good man who could forgive the whole world their trespasses before he could forgive himself his own.

I didn't know about Clay, but I knew what I believed. If I ever had the chance to write Connor's story, I'd write that our Father is a God of miracles, explain them as we will.

chapter 27

If Clay had been a beagle, his ears would have come up at whatever he thought he heard. But he was a Batguy, so just his head rose. He stared into oblivion until he was sure, and then he passed Connor from his lap into mine. In the next moment he was out of the cave and on the ledge, checking his lower pants pockets as he went. At last he found what he wanted, held it in both hands, and raised it to the skies rather like Rafiki had the new Lion King.

I knew Clay too well by now to think him insane. I set Connor on his feet and scrambled to the front of the cave after him. "What is it?"

"A helicopter," he said, lowering his hands. "Forest Service, I think. Probably checking on the status of that wildfire the lightning started." He frowned in discouragement, or perhaps disdain, and shook his head. "They were a mile from where the smoke was. More."

Now I saw what was in his hand. I put my hands on my hips, incredulous. "You've had chocolate *and* a mirror?"

Clay stuck the square of polished metal back in his pocket, probably figuring he was doing me a kindness by not letting me look into it. Or maybe he was thinking of himself. He probably wasn't willing to hike down the switchbacks barefoot to retrieve my mangled body when I flung myself from the cliff at the sight of what I'd become.

"Did they see you signal?" I asked at last.

"No," he said, "but they didn't see any signs of the brush fire, either." He looked toward the west. "That means they may make another wide circle before sunset." He appeared to consider his options. "We'll have to chance a signal fire. It's the best hope we have at this point."

He didn't add that it was probably our last hope—our *only* hope, and I was grateful.

He returned to the cave with me on his heels. "Do we have *anything* dry?" he asked after a few moments.

I looked around. I even felt my hair. Nothing had dried past damp. Every piece of wood in a ten-mile radius, even our clothes, were too wet to burn.

I watched Clay kneel in front of Connor. The little boy's clothes were dry. Still, it was already cold in the cave. I knew from painful experience that if Clay was wrong and the helicopter didn't return, it would be bitter cold before long.

"Connor," Clay said, "I really need your doll."

He should have asked for the T-shirt. Connor clasped the toy to his chest. "He's not a doll!"

Before Clay could argue I said, "Of course he's not. He's Woody."

Connor nodded but continued to eye Clay suspiciously.

"Woody is very brave," I told Clay. "He saved Buzz Lightyear." Clearly, Clay thought I was delusional. I knelt beside Connor with a smile. "I bet Woody would give Clay some of his stuffing if he knew it would help get your daddy to a doctor."

Connor looked from his doll to his unconscious father. "Would it help?" he asked Clay.

"It would help very much," Clay said.

Connor extended the toy, then pulled it back.

"I can fix him!" I assured the little boy, though I had never taken an actual stitch—or even held a needle—in my whole life.

"You can?"

"I'll make him good as new," I promised.

He handed over the doll. When I saw Clay reach for his knife, I took Connor back to the ledge to help look for helicopters. He'd been through enough without having to watch his best friend's innards being removed.

In another minute, Clay joined us. He sheepishly handed over a considerably thinner version of Woody and knelt on the ledge with a fluffy pile of filling. "Polyester," he said. "It would be better if it were cotton." But he was already working flint against steel. "At least we ought to get some smoke from it."

I contemplated Connor's crestfallen expression with concern. Unable to stand it, I looked down toward my feet. That's when I saw the remains of Clay's shirt hanging in tatters over my hips. He'd torn off the bottom two inches himself, but I could easily spare another six or ten.

I raised the grimy fabric to my mouth and gnawed a small tear into the fabric, then I tore the shirt off at my waist. "Let me see Woody," I said, holding out a hand. Connor passed him to me and I wadded up the fabric and used it to restore as much of the little cowboy's character as I could. Really, he didn't look too bad.

"Thank you!" Connor cried.

Wow. I was a heroine at last!

Connor took Woody back into the cave to rest with his father, and Clay looked up at me from the small, smoky blaze. "I'm impressed," he said. "I'd never have gotten that doll away from him without a battle."

I smiled. "That's because you haven't prepared yourself like I have."

"Excuse me?"

"You," I pointed out, "don't go to the movies. But don't worry." Then I sang a verse of "You've Got a Friend in Me" to show off.

Under the trying circumstances, Clay didn't crack a full-fledged grin, but I could tell he wanted to.

"It's not going to work," I worried.

In spite of Clay's careful ministrations, the fire for which Woody had given his all had burned fitfully for about fifteen minutes and then sputtered down to a few melted-looking ashes. Another forty-five minutes had passed since then and the Forest Service helicopter personnel hadn't seen the tiny column of gray-white smoke. Or if they had, they'd thought it too insignificant to check out. We'd sat on the ledge, mirror at the ready, but they didn't return.

"How long until sunset?" I asked.

"Not long," Clay said. "I better go down and get Connor that cactus I promised." As he rose, those ears of his went to attention again. I could see it. Then I really *could* see it. What he was listening to, I mean. From our buzzard's eye view, the two men who paused at the entrance to our gully were clearly visible. As visible, I realized in the next second, as Clay must be to them.

He fell on top of me and scooted us both into the mouth of the cave as the first shot echoed through the canyon. The bullet pinged into the rock wall, ricocheted at a downward angle, and cut a long, razor-sharp path across the back of Clay's shirt and into his flesh. Without so much as a moan, he sat up and pushed me farther back into the cave.

"You're hurt!" I cried out.

He didn't respond. I could see his mind working overtime to figure out our options.

What options? The words "like shooting fish in a barrel" came back to mind. Heck, killing us in here wouldn't even make good sport. Especially since these men didn't have handguns with silencers. They had rifles with scopes, and they no longer seemed to care who might hear them.

"How long until dark?" I asked again, frantically this time. This was my fault. If I had picked up the two guns like any good sidekick, Clay could at least shoot back.

"Doesn't matter," he said. "They have infrared goggles."

"Who *are* those guys?" I exclaimed. I'd thought this morning about being in a Stephen King novel, but Dean Koontz hadn't entered my mind. Just how desperate had Eliot Fuller become? How confident was he that there wasn't another human being within miles of this canyon?

"A helicopter!" Clay said suddenly, proving again that sonar has its uses. In another minute, I heard it too. He crawled toward the cave entrance.

"You can't go out there—" I didn't need a punctuation mark. It was provided for me by the sound of gunfire.

"My heck," Clay said. (If I hadn't been so petrified I might have been gratified to note that he'd picked up *something* from me along the way.) "Who *are* those guys?" He pulled his head back in the cave while he still had it. "They just used semiautomatics to shoot at the *copter*." He shook his head. "It doesn't make sense." Before I could agree wholeheartedly, he added, "Yes, it does."

"It does?"

In one fluid motion he rose, crossed the cave and pulled me to my feet. "You have to get Connor back inside the tunnel, Jill. They didn't see you. They don't know we have Connor. I'll rock up the entrance and you'll be safe." His honesty leaked out despite his intentions. "Safer," he amended.

Pressed tightly against his father, Connor whimpered. I probably did too. "I don't understand," I told Clay as he pushed me forward.

"Those men have one objective," he said grimly. "They need to kill me and the senator as quickly as they possibly can. It's Fuller's last hope. He must know we've signaled for help and that it's only a matter of time until it arrives. But he also knows that if there's nobody left to tell the truth, he'll get off scot-free. The authorities will look for a well-armed guerrilla group of kidnappers—maybe pin it on that underground militia the senator's spoken out against—and nobody, *nobody* will look for Eliot." He'd gathered Connor up on the way and had us both at the entrance to the narrow tunnel.

"The flashlight won't last much longer," he said, "but the bats will be leaving soon. Go as fast as you can, Jill. Take Connor back to the room where you found him and wait there. Wait a long time. A *very* long time. Don't come back out until you're positive there's nobody in this cave."

Nobody alive, he meant.

Clay kicked aside a rock. "Go!"

But the rock gave me an idea. "Wait!" I said. "I saw something in a movie we can use. When the Swiss Family Robinson was attacked, they climbed up a hill and threw rocks down at the pirates."

"Good for them," Clay said, putting pressure on my shoulder as if he would wad me up and push me through the hole if he had to.

He probably could have, too, but I wasn't going to make it easy. "We can—"

"I'll throw rocks if you want me to, Jill," he said. "I promise. Just—"

This time I heard the *chop, chop, chop* of helicopter blades as soon as Clay did. It was much closer. The sound was followed almost immediately by more gunfire.

"Is that pilot out of his mind?" Clay exclaimed. "One hole in the wrong place and—"

"It must be Dirk!" I cried. "NewsChannel 2's Guy in the Sky!"

Clay closed his mouth, then opened it again, then closed it.

"Dirk *is* out of his mind!" I told him, laughing and crying at the same time. "He's certifiable! He'd fly to Hades and back if he thought it would get him a gig with CNN." The more I thought about it, the surer I was. "*Plus*, he's Marine Reservist. He's only been home from Iraq eight months or so. He's a war hero, Clay. Shock and awe are his idea of a great time."

This cave was a really odd place in which to stage a debate, and the timing was even less fortuitous, but still we did it.

Clay countered, "No way would they let a news-copter pilot—"

"What are they going to do to stop him?" I interrupted. "Shoot him down?"

"The sheriff's department—"

"Knows a good deal when they see it. They use *you* for search-and-rescue."

"That's different. This . . ."

The sound of the chopper veering away and the stunning silence that followed stemmed his words. (Realization that the point is moot can end a debate faster than anything.)

"Get in the tunnel," Clay said. He raised a gentle hand to my cheek, which had the effect of staying my protest by freezing my vocal chords. "Jill, please."

It was a different tone of voice than I'd heard him use. I might not have recognized what it meant, but I couldn't ignore it, either. I leaned into his touch for just a moment, and then reached for Connor's hand. "Come on, honey."

"Daddy?"

"Daddy will be okay." I knew that lie *might* come back to bite me very soon, but I couldn't help trying to believe it myself.

Connor hugged Woody and looked doubtfully toward the dark hole. "Will Skimmy be in there?"

"I don't know," I said. "I hope so." But what I really hoped was that the brave chief would be out here with Clay to face the men who were coming to undo all the good they both had done today. I hoped that if something of Eskiminzin did remain in this place that had once sheltered him and his people, it would help Clay defend it now.

Peace, I thought, *like a stone.* Had there ever been a greater prayer uttered in the history of this land?

chapter 28

All my life I've known that I am a reactionary. That I am a coward. That I would rather hide than fight, whether for an object, a person, or an ideal. I never fought with other children for nursery toys; I let them have whatever they wanted. I didn't argue ideas in school; I kept my head down and waited for the bell to ring. I didn't even fight for my friendship with Shar; when the going got tough, I let her go. After all those years of her being my best friend—my sister, my other half—I turned away and told myself it was her fault, or at least her husband's, and there was nothing I could do about it.

Now I sat in a cramped little hole in the ground wondering if I was right about me.

I hadn't taken Connor back to the interior cavern. Maybe I would in time. Maybe I wouldn't. For now, I'd taken him as far as the spot where the tunnel widened enough for us to sit up. From here we could clearly hear what went on back in the cave.

The sounds told me that Clay stacked rocks against the small opening. His was a suicide mission. There was nowhere for him to go when he finished. The cave had only two exits. One was too small to escape through and the other was too big to defend. It was merely a matter of time before Connor and I would hear the gunfire that told us Clay and Alex were dead.

What then?

What now? I asked myself.

There wasn't time to form a panel or take the question to committee. I—the girl who never made up her own mind—had to decide.

"What would Lozen do?" I wondered aloud, realizing even as I spoke the words that *I* was no warrior princess. I was the spun-sugar variety of princess. The kind of princess who sits in an ivory tower looking pretty and waiting for a handsome prince to come along and change her life.

Or was I? What if the tower was under attack and the prince about to die? Like spun sugar, my world could dissolve, and I'd never care if I was pretty again.

But even that didn't give me the easy answer I sought. Going back to be with Clay would probably be suicide, but I didn't mind that. What I grappled with was deciding if it would also be murder. If I went back, and left Connor here alone, would I be sentencing to death a child that Clay was giving his life to save?

Not if I could do anything about it.

"Connor," I said, "listen to me." I turned on the flashlight so I could look into his face, but found him sound asleep. And why not? It was dark and he was exhausted. He trusted me and had no concept of the danger we faced.

I turned the flashlight back off and placed it in his little hand alongside Woody. Then I got on my hands and knees, ready to crawl back out the tunnel.

"Skimmy?" I whispered into the darkness. "Eskiminzin, sir? I'm counting on you to keep Connor safe until help comes."

I didn't count on Clay getting the hole completely blocked while I made up my mind what to do, but I should have. I pushed against the pile of rocks, but nothing budged. I pulled at the lowest stone, but I couldn't move it. Finally I grasped the highest, lightest stone and pulled. It came away in my hand. From that point on it wasn't too difficult to deconstruct a rock wall made hastily and without mortar.

Maybe there is something to that adrenaline theory of Clay's after all. It took much less time than I supposed it would to free myself. When I pushed aside the last stone that was in my way, I was rewarded with a picture-postcard view of the back of Clay's broad shoulders framed in the door of the cave against a spectacular sunset. I caught my breath.

He hadn't yet seen all there was to see in a sunset, he'd told me the night before. Somehow, I vowed, there'd be more time for him to look. Years and years and years more.

Clay turned as I scrambled from the rock heap. If I had been Lozen herself, he couldn't have looked more surprised.

"A quote from one of my favorite movies," I said before he could speak or I lost my voice to emotion. "Never give up! Never surrender!" Clearly he thought I'd lost my mind. But he was wrong this time. I'd only lost my heart. "I'm a warrior princess," I told him. "I came to rescue you."

Surprised, nothing. The man was dumbfounded.

At that point it dawned on me that he was also standing in the doorway. "Where are the gunmen?"

"Directly below," he managed. "They don't have a shot from there." But the implication was that it wouldn't be long before they would.

"Then shouldn't you be rolling rocks down on them?" I asked. When he didn't respond, I added, "You promised, Clay."

"I—"

"Here!" I rolled a medium-sized stone across the cave to get him started. "Toss it down," I urged.

Clay's wits began to return. He took a step toward me.

"There's no time to thank me," I said, rolling another rock right to the tips of his bare toes. "Save it for later. After we've beaned the bad guys."

"You saw this done in a *movie*," Clay said, in exasperation.

I picked up another rock. "I've seen it done in lots of movies. Not only did rocks work for the Swiss Family Robinson, Ewoks got a lot of mileage out of them, as did Ents, and—"

"Jillanne!"

I put my hands on my hips in true warrior princess fashion. "These are probably my last few minutes on earth," I said, "and I've already chosen to spend them with *you*. It seems like the least you could do, Clayton Eskiminzin, is to humor me."

A half dozen emotions flickered across his face. I filed away the ones I liked and forgot the rest. Then I rolled another rock, a big one this time. It didn't make it very far, but Clay walked over and picked it up. Then he went back to the mouth of the cave and shoved it out and over the lip.

We heard it fall, bouncing off the lower ledge, no doubt taking at least a small part of the path with it as it continued to roll to the bottom of the gully. Even from where I stood, I could hear a man below curse.

We had their attention.

The next look Clay gave me was one of stunned admiration. I filed that away too.

He dropped onto his stomach and crept toward the edge of the cliff. "Roll me a few of the smaller ones," he said. "We'll save the big ones for when they're higher. They'll do more damage then."

I don't think I've remembered to mention this yet, but I bowled in a junior league in high school. Even after all those years, I haven't lost my middle-seventies average. I kept Clay supplied with stones—more or less—and he kept launching them over the ledge. The cursing really heated up, but it didn't get any closer. We had slowed the desperados down for now.

But what would happen when we ran out of rocks?

Doing that mind-reading thing of his again, Batguy turned and looked back at our dwindling arsenal. The emotion that crossed his face was—I couldn't look; I knew what it would be.

"Go back in the tunnel, Jill," he said. "We need the rest of the rocks to cover it."

My heart hammered in my ears.

Or maybe it wasn't my heart, because Clay appeared to hear something too. So did the men below. But this time when the gunfire broke out, it sounded as if it might be coming from above as well as below. Directly above. Unless I missed my guess, NewsChannel 2's Guy in the Sky had returned, and this time he'd brought reinforcements.

The exchange of gunfire was terrifying. I covered my ears even though I knew that wouldn't block out the sound of a helicopter's fuel tank exploding above my head. But the firefight ended almost as soon as it had begun—and without an explosion.

A shaft of light came down from the just-dark sky and swept the gully, the cavern, and the canyon walls—back and forth, again and again. At last it moved to the entrance to the cave and stayed there.

"You okay down there?" an unfamiliar voice boomed.

Clay walked out into the light and waved his arm. Then he performed some other movements that looked like sign language to a giant.

"MedEvac is on the way!" the voice responded. "Stand by."

"Stand by?" I squeaked from my place at the back of the cave. "That's all they have to say to us? *Stand by*?"

"Get Connor," Clay said.

At least that was easier to do than standing by. I lay on my stomach at the entrance to the tunnel and saw a flicker of light no bigger than Tinkerbell moving steadily toward me.

"Can me and Woody come out now?" Connor asked.

"Yes!" I cried happily. "You can come out, Connor! Everything's okay now."

* * *

Twenty minutes later, I realized I had spoken too soon. Things were *not* okay. They were not okay *at all.*

"I can't do it, Clay," I said, pressing my back against the wall of the cave. "I *can't.*"

He stood and turned toward me. He'd just finished helping a paramedic secure Alex in a long aluminum-and-plastic cocoon. In another minute they would attach the contraption to the line the medical tech had come down on, and then airlift Teagler to a Tucson hospital.

It was a fine way to travel if you were unconscious. I wasn't. I was very conscious. Conscious of my terror.

"It's easy, ma'am," the medic said cheerfully.

I scowled at him. After this whole awful affair I had one nerve left, and he'd touched it. Trounced on it, in fact. I might have looked around for a spare rock to stone him with, but I was frozen, already envisioning myself at the end of that little silver cord, swinging wildly through the air before splatting against a canyon wall. People weren't meant to fly, especially at night. I'd seen bats do it and they didn't make it look easy—even *with* wings. "I won't do it," I told Clay. "I won't."

Batguy came close and put his hands on my shoulders. "You're scaring Connor."

I glanced guiltily at the little boy with the impossibly wide eyes.

"You *can* do this, Jill," Clay continued. "You can do anything. You're a warrior princess."

"Lozen spent her whole life on the *ground*," I pointed out, but in a whisper.

"Connor needs you to go with him," Clay said. "I need you to go. It's easy."

With his soft voice and earnest face he almost had me—right up until those last two words. "*Easy*?" I cried. "Easy for *you*—or Spider-man, maybe. You go with Connor, Batguy. I'm going to wait right here for the bus."

Clay's eyes crinkled into a smile, but his hands tightened on my shoulders. He pulled me away from the wall, turned me toward the entrance of the cave, and walked me to it.

We stood and waited as the tech attached the last two lines to Alex's gurney. With Clay's hands on my shoulders, escape was impossible. I could only dream of that dirty, black hole in the corner and rue the love that had caused me to make such a regrettable exit from it. Now there was nowhere to go but up. I felt my knees buckle. I *couldn't* go there. I couldn't.

When the litter was secured, the medic motioned with his arm to the MedEvac pilot above and gently pushed the cocoon off the ledge into the blackness. At first I thought it would fall, but it swung like a pendulum in a small arc, back and forth, and then hung suspended in the air before it was hoisted upward.

"That's my cue to exit stage right," the medic said, grasping the last free line. "See you around, Clay." He paused, embarrassed. "I mean, Mr. Montgomery. Sir."

Suddenly, Clay looked less anxious to return to civilization than I was.

"Daddy?"

Connor was pressed to my side, his arms wrapped around one of my legs. His eyes followed the helicopter that carried his injured father.

"The next one's for you, Connor," Clay told the little boy, as if hanging by a thread above a rocky canyon would be more fun than anyone could imagine.

On cue, another chopper appeared. Instead of a red cross it had *NewsChannel 2* lit up on its blue-and-white underbelly.

"You were right, Jill," Clay said, as if that would make me feel better. "That Dirk is some Guy in the Sky. He saved our lives."

"He only wanted to save *yours*," I muttered. "He knows it will finally get him on CNN. *I* could be splattered across the canyon walls and Dirk wouldn't think a thing about it. He doesn't even know my name. He calls me 'Babe,' which I can only hope means he thinks I'm as smart as the little pig who went to the big city to try to make good. Not that *you've* seen it."

Clay released my shoulders and took a cautious step back, but he remained between me and the tunnel, just in case. Then he knelt beside Connor. "Want to go for a ride, big guy?" he asked. He pointed above our heads to a descending sling that contained the sheriff's office sharpshooter (who had really saved us—Dirk merely flew well enough to save his own skin). "See that seat he's in?" Clay continued. "When it gets here, that man will get out so you and Sister Caldwell can get in. The guy in the helicopter will pull you up and take you right to your mommy. She'll take you to be with your daddy again. Okay?"

Connor's grip on my leg tightened into a tourniquet. "Can Woody come too?"

"Of course," Clay said. "Woody's always wanted to fly."

"That's Buzz," I told Clay between clenched teeth.

"Sister Caldwell likes to fly too," Clay said.

I grumpily wondered why the overgrown Boy Scout had picked now to drop honesty from his sterling code of conduct.

"Mr. Montgomery, sir," the officer said to Clay when his feet touched the ledge. "There's another chopper standing by for you. It will be right here, sir."

Although the guy didn't actually salute (or genuflect), he looked like he wondered if he should. I saw by his uniform that he wasn't from the sheriff's office after all. He looked military. Clay's grandfather must have convinced the governor to call out the National Guard. Or maybe this robo-cop was in the Special Forces. It was impossible to say just *who* might arrive when Henry Hamil Clayton was the one calling the shots. (I figure the only reason it wasn't Arnold Schwarzennegar himself was because he was busy running California.)

Clay had somehow unhooked Connor from my leg and gathered him into his arms. "Ready to go see Mommy?" he asked him.

The little boy nodded vigorously.

Clay turned to me but was prudent enough not to ask if I was ready to face death for the fifty-seventh time in two days. "Sit in the sling, Jill," he said.

I couldn't say any of the things I wanted to say, with one of my Primary children listening and all. I sat in the sling.

Clay placed Connor in my lap and began to secure the harness. When it was snug, he tightened it a little more, checked it again, and then ran one finger down the bridge of my nose with a sheepish smile. (I was too frantic to catalogue any of these tender actions at the time. Thank goodness my brain has an automatic recording, storing, and retrieval system of its own.)

Clay waved up at Dirk. "Think of it as a carnival ride," he suggested to me.

"I hate carnival rides!" I screamed as my toes left the ground.

"A swing," Clay called. "Think of it as a playground swing."

"I hate swings!"

"Jill!" he called up to me, "Just don't think!"

At last there was some advice I could live with.

Jill's Picks from Some Favorite Flicks

Even if something you see or hear in a movie doesn't happen to save your life the way it did mine, it can still inspire you. That's why I collect quotes from classic movies. (That and because they're a whole lot cheaper than Lladro, and lots more interesting than stamps.) Here are a few that went through my mind during my adventure in the wilderness:

To myself upon getting into the helicopter: "What would you do with a brain if you had one?" *(The Wizard of Oz)*

Upon reuniting with Shar and meeting Clay: "I always have a wonderful time, wherever I am, whomever I'm with." *(Harvey)*

What I should have told Clay to explain my impetuous actions at the top of the canyon: "Insanity runs in my family. It practically gallops." *(Arsenic & Old Lace)*

What I understood after the jeggo and rappelling down the cliff: "Nature, Mr. Alnutt, is what we are put in this world to rise above." *(The African Queen)*

What I wish I'd said to Clay after leaving the waterfall: "I'd love to kiss you, but I just washed my hair." *(Cabin in the Cotton)*

What I thought inside the cave with Clay: "Inside this room, all of my dreams become realities, and some of my realities become dreams." *(Willie Wonka & the Chocolate Factory)*

What I decided when I couldn't find out everything I wanted to know about Clay: "After all, tomorrow is another day." *(Gone With the Wind)*

How I felt when I thought Connor had been killed by the cougar: "Hearts will never be practical until they're made unbreakable." *(The Wizard of Oz)*

What I told myself sheepishly after listening to Alex's confession: "You know, people seldom go to the trouble of scratching the surface of things to find the inner truth." *(The Little Shop around the Corner)*

What I kept repeating to myself as I shimmied into the tunnel after Connor: "Do or do not. There is no try." *(Star Wars, The Empire Strikes Back)*

The first thing that came to mind when the snipers took a potshot at Clay: "Houston, we have a[nother] problem." *(Apollo 13)*

What I told Clay and meant with all my heart: "Never give up! Never surrender!" *(Galaxy Quest)*

What I think every time I look at Henry Clayton Montgomery Eskiminzin: "Was that cannon fire, or is it my heart pounding?" *(Casablanca)*

chapter 29

There was no emotion left in me. None at all. I lay atop Shar's warm, exquisitely soft bed and probed the innermost reaches of my psyche. I found no joy at being alive. No pride at what I had done. No satisfaction even that Connor was safe. There was nothing left inside me at all.

I rolled over and looked at the clock, but the time wouldn't register in my brain. Maybe I'd spent too long measuring time by how many more minutes I thought I might live for real time—that which was measured by clocks—to seem relevant.

Out in the hall, an ancient grandfather clock bonged twice. I figured it must be well after midnight and I must be tired. Was tired an emotion?

No, I decided. Tired was a state of being. A state of being alone. A state of being back in my old life. A state of being without Clay.

Suddenly my toes and my stomach and even my heart clenched. Maybe I felt emotion after all, and maybe the emotion was fear. If it was, it was worse than any fear I'd faced in the Galiuros Mountains. It was fear that I'd never see Batguy again.

After all, I hadn't seen Clay since he'd strapped me into the sling outside the cave and told me not to think. If only. Since I couldn't be with him, all I *could* do was think—about him, of course.

The only thing I remembered about the copter ride was clutching Connor tightly and keeping my eyes closed. And I remembered that Dirk called me Jill as he fired off a string of questions about Clayton Montgomery that I couldn't—wouldn't—answer. Sometime in the last two days the pilot had apparently learned my name, but it didn't do him any good. He might as well have been talking to Babe the pig.

Back at the ranch and on the ground at last, I spent an emotional few minutes with Shar before she and Connor were whisked away to have the child checked out by doctors before being allowed to see his father again. The senator was on his way into surgery, but was expected to make a full recovery. He'd already made a statement to authorities that had Eliot Fuller and his henchmen well on their way to indictment for abduction, blackmail, conspiracy . . . and just about every other crime in the legal alphabet. I'd stood and watched Shar's helicopter lift off toward Tucson and thought about how much Alex had been through, how hard the lessons he'd had to learn had been, and how different things could be now without Eliot Fuller controlling their lives. Very likely, Alex would retire from politics and he and Shar could build the family she'd always dreamed of.

Speaking of dreams, I'd done everything but grab hold of a cactus in order to be allowed to stay outside waiting for Clay's copter to arrive. Unfortunately, you couldn't see the cacti for the journalists, so I'd been hauled inside, examined by a doctor, and "debriefed" by county, state, and federal agents. As I answered the million-and-fourteen questions (some of them multiple times), my eyes remained focused on the door. I knew that any second that door would open and Clay would enter. Though it opened (and opened and opened), it was never he who walked through it.

Mr. Montgomery was fine, I was told, and having the wound on his back treated. Then I was told he was conferring with authorities. Then he was consulting with his family's press representative. Then he was talking to his family. Then he was simply "unavailable." More than one person assured me that Clay would see me when he was ready.

He was never ready.

At last the hour had grown so late and I was so far past exhaustion that the authorities released me. Shar's kindly maid took me upstairs to my friend's own suite of rooms, where there was a warm bath drawn and a clean nightgown laid out on the bed. The maid brought me real shampoo and real conditioner and real food. It made me cry—but not the happy kind of tears you would have expected in earlier chapters. Now I realized I could live on cactus for the rest of my life if the right person would give it to me.

I phoned my mother and woke her up. She assured me that she hadn't worried at all. (I knew that if news about us hadn't kept interrupting her soaps and sitcoms, she might not have noticed I hadn't come home from work. Too much "antidepressing" isn't good for anybody.) She said she'd seen me on the news, but why wasn't I the one reporting it? Wasn't that my job? I hadn't gotten fired, had I? Then she said that she'd seen video clips of the young man I was with and that he was very nice-looking and seemed very respectable. Everybody on TV said he came from a good family. Why didn't I bring a man like that home to meet her?

That made me cry.

I didn't call my "boyfriend."

I took the telephone into the bathroom in case Clay called me. I soaked and shampooed and repeated. Clay didn't call. I took a shower and manicured my nails. He still didn't call. I slathered moisturizer on my face and checked again to be sure the phone worked. It did. Clay didn't call. I examined my hair and snipped off some split ends. I rubbed an entire tub of shea butter into the deep crevices in my lips. Somewhere along the way I grew numb enough to go to bed.

But I put the phone under my pillow, just in case.

* * *

"I'm dreaming!" I mumbled to whomever or whatever woke me. "Go away!"

My words touched a familiar chord in my memory, and I shot up in bed. "Clay!"

"It's me, miss," the maid said from the bedroom doorway. "They asked me to tell you that you're needed downstairs in thirty minutes."

I looked at the clock and the numbers made sense. It was 5:00 A.M. I even knew who "they" were. "They" were Gene, the news director, and Bob, the producer of my morning show. I figured they had speculated—and salivated—all night over what I'd be able to dish today on Henry Clayton Montgomery. (NewsChannel 2's Reporter Barbie had never been much at reporting news, they must have told each other and everybody else who would listen, but boy had she succeeded in making it!)

And all I'd had to do was accidentally team up with a handsome, rich, romantic, publicity-shy legend-in-the-making and then practically get us both killed—numerous times—in order to make it to the big leagues. I should have thought of it before. I knew that at that very moment every network and affiliate in the nation—possibly the world—waited breathlessly to rebroadcast whatever sensational report I gave of our adventures on *What's Up, Tucson?* I could put our little station in the stratosphere and probably have a new job on *60 Minutes* or even *Entertainment Tonight* by mid-afternoon.

"Tell them I'm taking the day off," I told the maid. "Tell them I quit. Tell them I died and am even now being packaged for delivery to some buzzards I know!"

The maid deposited a garment bag and some boxes onto a chair just inside my door. Then she fled for her life.

I lay back down, burrowed into the fluffy white pillows, and pulled the expensive Egyptian linen over my head. Clay Eskiminzin hadn't called me. Henry Clayton Montgomery would never call me. Somebody call the buzzards. After all that trying to survive, I just wanted to die.

And I wanted to do it in peace. I wished that darned telephone would stop ringing.

"Oh my heck!" I said at last. I sat up, picked up the phone, and glared at the receiver. "What?"

"Jillanne Caldwell, what do you think you are *doing*?"

It was Gene. Big surprise there.

"I think I'm sleeping." That's what Clay would have said.

"I don't care if you think you're dying," he bellowed. "You can't keep Henry Clayton Montgomery waiting!"

I clenched Shar's fancy little phone so tightly I'm surprised I didn't snap it in half. With so much strength siphoning into my hand, there was none left for my voice. "What? What did you say?"

"It's already 8:15 in New York," he hollered, ignoring the question. "The network brass is going to have my—"

I knew Gene well enough to anticipate the words that came next, so I prudently moved the phone away from my ear. When I thought it might be safe I ventured, "What exactly *are* you saying, Gene?"

If it was what I thought he was saying, I was going to die for sure—of joy and ecstasy and that other emotion that is simply too exquisite to have a name here on earth.

Gene sputtered. Talk about somebody who must be squeezing a telephone. I was glad my neck was well removed from the vicinity of his fingers. "I'm saying there's one reporter here—one reporter in the whole *country*—who Clayton Montgomery has agreed to talk to. That reporter is you."

It was shock and awe all over again. Gene was shocked and I was awed. Awed, and so very, very happy. "I'll be right down!" I cried into the phone.

"Thanks *so* much," he said.

Sarcasm is wasted on some people. At that moment, I was one of those people.

Having no time to fumble with zippers, I tore open the garment bag. The clothes inside weren't mine. They were from the boutique that supplies our evening anchor, but the suit was beautiful and just my size. I had it on in three minutes and reached for the shoe box with one hand while my other worked on the last pearl button on the blouse. (Silk, of course.)

The shoes were my size too, but there was no way they were going on over the water balloon-sized blisters on my feet. I looked down at my tootsies in dismay. Except for being encased in silken pantyhose, those feet could have belonged to a Hobbit. I panicked until I remembered that feet don't show on the news. I tossed the high heels aside and reached for the next box.

Praise the heavens and pass the mascara, it was my makeup kit! My *own* makeup kit. I almost hugged it in delight. Okay, so I *did* hug it. (We are very close, considering that it's an inanimate object and all.) Then I rushed into the bathroom to Shar's vanity.

Big mistake. Shar's vanity has a mirror. A big mirror. With lights. Bright lights. I screamed loud enough for Clay to have heard me even if he'd been back in Maryland already.

* * *

"I can't do it!" I told Gene morosely. "I can't go on TV looking like this."

I'd sneaked downstairs to an empty hallway behind the staging area and beckoned for the news director to follow. I'd come down for one reason and one reason only. Since discovering in Shar's bathroom that I was too big a coward to commit suicide by drowning myself in the toilet, I figured the next best thing was to provoke Gene into killing me. Piece of cake. Already his fingers twitched uncontrollably. He couldn't wait to get them around my scrawny neck.

Scrawny, sunburned neck, that is. Its only saving grace was that it matched my sunburned, scratched, and swollen face. I licked my split, flaking lips and hung my head. Thanks to Shar's conditioner and blow dryer, my hair wasn't all that bad. Maybe if I parted my hair in back and combed it over my face—No. It would never work.

"I can't go on national television looking like this," I repeated. (I couldn't have gone on a local cable show broadcast only to insomniacs, but that was beside the point.)

Gene obviously agreed. I glanced up in time to see all the color drain from his face. But soon his neck turned a light red that deepened toward purple as the flush crept up toward his hairline. He stared at a spot just over my shoulder. Before the poor man could turn blue and topple over, a deep voice from behind me said, "Breathe."

The old "rooted to the spot" cliché took on a whole new meaning in my life.

"Mr. . . . Mr. Montgomery!" Gene exclaimed at last.

"Clay Eskiminzin," Clay said. The hand he extended past my elbow for Gene to shake was covered in fresh scabs.

At last I turned. Batguy looked worse than I did. Even the custom-tailored suit, white shirt, and designer tie couldn't distract much from the cuts and bruises on his handsome face. He looked like he'd been hit by a truck. Or maybe it was only a jeggo, a cliff, a long stretch of catclaw, a flash flood, and a stray bullet.

"Are you okay?" we said simultaneously.

Either we both were okay or we both lied.

"Then let's do this thing and get it over with," Clay said. Clearly, he'd rather wrestle the mother puma.

The man who'd approached with him said, "Remember what we've discussed with your grandfather, Mr. Montgomery."

"How could I forget?"

"As for the ground rules for this interview—" The Claytons' spokesman had attempted to step around Clay to get to me, but he didn't make it.

"She knows," Clay interrupted. To me he said again, "Let's do this and get it over with. I have a real life to get back to."

Suddenly, I couldn't breathe. I was confusing real life with reel life again. In reel life, Clay would have swept me into his arms just now and the music would have swelled and the final credits would have rolled while women used buttery napkins to dry happy tears from their eyes. But real life was different. In real life, Clay Eskiminzin was performing a last kindness to help me on my way. After that he and I would never even go to a movie together. I watched him turn to walk back toward the staging area and willed my heart to stay in one piece just one minute more. In one minute he'd turn the corner. When he was gone, it wouldn't matter if my heart broke because I wouldn't need it again anyway.

Clay stopped and turned. "Jill?"

Two minutes, I told my heart.

"Lights?" he prompted. "Camera? Action?"

"I can't, Clay," I managed. "Not looking like this. You know me. You understand."

"Yes," he said slowly. "I think I do know you, but I don't understand."

"I don't want to go on TV."

"I don't either."

"I won't do it," I insisted.

"Then neither will I. That was the deal I made with your network. You interview me or nobody does."

Gene gurgled as Clay walked back toward us, away from the staging area. I surmised that Clay was coming back to administer CPR to my boss, but he stopped where I cowered. He looked at me as if I were a jigsaw puzzle with all blank pieces. I bowed my head to make sure my silky hair obscured my wilderness-ravaged face. "I look . . . horrible," I murmured.

"Ah," Clay said as if the puzzle had just solved itself. He put a thumb under my chin and raised my face to his. His blue eyes smiled into mine as he leaned close and said into my ear, "If people only want to look at you, Jillanne Caldwell, that's their loss. Being beautiful outside isn't what you're all about."

While all the circuits to the possibly-complimentary-things-Clay-has-said-to-me file in my brain flashed and sparked and shorted out, he grasped my elbow. As he pulled me down the hall toward the makeshift set, I reviewed the precious words. I needed to write them down somewhere. With no marble pillars or gold plates available, I had to settle for carving them on the tablets of my heart. With him going back to his life—both lives—after this short interview, I'd have to live on those words for the rest of mine.

The producer almost cried with joy when we arrived—less than one minute before airtime. "Sit down, sir," Bob said to Clay, offering him a stool next to Dirk Hadden, the Guy Who Wasn't in the Sky today.

"I won't be here long enough to sit," Clay said, confirming my fears.

I stood next to Henry Clayton Montgomery, as expressionless as I was emotionless. Or maybe I wasn't emotionless. There was a good chance that if Clay hadn't still had a grip on my elbow I would already have been back upstairs crying my mascara off.

Dirk stood too and tossed his stool aside. There was no time to wire us, so Bob thrust a microphone into my free hand. I didn't raise it to the ready position. I didn't even look at it.

"Jill . . ." he began, then gave up. Every other day of our association when he wanted me to shut up, I wouldn't. Now on the one day in history that he wanted me to talk, it was apparent I couldn't do that, either.

"Warrior princess," Clay said from the side of his mouth as Bob counted down to air time. He released my arm and tried to rearrange the expression on his face from pained to patient. "Let's make Lozen and Skimmy proud. We owe them."

I nodded and tried to rearrange what was left of my face from hamburger to near-human.

The lights came up. Bob's arm went down for the cue. We were on the air.

They say if you fall off a horse you're supposed to get right back on. *(Wait! Wrong cliché!)* They say once you learn to ride a bicycle you never forget how. I guess it is true. With the microphone in my hand and Bob's finger almost in my face, I flashed my trademark smile—one everybody later said was just as perky as ever—and said, "What's up, Tucson? This is Jillanne Caldwell with Dirk Hadden, our very own Guy in the Sky, and a very special guest." I paused theatrically for the camera to include Clay. (As if our female cameraperson hadn't been focused on him exclusively since he entered the room.) "America, may I introduce you to search-and-rescue ranger Clay Eskiminzin."

I heard the gasps of shock and dismay from Gene, Bob, the Claytons' spokesman, and probably everybody else from coast to coast. But I also saw the genuine grin that split Clay's face. I was on a roll.

* * *

After Clay recited a brief, carefully rehearsed statement crediting Dirk and me and the sharpshooter and everybody else under the sun but himself for saving Alex and Connor, he politely answered enough of Dirk's questions to assure the guy a spot on CNN and then he was gone. (I had no idea where he went, but assumed it was either back to the desert or back to the gilded halls of his family home. Back to his life, as he had said.)

Unfortunately, *What's Up, Tucson?* was my life, so I spent the next two hours on the air chatting with journalists from Montreal to Moscow via satellite. When the show finally wrapped, I gathered up my few possessions and went in search of the front door. Or back door. Or any way at all out of that place.

As I paused before a large window to blink back the sunlight, Clay appeared from nowhere. He'd changed from the suit and tie into jeans and a khaki shirt with a Forest Service patch on the chest and the sleeves rolled up to his elbows. He looked better than anything I'd seen in a department-store window my entire life. I was through shopping for a husband. I not only knew I couldn't live without this man, I knew that if he didn't match everything—anything—I had in my life, I'd throw it all out and start over with just him.

He said, "Do you need a ride home?"

There were any number of news vans, at least four helicopters, and Shar's limo available to me. "Yes," I said at once. "I do."

Thank goodness he was a trained tracker and guide, and had grown up on an estate of his own. He led me through the huge house and down the steps outside with little more trouble than he'd had leading me through the wilderness.

Most of the press was still there in front, held back by a line of deputy sheriffs. Clay scarcely spared them or their camera strobes a second glance. "Strange business you're in, Ms. Caldwell," he told me. "Wonder what the big story will be tomorrow."

We walked toward a Department of Interior jeep that had doors, windows, *and* a roof. "Yeah," Clay said, "it's a little fancy. I don't drive it much." He pulled open my door. When I was seated he said, "Thanks for accepting the ride, Jill. I'd like to meet your mother." Although I knew he was trying to gauge my reaction, I was too mesmerized to react. I simply stared into his eyes. "And," he said, "your boyfriend."

"Who?" I murmured.

Batguy smiled. "Right answer." He circled the car, climbed into the driver's seat, and started the engine. As an afterthought (or maybe the first impetuous act of his life?), he leaned across the seats, pulled me into his chest, and kissed me in front of the photographers, reporters, heaven, and everybody.

That kiss was better in real life than all my fantasies and dreams combined. Clay kissed like he did everything else—with skill, deliberation, and all his heart and soul. This time when my toes curled, it wasn't from anxiety. At last he moved marginally away, cradled my face in his calloused palms, and said, "Just so you know."

* * *

If I were Zane Grey, I'd wrap this all up with us riding blissfully off into the sunset. But not only am I out of Mr. Grey's league, it was technically closer to sunrise. And we weren't on horseback. (Thank goodness. Add horses to the list of things I hate. After giant spiders, but before jeggos.)

And then forget the alphabet and start a new list with sunrise at the very top of things I love. Right after Clay. Everything on that list will have to come after Clay.

Sunset usually symbolizes the end—of a day, or a movie, or a story—but sunrise represents a new beginning. This one definitely did. It had so much hope and promise and possibility in it, it made me cry. I gazed over at the man of my dreams and uttered another silent prayer to the God of the Galiuros: *Thank you, Father.* Being right there right then with Henry Clayton Montgomery Eskiminzin made the entire universe seem hopeful and full of possibilities. I hoped that with Eliot Fuller gone, Alex and Shar could make a real home for Connor. I hoped that the first Eskiminzin had at last found his peace like a stone. And I hoped that one day his descendant and I would kneel across from each other at an altar in one of the glorious Mountains of the Lord to make promises to one another that would also be like a stone—steadfast and immovable and meant to endure the test of time. All time.

Just so you know.

about the author

A native of Arizona, Kerry Lynn Blair grew up in a home where the décor was American Indian-inspired, the family vacations were to Tombstone and Custer National Monument, and there was almost always a black-and-white western playing on the television. (Her mother watched to root for the Indians.) Today Kerry enjoys romantic comedies, classic flicks, and just about any other movie that doesn't have a horse in it. She's seen every Miss America pageant since 1966, and can almost always pick the soon-to-be winner during the Parade of States.

Kerry lives in Arizona with her husband, mother, and teenage daughter. Two of her still-very-eligible sons attend Arizona State University, and a third serves in the United States Marine Corps. This is her sixth novel for Covenant.

Always thrilled to correspond with readers, Kerry can be reached through Covenant e-mail at info@Covenant-lds.com or through snail-mail at Covenant Communications, Inc., Box 416, American Fork, UT 84003-0416.